"Hats off to Olivia Newport and the debut novel *The Pursuit of Lucy Banning*. The characters are compelling, and Chicago's history comes alive on each page. Readers will feel like they've been transported back to 1892."

—**Andrea Boeshaar**, author, Seasons of Redemption series

"Lucy Banning is my kind of heroine, pushing against the strictures of her times of the 1890s. Her love and caring wraps around your heart as it does those who need her and even to those who wish her harm. A fine read."

—**Lauraine Snelling**, author, Red River of the North series and Wild West Wind series

"Newport brings to life historical Chicago with fascinating insight into the wealthy families of Prairie Avenue, portraying the heart-wrenching disparity in the lifestyles of the elite and working class. She gives us a worthy heroine who struggles to break free of the constraints of her time and offers grace to those less fortunate. *The Pursuit of Lucy Banning* is a beautiful and sweet romance that will touch readers' hearts."

—**Jody Hedlund**, award-winning author, *The Preacher's Bride* and *The Doctor's Lady*

The PURSUIT *of* LUCY BANNING

A NOVEL

OLIVIA NEWPORT

Revell

a division of Baker Publishing Group
Grand Rapids, Michigan

© 2012 by Olivia Newport

Published by Revell
a division of Baker Publishing Group
P.O. Box 6287, Grand Rapids, MI 49516-6287
www.revellbooks.com

Printed in the United States of America

Library of Congress Cataloging-in-Publication Data
Newport, Olivia.
    The pursuit of Lucy Banning : a novel / Olivia Newport.
        p.   cm. — (Avenue of Dreams ; bk. 1)
    ISBN 978-0-8007-2038-4 (pbk.)
    1. Upper class women—Fiction. 2. Architects—Fiction. 3. Chicago (Ill.)—History—19th century—Fiction. I. Title.
PS3614.E686P87 2012
813′.6—dc23   2011051195

This book is a work of fiction. Names, characters, places, and incidents are the products of the author's imagination or are used fictitiously. Any resemblance to actual events, locales, or persons, living or dead, is coincidental.

The internet addresses, email addresses, and phone numbers in this book are accurate at the time of publication. They are provided as a resource. Baker Publishing Group does not endorse them or vouch for their content or permanence.

12   13   14   15   16   17   18   7   6   5   4   3   2   1

For my mother,
who always has her nose in a book

1

A week from Tuesday. Is that possible?

It wasn't that Lucy Banning did not want to view the new art exhibit at the up-and-coming downtown Chicago gallery. She did, keenly. But could she manage it before a week from Tuesday? If the expedition required her mother's co-operation, it would come with a price. Flora Banning would pounce on the exhibit to launch a social occasion. Floating through the gallery in her draped silk gown and overdone hat, nodding and smiling, she would scan for people who really "mattered" and expect Lucy to assist in this endeavor rather than pause to study the paintings.

Lucy had played the dutiful daughter many times. She pointed out Mrs. Field across the crowd and bantered with the mayor. She smiled coyly at the young man who offered to fetch a refreshing drink and listened to Mrs. Pullman describe the hand-painted table service for her dinner party for forty-eight guests. This time, though, Lucy actually needed to scrutinize the paintings. Her art history professor would be expecting an analysis. Lucy must prove herself insightful and articulate, a student worthy to occupy a chair at the newly opened University of Chicago.

Leo.

Leo would do it. Lucy exhaled in relief. Her brother genuinely enjoyed examining art. Siblings barely a year apart, Lucy and Leo had been close companions since childhood. Leo wouldn't ask any questions and he wouldn't hurry her, because he would be even more absorbed in the art than she was.

As the professor expounded on the particulars of what the paper must include, Lucy jotted notes, mindful that she enjoyed a rare privilege in being present. When the university opened just a year ago in 1891, its policy was to accept female students from the start. Lucy could hardly believe her good fortune—to have a prestigious college open right in Chicago and permit women to enroll. Both of her older brothers had gone East for their educations then returned to Chicago, and though Richard was only fourteen, the Bannings were already nudging their youngest son toward a time-tested institution as well. Much to Lucy's disappointment, her parents never seriously entertained further studies for their only daughter once she completed the requisite finishing school and toured Europe for most of a year. A wedding that would define her life had shrouded the last few years. Attending classes at the University of Chicago was not part of preparing to be a banker's wife.

Nevertheless, attending the university was precisely what Lucy was doing—at least, one class—despite Flora Banning's conviction that higher education was irrelevant for her daughter, and for that matter, all young ladies from fine families with good prospects. Flora's own sister held the opposite view. In fact, when Lucy shared her secret wish with her aunt, Violet encouraged her.

"But how can I take a university class without my parents knowing?" Lucy asked. "They're expecting me to marry Daniel. My mother wants to plan a wedding. I'm going to have to set a date soon, and then every minute of the day will be about the wedding."

"It's one class," Aunt Violet answered, "one step. Take this one step and see where it might lead. For the time being, no one needs to know. I'll help with any expenses."

While her parents and youngest brother were away at the family's lake house for most of the summer, Lucy had conjured up excuses to return to town frequently. Her work at the orphanage provided regular justifications. During those quiet weeks in the house without her parents, she applied, interviewed, and was accepted to the university. While her private self did all this in Chicago, her public self formalized her long unofficial engagement in Lake Forest. Now in mid-October, she was several weeks into her art history class and facing her first major assignment. Only two people knew the truth of Lucy's whereabouts on Tuesday and Thursday afternoons: Aunt Violet and Violet's Irish coachman, Paddy, who with her blessing sometimes conspired to solve Lucy's transportation challenges.

The student next to Lucy leaned toward her. "Did you get that third point? He's talking too fast."

Lucy pointed with her fountain pen to the notes she had just written: (1) composition, (2) uniqueness of palette, (3) use of light. The young man—not more than seventeen, Lucy thought—quickly copied what she had written. She wasn't surprised that he had only sparse notes on his paper. From the first week, it seemed he was in over his head. Lucy could only imagine what his other classes were like. Once again, she had to swallow the injustice: a young man lacking talent could openly attend university, but a woman with a keen mind had to sneak around.

Her parents believed Lucy spent three afternoons a week volunteering at St. Andrew's Orphanage. So did all her brothers. So did Daniel. So did the household staff. Lucy did in fact go to the orphanage once a week, and the endeavor gave her good reason to select sturdy clothes without the usual flamboyance of the families who lived on Prairie Avenue. She fashioned her dark hair in a practical style that would not come undone while caring for small children or sorting files in the cramped office. To fight the odds she might be recognized as a Banning while roaming the university campus, Lucy wore the same unadorned garb to school as she did to the orphanage. Her mother sighed at the whole business. Lucy had trunks and racks full of European fashions, yet three times a week she left the house looking like hardly more than a ladies' maid.

Today Lucy wore a nondescript gray flannel suit and a functional broad-brimmed black hat tipped strategically to hide her face. She remembered the day she brought the suit home.

"What is that thing?" Flora Banning had asked.

"I've been shopping."

"Shopping? Don't tell me you bought that rag off the rack."

"It's from Mr. Field's store. He deals with some quite capable dressmakers."

"We have a dressmaker," Flora reminded Lucy. "I'd like to be there when you explain this to her."

"I need sturdy, practical clothes to wear to the orphanage. Lenae would be insulted if I asked her to make something so plain."

"Everybody knows she makes your dresses. She'll be insulted that her client would wear something so plain under any circumstances."

"I won't tell if you won't tell." Lucy managed a light laugh as she carried her new suit up the stairs to her mother's consternation.

Lucy's figure was never quite as slim as her mother thought

it should be, but her corset did its job. The suit was well made of good quality cloth and the tailored style was current, but nothing about the ensemble would bring particular attention to the young woman who slipped into class at the last moment and sat in the back of the lecture hall. When class was dismissed, Lucy generally fidgeted with her textbook and satchel, managing to pass enough time to find the halls sparsely populated as she left the building. Today was no different. She was the last to leave.

In the corridor, Lucy schemed as she walked. An art exhibit in itself was a cultured enough event that Flora Banning would not, in principle, object to Lucy's attending. However, Lucy needed an escort for such an occasion, and the last thing she wanted was for Daniel to take her—or to explain to her mother why she did not even ask Daniel. She had to get Leo to go with her.

Lucy rounded a corner and came to an abrupt stop. As the flush rose in her cheeks, she realized it was too late to backtrack. Leo had spotted her. Even if she donned clothing meant to make her look as inconspicuous as possible, Leo would never overlook her. Most of the time Lucy was grateful for his ability to pick her out of a crowd of thousands, but not today. What was he doing leaning casually against a wall outside her classroom chatting with a young man Lucy did not recognize? As Leo lifted his eyes and smiled, the man turned and followed Leo's gaze.

"Lucy! What are you doing here?" Leo's green eyes, matching her own, quizzed.

Lucy laughed as she stepped forward to kiss her brother's cheek. "I might ask you the same thing. When you gave me a tour of your research office, I'm quite confident it was in a faraway wing of the university. The walk from there to here would qualify as a daily constitutional."

Leo's field was manufacturing technology. Why had he wandered to the fine arts department on this afternoon? Why at this moment?

"I'm just giving my friend Will here a tour of the university," Leo explained. "Lucy, this is my friend, Will Edwards. Will, this is my little sister, Miss Lucy Banning."

Lucy shook Will's hand. "I'm happy to meet you. What is your interest in the university, Mr. Edwards?"

"I'm an architect." His eyes, cobalt blue, glowed, and Lucy's heart beat just a little faster. "I've recently joined a Chicago firm that played a part in the design of the university. I thought it might help me fit in better if I looked at some of the recent projects."

"Will's firm is also working on the Expo," Leo said. "Burnham and Root have subcontracted them."

"A lot of firms have small commissions," Will added.

"That's wonderful!" Lucy said. "I can't wait until opening day. Just imagine: a world's fair here in Chicago." She glanced from one man to the other and found herself returning Will's friendly smile. *Stop gawking!* Lifting her chin a notch, she asked, "So tell me, how do you two know each other?"

"Princeton." Leo's answer came quickly, before Will could take a breath.

"Oh, you're college friends, then."

Will fidgeted. "Not quite. Your brother is not referring to the famous College of New Jersey in Princeton, but merely to the town that hosts the famous institution."

"You spoil my fun, Will," Leo said. "Why can't you just be a Princeton man?"

"I'm afraid I don't understand," Lucy said.

Will smiled again. *Those eyes.* Lucy had to break the gaze before her mouth fell rudely open in fascination.

"I did not attend the College of New Jersey or any other

college," Will explained quietly. "I was engaged in an internship with an architectural firm in Princeton, New Jersey, when I met your brother at a party to which I should never have been invited."

"I'm sure I don't know what you mean, Mr. Edwards. Any host would be happy to have you." Looking at Will's face, Lucy could hardly remember what Daniel's looked like. She had never seen such thick honey-colored hair on a man. His square jaw dimpled delightfully on one side.

"My background is considerably more humble than yours," Will said without apology, "a fact that your brother kindly insists on overlooking."

"With good reason, I'm sure." Lucy turned to her brother. "Leo, I was thinking I would like to take in the new art exhibit downtown. Perhaps you could find the time to go with me."

Leo's eyes lit up. "I'd love it!" Then, "Will, join us, won't you? No need to rearrange your schedule. They're open in the evenings."

"I wouldn't want to impose." Will turned his head slightly in hesitation.

"It's no imposition," Lucy assured him. And it wasn't. She smiled again at both Leo and Will and collected herself. "I ought to be going."

"What's the hurry?" Leo asked. "Are you meeting Daniel?"

Lucy bristled ever so slightly. "Just for some quick tea. He has a business engagement this evening. See you for dinner, Leo?"

"When the alternative is facing the wrath of Mrs. Banning, appearing for the Thursday family dinner is clearly the rational choice."

"Then I'll see you tonight." She stepped away from them to continue down the hall.

"Wait a minute," Leo protested, reaching for her arm to

stall her progress. "You never told me what you were doing here."

Lucy looked him in the eye. "Mr. Emmett asked me to do an errand."

"The director of the orphanage?"

Lucy nodded. "He has a very bright boy in his care and he is hoping to arrange a scholarship for the young man to enroll in the art department at the university next year."

Lucy regretted that she could not be forthcoming with Leo, but she was telling the truth. Phillip Emmett had asked her to use her family's influence to speak for the sixteen-year-old boy. What she didn't mention was that she had dispatched this errand two weeks ago, and she had not worn a gray flannel suit when she did it.

"Well? Did it work?" Leo asked.

Lucy shrugged. "We're awaiting a final decision, but it would seem that the Banning name does count for something." She turned to Will. "It was very nice to meet you, Mr. Edwards. I hope to see you again."

"You will," Leo reminded her, "at the art exhibit."

"Oh yes, of course. Until then."

Lucy made her way to the end of the hall and down two flights of stairs. Outside, she walked more quickly than necessary away from the building. *You are a weak-kneed chicken,* she told herself. How long would Leo believe her story about the orphanage? She paused to lean against a tree, gazing back at the university's main building in waning afternoon light. Gothic stone spired at the corners as if the building were as old as Oxford or Cambridge, rather than a recent structure erected at the behest of John D. Rockefeller on land donated by Marshall Field, the Bannings' Prairie Avenue neighbor. She counted the familiar four rows of windows that lifted the eye to the turrets seeming to stake the building firmly in place.

Clearly the founders of the school did not intend for it to go anywhere anytime soon. It was a fortress of learning, of history, of tradition, even though its doors had opened just a year ago. And somehow Lucy Banning had penetrated the fortress and earned a seat in one classroom. At that moment, though, continuing her quest seemed like throwing a feather at the building and expecting to chip the stone. What was the point? Taking one secret class at a time would mean years and years to earn a degree.

Lucy would much rather have taken a leisurely carriage ride to visit Aunt Violet, who undoubtedly would know what to say to stir up Lucy's momentum. Instead, though, she was to meet Daniel in less than half an hour, and Paddy was not available to whisk her downtown.

Her university escapades could not be a secret forever. One of these days she was going to have to tell Daniel the truth.

2

*C*harlotte Farrow hustled to keep up with Mr. Penard, the butler and clearly the person who kept the Banning household humming. She had arrived at the massive home less than twenty minutes ago and already Penard was giving detailed descriptions of where she was and was not allowed to tread and what she was and was not allowed to touch. It seemed to Charlotte that this grand tour of the spacious home was meant to put her in her place. So far, since leaving the kitchen, Penard had not indicated she was permitted to enter a single one of the rooms she viewed without specific approval from him and only for a particular, limited purpose.

Standing stiff-backed in the middle of the parlor, Penard paused. "Mr. and Mrs. Banning are fond of retiring to this room in the evenings after dinner. You may hear Miss Lucy playing the Steinway. Mr. Daniel is especially fond of listening to her play." Frowning, he pointed at the intricately woven rug beneath his shiny shoes. "Be particularly mindful of the carpets. They are irreplaceable. Mrs. Banning commissioned them from William Morris, and should you cause a stain, you would of course lose your position."

Who is William Morris? Charlotte wondered. She had never been in a room filled with items whose value was their beauty, not their usefulness—carved trays, porcelain minia-tures, glass vases, and dozens of other objects that existed to dazzle the eye.

"Of course, sir. I'll be careful," Charlotte said.

Stepping into the parlor was like stepping into one of the paintings on the wall. The room was large and meticulously appointed. Miniature statues adorned intricately carved dark wood end tables. Every small item on each side table seemed angled for particular effect. Charlotte knew without being told that the paintings were masterpieces. If Mr. Penard were to say the wallpaper was hand painted, she would not doubt it. The carefully selected green and gold settee and chairs, in coordinated but not identical patterns, were surely made specifically for the room with restrained extravagance.

Penard continued his lecture. Charlotte wondered how much he expected her to remember because she was sure she wouldn't recall much.

"The Bannings have been on Prairie Avenue longer than many of their neighbors," he explained. "They came a few years after the Great Fire. Things were never the same on Washington Street after that disaster."

Charlotte nodded as if of course she knew all about the demise of the old neighborhood. At least she had heard of the Chicago Fire of 1871.

"As you become familiar with the neighborhood," Mr. Penard said, "you'll find that the Banning home is actually modest. Many homes have far more than the 17,000 square feet we serve here."

Penard led the way out of the parlor and into the hall, continuing with a roving lecture. Charlotte would not risk asking questions, but she did try to store some basic facts about the family, which seemed more relevant to her than the neighborhood architecture.

Charlotte had only seen part of the first floor, and already she estimated the mansion could hold two dozen farm cabins like the one she grew up in. She had lived most of her twenty years in perpetual overcrowding, with her grandmother in the kitchen and younger brothers underfoot. Where she had been in the last year, she wanted to forget.

Six weeks ago she would not have imagined she might be walking the floors of a home like the Bannings'. Charlotte resolved Penard would never learn the truth about the more than questionable references she had provided three days ago—or anything else. She was here now, and the vise in her stomach would not keep her from doing her best to please Mr. Penard. He would have no cause to reconsider the decision to employ her. Charlotte knew her way around a kitchen, even if the Banning kitchen alone was larger than her family's home. Her mother, as poor as she was, had a copy of *Mrs. Beeton's Book of Household Management*, and Charlotte had read it more than once for lack of anything else to peruse.

"You'll find that the Bannings have admirable neighbors." Penard ran a white glove along the bottom edge of a painting in the hall and inspected for dust. "Many of the homes are in the Italianate or Second Empire style, like this one, though the Glessners were more daring when they built their home. Its Romanesque flair does not sit well with all the neighbors, but you will discover that Mrs. Glessner's interest in Arts and Crafts is having some effect on Mrs. Banning."

Italianate? Second Empire? Romanesque flair? Arts and Crafts? Charlotte didn't know what to call the architecture or decorating. She only knew she had stepped over the threshold into another universe.

Penard continued his quick steps, Charlotte keeping a respectful distance behind him. "Take care not to gawk at the neighbors, since many of them are well known. Marshall

Field has forged new standards for retail stores. Philip Armour could feed the nation with his slaughterhouses and meatpacking plants. And as you know, George Pullman's sleeping car revolutionized train travel."

Charlotte had never been in a store other than the local mercantile at home. Until the day she stole away to Chicago, she only imagined what it might be like to travel by any method other than a horse and carriage. She was too terrified, sitting bolt upright on the hurtling journey, to wonder whether the train she rode had sleeping cars.

Penard gestured that they would continue down the hall. "The Glessners are perhaps the most amiable neighbors, despite the dubious architecture of their home. Their son George is the same age as Miss Lucy and they've known each other socially for years. John Glessner understood that the future lay in improved farm equipment. His tools and machines are all over the country now."

If that was true, Charlotte's own father probably owned something designed by John Glessner, she realized.

"Mr. Banning represents the legal interests of a wide spectrum of businessmen," Penard said. "Occasionally he will bring clients to dinner, and I will expect you to show the greatest respect."

"Of course, Mr. Penard."

"This is the master suite." Penard opened the door only briefly. "Although it's unusual, they prefer the ground floor because Mrs. Banning has a weak knee."

"Yes, Mr. Penard." Charlotte nodded, confident this was the only response the butler expected.

He led her farther down the hall. "This is Mr. Banning's study. He does not like anyone touching his things. You will not enter either of these rooms without explicit permission."

"Yes, Mr. Penard." The study was filled with knickknacks

and memorabilia, some of value and some that looked to be junk even to Charlotte. She had a fleeting doubt whether even Mr. Banning himself would notice something out of place amid the cluttered arrangement.

They retraced their steps down the hall to the foyer, then Penard led her up an expansive marble staircase, barely slowing his steps enough for her to lift her skirts. "I want you to know your way around the house, but you will of course not use this front staircase when the Bannings are home."

"I wouldn't think of it."

Penard's expression left no doubt in Charlotte's mind what the consequences might be if she infringed.

"The children's rooms are up here, though only Mr. Richard can still be called a child, and only just barely. Richard is fourteen. Miss Lucy, Mr. Leo, and Mr. Oliver are grown and engaged in various pursuits." He gestured vaguely down the hall to the left. "The boys have their rooms here. They will not call for you, but Miss Lucy may have need of your attentions from time to time." He gestured in the other direction. "Miss Lucy has recently chosen a larger suite of rooms at the far end of the hall across from the old nursery."

"Yes, Mr. Penard."

"The other rooms are guest rooms. Miss Lucy's fiancé prefers the corner room with windows opening on the front of the house. He frequently stays a night or two during the week. The Bannings consider Mr. Daniel a fourth son."

"Yes, sir."

As they walked the hall toward Lucy's suite, Charlotte wondered if Lucy ever regretted being in such an isolated part of the house. Perhaps she was a quiet sort or needed a place to withdraw. Charlotte knew that feeling, though she'd had to go outside to the creek that flowed through their land to be alone.

They descended a narrow rear stairway just past Lucy's rooms. "If you have cause to come upstairs, you will use this stairwell," Penard instructed. "These stairs also lead up to the third floor servant quarters. Have you seen your room?"

"Yes, Mr. Penard. Mrs. Fletcher showed me as soon as I arrived." She had left her few possessions there, along with the only thing that really mattered.

The stairs going down led directly into the kitchen. "I will leave you with Mrs. Fletcher now," Penard said. "You will have little need to be in the rest of the house, but I thought it useful for you to have some general bearings."

"Thank you, Mr. Penard. You've been a great help."

Charlotte had been forewarned she would encounter the family at dinner that evening. There would be no formal introduction, of course. She would merely be there to serve and clear dishes and to remain as unseen as possible. That's exactly what Charlotte craved—to remain unseen. If no one noticed her, no one would ask questions, and she would not be forced to deceive anyone—at least not any further.

Penard pushed through the door leading from the kitchen to the butler's pantry, leaving Charlotte behind exhaling air she had not realized she was collecting in her lungs. Involuntarily her shoulders drooped. She attempted a smile for Mrs. Fletcher, the cook, searching the unfamiliar wrinkled face for some sign of temperament. If the wrinkles around her gray eyes were any indication, Mrs. Fletcher was a good ten years older than Charlotte's own mother. A tight bun kept her gray hair out of her face, and the stoop of her shoulders told Charlotte that during her younger years, she had stood an inch or two taller. Mrs. Fletcher wore a dark dress under a white apron. She absently wiped her hands on a towel, then tossed it over her shoulder as she inspected her new maid. The image struck Charlotte as severe, and she hoped for warmth beneath the uniform. As they stared at each other, Charlotte was relieved to see the older woman's eyes soften.

"Did Mr. Penard discuss uniforms with you?"

"No, ma'am."

"Do you have a uniform?"

"Not precisely. I do have dark dresses."

The cook sighed. "I have told that uppity fool time and again that the girls he sends me need to have proper uniforms with a crisp white apron for evening service."

"I'm sorry . . ." If Penard had known she didn't have uniforms and refused to hire her, where would she be now?

"With your references, he probably assumed you were bringing uniforms. That's often done, you know."

"Yes, ma'am. At my former place of employment—"

"Never mind." Mrs. Fletcher waved one hand. "There's no time for your story now."

Charlotte was grateful to be interrupted, because she had no idea what would have come out of her mouth next.

"You look about the size of the last girl we had," Mrs. Fletcher observed. "She left in a mysterious hurry and didn't come back for her things—at least not yet. I'll find her uniform and put it in your room while you get started peeling potatoes." She pointed to a mound of spuds on the worktable and turned toward the stairs.

"I don't want to trouble you." Charlotte quickly stepped in the cook's path. "I'm the one who arrived unprepared. Perhaps you can just tell me where the apron is and I'll fetch it."

"You don't know your way around up there yet," Mrs. Fletcher countered. "It'll be easier just to find it myself and put it on your bed. I'll show you where things are after dinner."

"Please, I have to learn my way around," Charlotte persisted. "Just point me in the right direction and I'm sure I'll find it. I'm quite resourceful, I assure you." Charlotte held her breath, waiting for some sign of relenting.

Mrs. Fletcher sighed. "Well, all right. But don't dillydally. I'm expecting you to peel those potatoes soon."

"And I will, I promise, as soon as I find the uniform."

The older woman eyed the young maid for a moment before speaking. Charlotte forced herself to breathe normally. If Mrs. Fletcher went in her room, her new life might come to an end before it even began.

"Go up to the servants' quarters," Mrs. Fletcher finally said, "and you'll find an empty room at the end of the hall, on the left. There's a green trunk. I think the apron is in there, though it may need pressing before dinner."

"As soon as the potatoes are peeled, I'll press it." Charlotte forced brightness into her face. "I'll run up there right now and find it." She turned and scampered up the stairs before the haggard cook could reconsider. Prior to proceeding to the empty room, Charlotte paused at the closed door to her own room and listened carefully. Satisfied, she let herself expel an anxious breath and went in search of the green trunk, wondering if she would ever breathe normally again.

In the unused room, which was hardly bigger than the space required to hold the three unmatched trunks Charlotte found there, she sank to the floor and put her head on the green trunk. *What have I done?* she wondered. *I'll be found out and they'll turn me out.*

The thought of going back was all Charlotte needed to snap out of her despair. She could not go back. They would not find out. She had to deal with one moment at a time. Charlotte opened the green trunk and found it held several dresses. Most of them were more frayed than her own, and Charlotte pitied the girl who left them behind. Charlotte had brought two worn carpetbags into the house. One of them held three dresses and an extra set of under things. The other bag no one could see. Closing her eyes briefly, she prayed for the gift of a little more time—and the gift of silence.

Charlotte found the maid's uniform. The apron was worn thin but was spotlessly white and wrinkled only where it had been folded. Charlotte crept back to her own small room, which was squeezed in between those of Mrs. Fletcher and the ladies' maid who served both Flora Banning and her daughter Lucy. She silently laid the uniform on the bed. Then she peered into the second bag, relieved to find the contents undisturbed.

This arrangement couldn't last long. Charlotte knew that. But for this moment, everything was fine, and this moment was the only one she had. With another silent prayer, Charlotte asked for a reprieve of just ten minutes. She was sure that was all she needed right now as she reached for the top button of her dress.

3

*L*ucy hoped Daniel was not waiting for her outside the teahouse. If he saw her getting off a streetcar, she would never hear the end of it. Daniel would likely hire a carriage to be at her disposal around the clock. Then her parents would wonder why that was necessary when the family had several carriages and drivers of their own and Aunt Violet was generous with hers. All Lucy wanted was to go from one point to another as efficiently as possible, and sometimes the streetcar or train met that fundamental requirement. In her plain gray suit, she fit in with the crowd availing themselves of public transportation. She was determined that someday she would even ride a bicycle.

Daniel rarely suggested meeting for tea anywhere but the shop convenient to the bank where he worked. Its location and luxurious ambiance made it popular with the families in his parents' social circle. When Lucy and Daniel met there, they nearly always ran into someone Daniel knew. Lucy was not so naïve that she didn't notice how much this pleased him. Today Daniel was not likely to be happy to see her wearing her "orphan rags," but even if Paddy had been available, she would not have had time to go home first to change.

The streetcar stopped at its usual corner and Lucy

descended its steps, glancing across the street and exhaling relief when she did not see Daniel standing outside.

Lucy had never not known Daniel Jules. He was there in her earliest memories and all the family stories. The Bannings had known the Juleses since before either couple married. Daniel was the first arrival of the new generation, and, it turned out, the only one for Howard and Irene Jules. Flora and Samuel, who married two years after the Juleses, promptly produced Oliver, then Leo. By the time Lucy arrived in the Banning household, Daniel Jules was seven years old. After three boys between the two couples, a little girl had no escape from inflated attention. Before her first birthday, the mothers were scheming for a wedding two decades off.

When Lucy was four and Daniel eleven, both families built lake houses on adjoining lots outside Lake Forest, beyond the northern boundaries of Chicago, as a summer reprieve from soaring temperatures. Daniel, Oliver, Leo, and Lucy spent their summers together, the boys turning brown and Lucy progressively compelled to protect her ladylike fair coloring under a wide hat or an umbrella. Each fall the boys returned to the Harvard School for Boys on Indiana Avenue, the same school her youngest brother, Richard, now attended in the shadow of his brothers. Lucy went to the Holman-Dickerman French and English Day School for girls, an honored establishment that prepared young women for refined lives.

Crossing the street, Lucy twisted the ring on her left hand as she remembered the night she realized she was going to marry Daniel Jules. She had been eight years old and had snuck past her nanny, who was distracted with a fussing baby Richard. At the bottom of the stairs, she heard her parents' voices in the parlor.

"I'm so glad Howard and Irene agree," Flora said. "They've

been enchanted with Lucy since the day she was born. Just think, someday we'll all be in-laws!"

"Daniel is a good match for Lucy," Samuel said. "Howard will make sure he's well established."

"He's just enough older that he can be in a good position by the time Lucy is old enough to marry."

Lucy sat on the bottom step. *I'm going to marry Daniel.* It made perfect sense—and she was relieved to think she would not have to worry about finding someone to love and marry. All she had to do was grow up.

As a young teenager, Daniel often managed to meet her at the carriage that carried her home from school with one of her brothers in tow. When she was herself a teenager and he a college man, he attended to her wishes whenever he was home. Daniel first kissed Lucy one summer at the lake. Even now Lucy looked back on that moment as one of sweetness.

Daniel spent the years waiting for Lucy to be ready to marry by establishing himself in the banking industry. Though his father was wealthy enough to support several coming generations, he insisted Daniel prove himself worthy of the daughter of his dear friends by embarking on his own fortune. So far Daniel had done fairly well. Lucy didn't know the details—just as her mother didn't know the details of her father's finances—but Daniel and his father supplied sufficient offhand remarks for Lucy to be certain that when she married Daniel she would be well taken care of.

And now she had grown up, she was engaged to Daniel Jules, and everyone was eager that the two families be linked forever by their union. Flora and Irene were ecstatic at the thought of sharing grandchildren.

When she turned nineteen, Lucy knew her parents believed she was ready for betrothal. They had allowed her a couple of years after leaving school to accept frequent social engagements where she conversed and danced with other young men. For a few months, she was frequently on the arm of George Glessner—but always assuring Daniel that it meant nothing. She also honed her skills at the piano with private study that gave her the confidence to gladly respond to requests to play at parties. However, this was merely training ground for being an accomplished wife to a bank executive. Though she knew she would marry Daniel eventually, Lucy endeavored to buy more time.

"Once I'm married and have a household of my own to run, I will have to focus on that," she had told her mother as they sat in the parlor with needlework one afternoon. Lucy was embroidering a tablecloth for her own trousseau. "I do want to marry Daniel, but first I want to try to do something that really matters."

"You speak of marriage as if it doesn't matter." Flora lifted her eyes from the detailed stitching along the edge of a handkerchief and looked at her daughter over her glasses.

"It's the orphanage, Mother. I think I can really do some good there, but I have to be free to spend time every week. I can help organize the office, or teach, or perhaps even find permanent homes for some of the children. Is that not worthwhile? So few people are willing to commit themselves."

"How long?" Flora asked.

Lucy rapidly gauged her mother's mood. "Three years."

"One."

"Two, then."

Daniel had been patient enough considering the circumstances. He himself was still absorbed in establishing independent finances. As long as he could see Lucy as freely as he liked, he was content to wait.

However, now that she was twenty-one, her parents expected Lucy to direct her attention to her future. Daniel was already interviewing architects to design the home they would live in. He had his eye on an empty lot not too far away from Prairie Avenue. It would be their first home, Daniel reminded Lucy, until he was able to build her the mansion she deserved.

Will Edwards waved through Lucy's mind as she involuntarily wondered whether Daniel would consider using his architectural firm. It would certainly bode well for Will's future if he could attract a client such as Daniel Jules.

The engagement had become official last July 4. Both families celebrated Independence Day at the lake, and in the middle of the festivities, Daniel produced a stunning sapphire ring. Lucy recognized the stone as one that belonged to Daniel's mother. He'd had a new setting designed for it with diamond accents on sterling silver. Her parents were right. It was time for her to plan for her future.

A series of three horse-drawn carriages seemed in no hurry to clear the intersection, confirming in Lucy's mind the efficiency of the streetcar. When they finally did, Lucy lifted her skirts slightly and proceeded to cross the street.

Inside the teahouse, Daniel sat at a table against the wall, facing the door. It was his favorite table. From that vantage point he could see who was coming and going and lift those glimmering brown eyes or dip his head in acknowledgment of anyone he knew—and it seemed to Lucy that Daniel knew everyone in Chicago. He stood as she entered and pulled out a chair for her. She settled into it, set her satchel at her feet, removed her gloves, and smiled at him as he took in her gray clothing.

"I was scheduled to go to the orphanage," Lucy said, before Daniel could object to her plain appearance. It was only a half-lie. As far as her family was concerned, she was scheduled to go to the orphanage. In the past, before the term started at the university, she would in fact have been at the orphanage on a Thursday afternoon.

Daniel glanced down at the satchel that held her art history textbook and lecture notes. "Are you now bringing work home from the orphanage?"

Lucy waved a hand. "Oh, it's just some odds and ends of supplies. I'm never sure what will come up. It just seems easier to carry a satchel and be prepared."

"It makes you look a bit like a schoolgirl."

Lucy leaned toward him and gave a wry smile. "As I recall, you didn't mind walking a schoolgirl home on a fine afternoon when you were home from college."

He smiled at last and she saw the pleasure spring in his eyes. "True enough." Pleasure evaporated as quickly as it flooded in. "But I do wonder about the amount of time you spend at the orphanage. Are you sure it's necessary? I rather expected that as our wedding approached, your involvement there would taper off."

"Mr. Emmett needs my assistance," Lucy assured him. "He has a young man in his care who deserves a university education. The Banning name may be helpful in attaining that."

"Emmett has hundreds of orphans. Surely he can't expect you to give personalized attention to every one."

"Don't they all deserve attention?" Lucy challenged.

Daniel shrugged. "I'm not completely unsympathetic to their plight. As you know, my family contributes substantially to St. Andrew's. But how realistic is it to fill this boy's head with dreams of going to the university? He could go into service with a good family and start earning his own way. We could take him on ourselves once we're married if you like."

Lucy bristled. "Perhaps he doesn't want to go into service. Perhaps he wants to attend university."

"Some people have more limited choices than others. It's the way of the world."

"Maybe it's a bad way for the world to be."

Daniel leaned back and examined Lucy. "I'm not quite sure where this is coming from, my dear. It's unlike you."

If only you knew. "Never mind. I suppose I'm just in a bit of a funk."

"A good pot of tea will help." Daniel signaled the waiter and ordered tea and sandwiches. "I think I've settled on the sketches for our house. We do need to set a date for the wedding that allows enough time for building."

"Perhaps we should wait until the building is under way and we're sure how long it will take," Lucy suggested.

Daniel shook his head. "The crew will work more efficiently if they know there's a deadline."

"Yes, I suppose so. Leo has a friend who is an architect, you know."

"No, I didn't know." The steaming tea arrived. Daniel rearranged some dishes while Lucy poured.

"I only just met him, but he seems quite nice. Perhaps he could have a look at your sketches."

"Where did you meet him?"

When will I learn to be more careful? Lucy had set her own trap. She picked up her teacup to take a sip. "I was at the university on orphanage business and ran into them," she finally said.

"Oh, well, if he's a friend of Leo's, I suppose he could have a look, though I'm fairly certain of whom I'd like to hire. Back to the question at hand."

"The question at hand?" Lucy echoed.

"The wedding date. How would you feel about midsummer?"

"Midsummer?" That was nine months away, and she

couldn't possibly wait that long to tell him the truth. The last thing she wanted to do was hurt Daniel, though.

"I suppose we should consult our mothers," Daniel said. "It's likely they already have a date picked out and just haven't told us!"

Lucy laughed nervously. "Yes, I suppose so." She let the moment go. The time was not right.

"Would a date in July give you enough time to plan the wedding?"

Lucy chuckled again. "Another question for my mother. But I would imagine so."

"I'll have a word with your mother," Daniel offered.

Lucy picked at a cucumber sandwich as her sapphire ring caught the afternoon light streaming through the window. This couldn't go on much longer, but a lot of people would be unhappy with the truth.

4

"Thank you." With a smile, Lucy pressed a coin into the hand of the cab driver as he helped her down. Daniel had put her in a carriage to carry her safely home after their tea.

The neighborhood was quiet as the carriage pulled away and Lucy surveyed her surroundings. The Pullmans had houseguests, Lucy knew, so she was not surprised to see a couple of extra coachmen tending to carriages under the broad porch at the front door across Eighteenth Street. The brownstone-covered massive home seemed as impenetrable as the Pullman business empire. Lucy had last been inside the Pullman home the previous spring for a dinner party. She'd spent several hours in the opulent dining room and parlor that evening, and more than one dinner guest had referred to the two-hundred-seat theater and the two-lane private bowling alley of the home. Lucy had managed to swallow her wonderings whether the Pullmans were looking for a life in which they never had to leave their fortress. In comparison, the Bannings lived simply, and perhaps even were the "poor neighbors."

Certainly the Fields were not the poor neighbors, nor the Kimballs, whose new home on the corner of Eighteenth and Prairie had been completed only in recent months. Lucy had watched it go up stage by stage, passing by it every day. The neighborhood rumor—no one knew for sure—was that the owner of the Kimball Piano and Organ Company had a Steinway in his parlor. A Kimball piano would have been a cheap insult to the Rembrandts that hung on the walls. Across the street from the Kimballs, the Glessners were the neighborhood rebels. They refused to erect a home that fit into the unspoken code of European design, opting instead for granite stone architecture that embraced a free American spirit. Inside, Mrs. Glessner flagrantly defied the rules for decorating and welcomed the friendly atmosphere of the Arts and Crafts movement with its warm tones and practicality even in exquisite craftsmanship. Flora Banning acquired select pieces from the Arts and Crafts movement, but Mrs. Glessner embraced it full on.

Lucy turned to face the solid oak front door of the Banning mansion two doors down from the Kimballs. With lips together, she inhaled deeply, then opened her mouth and exhaled slowly. The weight in her shoulders eased. She should never have let slip to Daniel that she had met Will Edwards at the university. At least Daniel was not coming to dinner tonight, nor would he be calling for her later. A business dinner would consume his evening. The staff would undoubtedly set a place for him just in case. Over the years they had grown used to Daniel's presence in the Banning house and seemed prepared for his needs regardless of when he turned up.

You can't stand on the sidewalk forever, she told herself. Her family may not have been the richest on the block, nor the most daring, nor the most creative, but they were her family. Dinner would be served promptly at eight o'clock, and Lucy could not appear in gray flannel. She picked up her skirts and climbed the handful of steps that led to the front door and entered the expansive foyer.

Penard, his wrists crossed behind his back, paced in front of a stiff lineup of the household staff. The round dark mahogany pedestal table, anchor of the foyer, separated butler from staff. Taking in the startling scene before her, Lucy instinctively caught herself from letting the door slam.

"As you know well," Penard was saying, "my position as butler of this household makes me accountable for every item within its walls. Mr. Banning is seriously distressed that some items have gone missing from his private study. I have admonished each of you repeatedly not to enter that room without specific permission from me, and I have extended no such permission to any of you. You can understand my concern that some items of sentimental value to Mr. Banning have disappeared."

As if on ominous cue, the seven-foot grandfather clock bonged six times.

Lucy skimmed the expressions of one stricken servant's face after another. As much as she might like to, she could not get involved. Running the household was Penard's purview. Her parents had trusted him for fifteen years. Mrs. Fletcher, the cook, had been with the family for years as well and was above reproach. The other staff tended to rotate every year or two. Lucy so far had found Archie Shepard, the footman and assistant coachman, to take his responsibilities seriously, and Elsie, the ladies' maid she shared with her mother, to be delightfully personable. Bessie, the parlor maid, said no more than she had to but anticipated her tasks and the family's needs with almost befuddling accuracy. The kitchen maid, Kate, had left abruptly a couple of weeks earlier, but Lucy assessed her to be simply highstrung, not the sort who had any point to prove by stealing knickknacks. She wondered whom Penard could suspect among this lot.

Lucy's eyes moved to the young woman at the end of the lineup. *She must be the new kitchen maid*, she thought, *and Penard is going to scare her off before she even catches her breath*. The woman, who was around Lucy's age, stared at her feet during the entire dressing-down. Holding her satchel closely, Lucy inched away from the door and toward the marble stairs across the foyer.

Penard pivoted and paced in the opposite direction. "I need not remind any of you that you serve in this house at my pleasure. The Bannings give me authority. If I do not recommend you, you do not work here. It's that simple. For the moment, I will refrain from making specific allegations, but be warned that I will be watching carefully. I will know everything that happens in this house."

The new kitchen maid twitched, and her eyes rose momentarily to Penard.

"Charlotte, do you have something you wish to say?" Penard glared at the maid.

"No, sir." The maid's eyes went back to her feet.

"If I discover that you are withholding anything from me, you have my assurance you will regret it."

"Yes, sir, Mr. Penard."

Lucy flinched on the girl's behalf. Clearly she was unnerved. Was it really necessary for Penard to speak to her this way on her first afternoon of employment?

Still, Lucy knew she ought to go upstairs to choose a gown for dinner and let Penard sort out whatever was amiss. Her foot was on the first marble step when her father burst into the foyer.

"Well, Penard, what have you discerned?" Samuel Banning boomed.

Lucy cringed. She knew that intonation well: her father had given up even trying to be polite. Involuntarily, she turned to see how Penard would respond.

"I have taken appropriate action, Mr. Banning," Penard said. "I'm sure we have put an end to things."

Samuel Banning pointed at Charlotte, the new maid. "Who is this? I don't recognize her."

"This is Miss Charlotte Farrow," Penard responded evenly. "We have engaged her services as a kitchen maid. She has just arrived to take up her post."

"Was she here yesterday?" Samuel snapped.

"Only briefly, sir, for an interview."

"Why didn't I meet her?"

"You had not yet come home from the Calumet Club, sir. After I interviewed her and recommended her, Mrs. Banning gave her approval."

"If she was here yesterday, she could have done it," Samuel said. "I want to see her bags."

By now Charlotte was visibly quaking, and Lucy could no longer resist the urge to intervene. "Father, please. I've only just got home, so I'm not sure what is causing such a stir, but I'm certain we can sort it out calmly."

"You wouldn't say that if it were your items going missing. My brass paperweight is gone."

"The one shaped like a gavel?"

"Yes. It's the only brass paperweight I have."

"It's not the first time you thought something was missing, Father," Lucy reminded him. "Remember last spring when you were sure Richard took a book from your library of first editions? You were quite distressed, as I recall. But it turned out you loaned it to Daniel's father. You didn't even recall you'd given it to him until he returned it a few weeks later."

"This is not the same at all," Samuel said. But the wind had gone out of him.

Lucy glanced at Charlotte, who was so pale Lucy thought she might faint.

"Father, let the staff go back to work." She spoke quietly. "I'm sure if we put our minds to it, we can figure out what happened."

"That's what your mother says." Samuel raised rather than lowered his voice. "But if one of her precious pots went missing, she'd sing a different tune."

"I would sing exactly the same tune." Flora Banning appeared in the broad arch that led from the parlor to the foyer. "Penard has a spotless record hiring staff, as you well know. No one he has brought into our employ has ever given you cause to think twice."

"Things change. This new girl—"

"She's only been here a few hours, Samuel."

"But yesterday—"

"She was in the parlor for all of ten minutes and then left directly by the servants' entrance. She was nowhere near your study."

Lucy glanced at the maid, who seemed visibly relieved.

Flora turned to Penard. "You may dismiss the staff, Penard. I'm sure they all have better things to do."

Penard nodded his head almost imperceptibly, and the staff dispersed.

"Samuel, for goodness' sake," Flora said, "it's a paperweight. It's nothing of value."

"That's hardly the point, Flora."

"I'm sure you've just misplaced it. You're not in court. There's no need to put anyone on trial. Stop acting like a foolish old man." Flora's eyes brightened as she looked at her daughter. "Lucy, dear, you're home."

Lucy stepped over to kiss her mother's cheek, one hand behind her back with the satchel.

"Have you been with Daniel in that outfit?" Flora asked.

Lucy sighed. "Yes, Mother. I had no time to come home and change. It's a perfectly good suit."

"It's drab and off the rack. It's a good thing Daniel is as fond of you as he is. I'm surprised he allows you to dress the way you do sometimes."

Lucy's eyes flared but she held her tone. "It's hardly Daniel's decision how I dress for an afternoon at the orphanage, is it?"

"You're going to be his wife soon. Your appearance will reflect on him."

"I promise I'm not going to get married in a gray flannel suit."

"Goodness, I should hope not," Flora said. "Have the two of you settled on a date?"

Lucy let her gaze drift away casually. "Daniel suggested mid-July."

"In the middle of the summer heat! Oh, I don't know, Lucy."

Lucy shrugged. "It's just a suggestion. We haven't decided anything."

"Perhaps I'll have a word with his mother. We don't want to let it become an urgent question."

Lucy smiled. Daniel was of course correct that the mothers would have strong opinions. "The only urgent question I'm facing is what to wear for dinner tonight." She looked from one parent to the other, then took her sulking father's elbow and turned him around. "Why don't the two of you relax in the parlor? Perhaps Mrs. Fletcher can have Bessie bring you some refreshment."

"I'll call for her," Flora said, taking her husband's other arm.

"I had hoped Aunt Violet would be here," Lucy said. "It's Thursday."

"She telephoned this afternoon to say she is otherwise engaged," her mother explained.

"Then I hope she's enjoying herself." Lucy's words masked her disappointment. *Aunt Violet, where are you when I need you?*

By the time Lucy left her parents in the parlor, Flora was talking about the redecorating that should be done before the wedding. As she turned back toward the stairs, across the foyer Lucy saw movement in the dining room. She paused long enough to see it was the new maid beginning to lay the table for dinner. The girl looked up just long enough to catch Lucy's eye before busying herself with the china.

Something's wrong, Lucy thought, *but not what Father thinks.*

5

She had only a few minutes. The table was set for dinner, the potatoes were peeled and roasting, the uniform was crisply ironed and laid on her bed, and dinner for the family was thirty minutes away. Charlotte gulped down her own meal around the kitchen table with the rest of the servants, an unadorned version of what the family would enjoy, yet more than she had eaten in one sitting—or one day—in over a week. She had been resisting the temptation to admit she was hungry for so long that she hardly knew what to do when presented with platters of steaming food. Charlotte ate heartily but hurriedly, grateful for Mrs. Fletcher's suggestion that she use the brief interval before serving dinner to unpack her few personal belongings and transfer them to a narrow chest of drawers opposite her bed.

Charlotte took the stairs quickly, glanced around the hallway upstairs—though she already knew all the servants were downstairs and the family would never come to the servants' quarters—and ducked into her room. Getting settled was not on Charlotte's mind. The second carpetbag, left open slightly in a narrow closet, was her focus. The closet, barely wide enough to contain the bag, had only a muslin curtain to separate it from the room that held nothing beyond a bed, the chest of drawers with a chipped washbowl, and a spindly bedside table. A candle rested on the table, no doubt to supplement the dim electric lightbulb in the center of the room. The sparse décor reminded Charlotte she was not expected to do anything but sleep in this room. Three strides took her to the muslin curtain, which she pushed aside to reach into the bag.

The baby cooed when she picked him up. Charlotte couldn't help but smile.

"Oh, you've been so good," she whispered, "such a quiet little baby. How did I get so lucky to have you?"

He was only three weeks old, but already his eyes seemed to fix on her in recognition and pleasure. Of course, hers was virtually the only face he had ever seen. His birth had been mercifully quick and was over before anyone but one other young woman realized it was happening. Charlotte did not indulge in any lying-in period. There was work to do the day after the birth. And he had come several weeks early, cutting short her planning time for what came next. She had to make rapid adjustments and disappear.

"Dear little Henry, you must be hungry," she mouthed hoarsely. "Let's fill up your little tummy."

Sitting on her bed with her back against the wall, Charlotte unbuttoned her dress, then unlaced her corset. She sighed as she felt the milk begin to flow. Henry was already an efficient eater and fed quickly. So far, he was eating and sleeping, eating and sleeping, and blessedly quiet in between. They both had been awake most of the previous three nights, which put Henry in a routine of sleeping most of the daytime hours. Charlotte knew this could not last long, however. She could not go back where she had come from, but she couldn't possibly keep Henry with her much longer. And she couldn't keep staying awake all night and working all day.

She had to find a place to board Henry. She knew that, but it broke her heart to even think of it. How could she possibly leave him? But she couldn't keep him here, not much longer. The immediate dilemma was that she would not have even a few hours off in the foreseeable future. How was she to find someone to look after Henry under such constraints?

If she thought of how numerous her problems were, Charlotte would dissolve into despair. So she didn't think of how numerous her problems were. She concentrated on each moment as it came.

She had escaped.

She had found a job.

For now, Henry was quiet and easy.

Tomorrow was soon enough to fret about tomorrow's challenges.

First she had to get through this night, serving this first dinner to the family, facing the first early morning call.

Henry was drifting off already. Charlotte brushed his face with a finger to rouse him and shifted him to the other side. He had to be full enough to sleep through the time it would take to serve dinner and clean up. Mrs. Fletcher seemed kind enough despite a brusque manner, and while the admonishment in the foyer had rattled her, Penard did not truly frighten Charlotte. He was nothing compared to what she'd left behind. Nevertheless, she wanted to please Mr. Penard and Mrs. Fletcher when she served dinner for the first time.

The baby was full. By the time Charlotte changed him and sorted out what to do with his wet diaper, he was asleep again. Gently, she laid him on the quilt that cushioned the bottom of the carpetbag. Her grandmother had made that quilt twenty years ago when Charlotte was a newborn herself. It was the only thing—other than Henry and her grandmother's Bible—that she'd brought from home.

Home. Could she even call it that?

A knock on her door made Charlotte gasp and she glanced at Henry, her form still crouched over him and her dress undone. When she heard the doorknob turn, she straightened abruptly and stared wide-eyed while fingering her buttons.

"Mrs. Fletcher wants you." It was Bessie, the parlor maid.

"Yes, of course, I'll be down in a moment," Charlotte answered.

"I rather think she means right now."

"Shouldn't I put my apron on first?" Charlotte snatched the apron off the bed and stood in front of the closet as she put her arms through the holes.

Bessie chuckled. "She'll be wondering what you've been doing all this time. You're not going lazy your first day on the job, are you?"

"She sent me up here to get settled—"

"And now she wants you back. It's been nearly thirty minutes!"

"I hadn't realized." Charlotte fussed with the lace collar on her apron as if to spread it more evenly. "Of course I'll be right there."

Bessie pivoted, and Charlotte listened to her steps clumping down the hallway as she let out her own breath. After one more reassuring look at the slumbering baby, she made her way down the stairs and presented herself to Mrs. Fletcher.

⁓

Lucy shed the gray flannel suit in favor of an ivory silk gown printed with delicate blue tulips, which Elsie had come to button up the back. The sleeves came three-quarters of the way down her arms and culminated in gathered lace elegant for any occasion. It would certainly do for dinner. Occasionally Lucy longed for her younger years when she ate with Nanny in the nursery and the evening meal was not such a production. Nanny had left them the year before. Now that Richard spent his days in school and was old enough to come to the formal table and sit in the parlor in the evenings, Nanny decided to retire and live with her sister and brother-in-law. Although Lucy hadn't needed Nanny's services for years, she still missed her. Other than Aunt Violet, Nanny had been the only one who looked at Lucy as if she were a real person.

Her stomach registered its protest again. At lunch, Lucy had overheard her mother approve the dinner menu: watercress soup, roast pork and potatoes, baby carrots, cranberry-walnut salad, and baked apples. Lucy had to admit it sounded appealing.

Lucy thought about calling Elsie again to come tidy her hair and pin it up more securely for the evening, but just as she reached for the annunciator button, she decided to attempt the task herself. There was no time to wait for Elsie—it was nearly eight. She had consumed the time she should have spent primping by devouring a chapter in her art history textbook, and now she was compelled to hurry. Gazing at herself in the mirror, she concluded her hair was far from a disaster and simply needed some gentle redirection. Lucy stabbed a couple of pins against her scalp, pinched her cheeks pink, and stepped out into the hall. Her mother did not take it well when family members were late for dinner.

Outside her room, Lucy caught the swish of black and white at the end of the hall on the servants' staircase as someone moved from the third floor to the second floor and down toward the kitchen. The door from the family quarters to the staircase was not supposed to be standing open. If Penard discovered it, someone would get a verbal thrashing. Lucy took a few steps to close the door herself, and as she did, glimpsed the back of the new maid hurrying down to the kitchen.

What had Penard said her name was? Charlotte? Yes, that was it. The girl had blanched at Samuel Banning's insinuations two hours ago. Even though Lucy thought her father's accusations unfounded, she felt an unsettling breeze about the new kitchen maid.

"Show time," she told herself. Lucy glided to the other end of the hall and descended the marble steps with her best finishing school posture and polish.

6

*L*ucy put a smile on her face as she entered the parlor, expecting to see her parents seated in their favorite floral-patterned William Morris side chairs awaiting word that dinner was served. Instead she stared into the welcoming blue eyes of Will Edwards as he stood in front of the oak bookcase with glass doors.

"Mr. Edwards! How nice to see you." Lucy resisted the impulse to reach up and press a stray curl on Will's forehead into place, wondering nevertheless what his skin felt like. *Where did that come from? Stop it!*

"Likewise, Miss Banning."

Refusing to blush, Lucy turned to Leo and gave him the sort of look a little sister gives her brother.

Leo grinned. "You said Daniel was not coming for dinner. I thought it was foolish to let the extra table setting go to waste."

Lucy nodded at Will. "Of course I'm delighted you could come to share our meal, Mr. Edwards. I hope Leo has given you fair warning about the eccentricities of the family."

"If his sister is any indication, I am sure to be in for a treat." His cheek dimpled when he smiled.

Lucy wished she had rung for help with her hair after all.

Her gown swished as she crossed the room and sat on the settee.

"I look forward to our dinner conversation," Lucy said. "It's time we had a fresh voice at our table."

Leo jumped in. "Will has some entertaining stories, but I've paid him well to rearrange his memory to remove me from them."

Both Will and Lucy laughed.

"I would imagine your sister has some Leo stories of her own," Will said. "As I recall, you were already an accomplished prankster when you arrived in Princeton."

"Ask me sometime about the lake house and the summer Leo was twelve." Lucy smiled slyly.

"No!" Leo said, laughing himself now. "You will *not* tell that story."

"We shall have to find a moment alone," Will said, "so you can fill me in on the details of the lake house and the summer Leo was twelve."

Now the blush overcame Lucy's willpower, and Will too seemed to retreat momentarily. But in a few seconds Lucy was laughing again.

"What's so funny?" said a voice from the arched doorway.

Lucy looked up to see her parents entering the room. She glanced at Will.

"Oh, nothing," she said. "Mother, Father, I wonder if you've met Leo's friend, Mr. Will Edwards."

Flora Banning glided across the room and shook Will's hand, simultaneously giving Leo a questioning look.

"Will is a friend of mine from Princeton," Leo said.

"We're always delighted to meet a Princeton man," Flora said.

"I'm pleased to meet you also, Mrs. Banning," Will said. "Actually, I—"

Leo cut him off, which made Lucy chuckle again. "Oh,

Mother, let's not go picking at all the Princeton connections," Leo said.

"Will is new to Chicago and Leo thought he could use a good meal," Lucy added.

"Of course, Leo's friends are always welcome." Flora's eyes continued to inspect her unexpected guest.

Samuel Banning failed to take the hint. "Did you graduate with Leo?" he asked.

Will took in a breath as if to answer, but it was Leo who spoke. "Will wasn't in my class. I imagine dinner must be ready. I wonder where Oliver is."

"I'm right here." Oliver, the tallest of the Banning sons by several inches, stood in the doorway with fourteen-year-old Richard right behind him.

The grandfather clock in the foyer began the sonorous process of striking eight as Leo introduced Will to his brothers. Momentarily, Penard appeared, bowed slightly, and announced dinner was served. Samuel indicated that his wife and daughter should lead the procession to the dining room, and Flora put her arm through Lucy's.

In the hall, Flora leaned in and whispered, "Lucy, dear, I'm not entirely sure who this friend of Leo's is, but it seems unseemly that you should be laughing with him."

"What are you talking about, Mother?"

"You might think me an old biddy, but I saw the way you looked at Mr. Edwards."

Heat rose in Lucy's neck. "We were merely teasing Leo. I've done nothing untoward."

"I can't help but think you would behave differently if Daniel were here tonight."

Laughter escaped Lucy's lips. "I assure you, Daniel knows all the old stories about Leo. He features prominently in most of them."

"Nevertheless, I feel I must remind you that you are an engaged woman."

At the double pocket doors leading to the dining room, Lucy disengaged from her mother and walked around the lavish table to her usual spot. She gestured to the chair next to hers. "Mr. Edwards, the extra seat to which my brother referred is here. Perhaps you would be so kind."

The centerpiece featured six ivory candles in gold candlesticks, three at each end of the table, linked by a copper-leafed vine. A dark blue damask tablecloth underlay ivory dishes with scalloped edges and delicate painted blue-flowered trim. Each place setting showcased plates and soup bowl stacked neatly and perfectly centered. Flanking the dishes were forks to the left and knife and spoons to the right, all sterling silver. Bread and butter plates awaited the fresh rolls whose scent wafted from the kitchen and filled the adjoining rooms. Crystal goblets shimmered as the water caught the flickering candlelight in the otherwise dim room.

Will held Lucy's chair for her, then took his own on her left. Richard slid into his chair on Lucy's right, and Leo and Oliver were seated across from them. Samuel held his wife's chair at one end of the table, then strode to the other end for his own. Lucy almost wished Will were seated across from her, where she could more easily admire his features.

Samuel Banning lowered his head to give thanks for the food. Lucy was grateful for the coming meal, but at moments like this she often calculated how many orphan stomachs could be filled with the food that no doubt would be left over or pushed to the edges of the Banning plates. Silently, she enriched her father's prayer with one of her own.

As soon as Samuel said "Amen," the footman appeared with the soup tureen. With the skill of daily experience, he ladled the watercress soup into bowls without splattering. As he did so, Penard placed rolls on the bread and butter plates. Soup spoons and butter knives began to clink.

"Mr. Edwards, how are you finding Chicago?" Lucy asked. "I don't believe Leo mentioned how long you've been here."

"I just arrived this week," Will responded. "It's certainly a change from New Jersey, but Chicago seems to be quite the up-and-coming city. I can see the attraction for all the people who are moving here."

Flora Banning set her fork down harder than etiquette would suggest. "Our families have been here for decades," she said. "We're looking forward to launching yet another generation. Did Lucy mention she is engaged to be married?"

"Mother," Lucy protested.

Will took it in stride. "I understand from Leo that she is to marry Daniel Jules, a dear family friend," he said. "I wish them every happiness." He turned and smiled at Lucy.

"I would like to know more about the work you'll be doing," Lucy said. She busied herself with a spoonful of soup while he answered. Will described some of the experience he had with the New Jersey firm and how he had come to be recommended to the firm in Chicago. Though young, he had developed a specialty in helping to design buildings for public use, and he thought a young, growing city such as Chicago would provide plenty of opportunities for creativity.

Charlotte appeared to remove the soup bowls. Something in Lucy inclined her to try to catch the maid's eye, but she restrained herself. It was the girl's first day, after all. It would not bode well if Penard perceived she did not achieve the goal of being smoothly unnoticed in her service.

Roast pork and potatoes came next, followed by baby carrots and the cranberry-walnut salad. By the time the baked apples appeared, conversation had turned to the coming World's Columbian Exposition, a topic of common interest.

"I understand from Leo that your family is quite involved in the fair," Will said.

"My father is on the board of directors," Lucy offered. "It's been quite a consuming task."

"I can only imagine the challenges," Will said. "Mr. Banning, I would be interested to hear what has been the most pressing issue in presenting the fair to the world."

"Ferris," Samuel said.

"Sir?"

"George Ferris," Samuel said. "A young engineer. He has some wild idea about building an enormous wheel that would take people in cars around the circle."

"That sounds fascinating!" Will and Lucy spoke simultaneously.

Samuel rolled his eyes. "The engineers and architects at the Saturday Afternoon Club think he's out of his mind. They say it can't be done. I am neither engineer nor architect, but if anyone were to be injured on such a contraption, the legal ramifications would be enormous."

Will looked thoughtful, forgetting about his baked apple for the moment. "What a feat that would be! I haven't seen the plans, of course, but I imagine it calls for some elements of physics that have not been tested in the general population."

Leo jumped in. "As a machine engineer, I would love to see those plans. People have got to understand that the future of machines is going to break new ground in all aspects of life."

"Perhaps I'll arrange for the two of you to inspect the plans," Samuel said. "The committee has not yet made any final decision."

Will nodded. "I'd be honored, sir, even if only to satisfy my own curiosity about how Mr. Ferris would support such a structure architecturally."

Flora pushed away her empty dessert plate. "I heard the

White Star Line is planning to exhibit at the fair. Lucy, that would be a lovely opportunity for you and Daniel to plan a honeymoon sea voyage to Europe on an exquisite ship."

Lucy smiled politely. "We haven't even set the wedding date, Mother. Daniel and I have not discussed the honeymoon yet." She turned to Will. "Mr. Edwards, will you be attending the fair's dedication next week?"

"I hadn't thought about it," he answered.

"Oh, you must come," Leo urged. "The fair won't open until spring, unfortunately, but the dignitaries are going ahead with the ceremony next Friday in spite of the delays. Your firm is involved. I'm sure they'll be represented in the crowd."

"I will make a point to inquire."

Lucy hoped Will's enthusiasm was genuine.

"Father is not the only one who has been busy with the fair. Lucy has been involved in the women's exhibit," Leo said.

Will turned to Lucy. "I'm delighted to hear that. I'm pleased to know there will be a special hall dedicated to the achievements of women."

Lucy brightened. "Perhaps you've heard of the architect for our building. Sophia Hayden is the first female graduate of the Massachusetts Institute of Technology with qualifications in architecture."

"I have heard of her," Will responded. "She was barely out of college when she won the competition to get the commission."

"Just twenty-two years old," Lucy said. *Only a year older than I am. What do I have to show for myself?*

"Lucy has time for such things now," Flora said, "but she may be a married woman by the time the fair opens."

"Married or not, I will fulfill my commitment," Lucy said.

"And what is your commitment to the women's exhibit, may I ask?" Will said.

"Nothing very exciting, I'm afraid," Lucy responded. "The women who are contributing to the exhibit are true artists. The best I have to offer is to help with correspondence and practical arrangements."

"That is a gift as well," Will commented. "Many people would be overwhelmed with such a task."

"In truth it's simply a matter of being persistent," Lucy said, "and keeping track of the details."

Flora spoke. "It's a skill that will come in handy when you finally begin planning your own wedding."

Lucy lifted her eyes and glanced around the table. "Perhaps we should have our coffee in the parlor."

Samuel scooted his chair back. "You have my vote." He glanced at Penard, who stood against one wall, and the butler stiffly turned toward the parlor to arrange service.

As the family and their guest rose and began to drift toward the parlor, Charlotte appeared and began clearing away the last of the dishes. Lucy watched in her peripheral vision as the young maid stacked dishes—and as a dessert plate escaped her grasp and tumbled to the floor. Lucy winced on Charlotte's behalf and turned ever so slightly to see the outcome. Thick carpet under the table prevented any serious damage, and Penard stepped over to both help with the plates and scold the maid.

The incident did not escape Samuel's notice. "I hope Penard knows what he's doing hiring that girl," he muttered.

"It's just nerves," Lucy speculated. "It's her first day."

Lucy paused long enough to see Penard shoo Charlotte toward the kitchen. The starched white apron disappeared behind doors to the butler's pantry that Lucy rarely transgressed. Lucy had seen servants come and go over the years—most of the lower-level servants didn't last two years before moving on—but something about Charlotte tugged at Lucy. If

Charlotte had been a girl at the orphanage, Lucy would have followed her to be sure she was all right. However, she could count on one hand the times she had been in the Banning kitchen. Even her mother rarely went through those doors.

"Miss Banning? Are you coming?"

Lucy turned to Will's cobalt eyes and irresistible—*I must resist*—dimpled cheek. "Yes, of course."

7

$\mathscr{I}$f not for the grace of alertness pulsed by anxiety, Charlotte would have been unconscious. Henry had, predictably, been wide awake much of the night, and Charlotte didn't dare let him feel even a moment's discomfort lest he cry. The walls were thin on the servants' floor, demanding she anticipate his every need and satisfy it before he had reason to protest. Catnaps were all she could hope for. She tended to his wriggling in the shadows of the moon for fear that turning on the electric light, or even lighting a candle, would attract the attention of an insomniac—or nosey—neighbor. With each rousing Charlotte glanced out the window to judge how soon the morning light would break. Knowing she must be up and ready to work before sunlight, she fed the baby freely in the predawn hours to begin another day of hoping, praying, he would stay full enough to sleep and the other servants would have little reason to be upstairs during the day. When she heard Mrs. Fletcher stirring in the room next door, Charlotte tucked her slumbering son in his carpetbag bed.

By the time Mrs. Fletcher appeared in the kitchen, Charlotte was cracking eggs in a porcelain bowl. Minutes later, she carved slices from the ham stored in the oak icebox, and soon after that she was arranging plums and apricots in a bowl. The cook gave an almost imperceptible nod of approval at Charlotte's prompt initiative and lit the stove to heat the griddle for French toast.

"Good morning," Charlotte said. "When will the family come down?"

"Mr. Banning will be first," Mrs. Fletcher answered, "then young Richard. They'll leave the house together in a carriage that will deliver young Richard to school and take Mr. Banning to his office downtown. The others will follow soon enough, though Mrs. Banning will likely call for a tray in her room. But before that, the staff will need their breakfast. You'd better lay the table in here for the staff, then in the dining room for the family."

"Yes, ma'am."

"Don't forget a place for Mr. Daniel. He came in late last night, rather than go all the way home to Riverside."

"Yes, ma'am."

⁓⁓

When Lucy arrived in the dining room, she was wearing a dark navy woolen dress with crimson satin trim around the collar and cuffs, the only ornamentation of her garb.

Daniel looked up from his financial newspaper. "Another of your orphan frocks?"

"Good morning to you too," Lucy responded. "I hope you slept well."

Daniel leaned back in his chair and smiled. Lucy recognized the smile for which she had fallen so many times over the years, a curve of the lip meant to cut through her irritability and make her see things his way. *It's not working this time.* She inspected the scrambled eggs on the buffet.

"I'm sorry," Daniel said. "It was rude of me to greet you that way. Let's start over."

"All right." Lucy sat down next to Daniel and leaned in slightly for him to kiss her cheek. "Good morning, Daniel."

"Good morning, Lucy. What a flattering color your dress is."

Charlotte stood by ready to serve. Lucy glanced at the maid. "I'd love some eggs and fruit," she said.

Charlotte moved smoothly to the buffet to prepare a plate and momentarily placed it before Lucy.

"I rather hoped we could have a day off today." Daniel cut a bite of ham. "I sealed an important deal last night and I'm in the mood to celebrate."

"I'm glad your meeting went well," Lucy said. "Charlotte, may I have some coffee as well, please?"

"So how about it?" Daniel asked. "You could put on one of your new silk suits and we can make a day of it. Perhaps we'll even find time to talk about the wedding without interruption."

There's that smile again.

Lucy swallowed the bite of egg in her mouth. "Daniel, it's Friday."

"Yes, I know," he said, "one of your regular days at the orphanage. But surely they can do without you for one day. You give them so much of your time."

"I've made a commitment. Mr. Emmett is expecting me."

"You can phone and beg off."

"The orphanage has no telephone."

"Then send a message. Your footman can take it."

"It's not that easy, Daniel. The day has been arranged with the assumption that I would be there to perform certain tasks."

"Surely they can wait until Tuesday."

Lucy of course could not explain she would not be at the orphanage on Tuesday because she would be attending an art history lecture. She couldn't possibly tell Mr. Emmett the work would have to wait a full week.

"Why don't we spend the evening together?" Lucy brightened her tone. "We can take a carriage ride out to the lake and have dinner on our own downtown."

Daniel sipped his coffee. "I'm not sure I like coming in second to your orphans."

"They're not 'my' orphans," Lucy said quietly. She set down her fork and swallowed the indignation that welled within her. "They're children who have no parents or who cannot live with their parents for whatever reason. They're human beings who need help. And I promised to help today."

"I'm afraid I don't understand why you must be so personally involved with these street urchins," Daniel said, "but I will respect that you want to keep a promise. I only hope you have the same passion for keeping your promise to me."

"Daniel—"

He threw his napkin on the table and pushed his chair back. "Perhaps I will go into the office today after all. I'll see you tonight for that carriage ride. Please remember to allow time to change your dress." He left the dining room without looking at Lucy again.

Lucy sighed and pushed her plate away. "You can take this," she said to Charlotte. "I've lost my appetite."

<hr />

Lucy chose to dismiss the carriage driver and walk the last few blocks to St. Andrew's Orphanage. She wanted the morning exchange with Daniel out of her system before she entered St. Andrew's, and walking always energized her. When he wanted to, Daniel could turn on the charm like no one else she had ever met. What did he have against innocent children?

"Miss Banning!"

Lucy turned toward the voice. "Mr. Edwards! How nice to see you." Breakfast conversation faded immediately.

Will fell into step with Lucy. "Where are you off to on this fine morning?"

"St. Andrew's," Lucy said. "Fridays are a regular day to volunteer."

"Leo told me you offered your time three afternoons a week."

"On Fridays I often spend the entire day." She had to, with so much left undone during her absences on Tuesday and Thursday afternoons.

"I admire your generosity," Will said. "I'm sure you could find any number of ways to spend your time."

"I enjoy the children."

"I imagine they enjoy you as well."

Lucy smiled. "It is rather a mutual admiration society."

"I'm not in a position to make a substantial financial donation," Will said, "but I'm not afraid to roll up my sleeves and do whatever needs to be done. I hope you will not hesitate to call on me if you feel I can be of assistance."

"What a lovely offer, Mr. Edwards. I shall be sure to pass it on to Mr. Emmett, the director."

"I hope you will feel comfortable calling me Will. Leo has told me so many stories about you the last few years, I rather feel I know you quite well already."

"If only Leo had honored me with as many stories!" Lucy laughed gently. "I feel at a disadvantage."

"I'm sure Leo can remedy that if you only ask."

"Perhaps I will." Lucy paused and glanced across an intersection. "This is my corner."

Will bowed slightly. "My streetcar stop is another four blocks. It was my pleasure to walk these few steps with you, Miss Banning."

"Lucy, please. And the pleasure was mine."

Will watched as Lucy crossed the street and climbed seven steps to the red front door of St. Andrew's Orphanage. As her blue dress disappeared across the threshold, he reluctantly turned to continue his saunter to the streetcar. Will had enjoyed Leo's friendship for three years, including accounts of his boyish escapades with his sister only a year younger. But now that Will had met Lucy Banning for himself, he was not sure what to make of her. She seemed every bit as spirited as Leo always led him to believe she was. Will had known Lucy would marry a family friend long before he ever imagined meeting Leo's family in person. The move from New Jersey to Chicago had been unexpected and swift. His encounter with the Bannings had amounted to one dinner, decided on short notice, and Will had little reason to think it would amount to more than an occasional crossing of paths.

Samuel and Flora Banning had lived up to Leo's descriptions of them, and Oliver and Richard were no particular surprise. But Lucy was another matter.

Lucy Banning was an engaged woman. But Lucy Banning was unlike any engaged woman Will had ever known.

"Good morning, Jane." Lucy greeted the eleven-year-old who often helped her with the clerical records in the office. Jane had come to St. Andrew's when she was eight after the sudden death of both of her parents. By the time Lucy met her two years later, Jane had a hard edge about her. Lucy was determined to sand it down and transform that perpetual sulk into at least one smile with each visit.

Jane's dark braids draped forward on her shoulders against the yellow cotton of her dress, a garment Lucy knew had been worn by at least two other girls before it came to Jane.

Brown eyes brooded under thick eyebrows as the girl sat on a wobbly wooden chair awaiting instructions.

"Are you caught up on your lessons?" Lucy asked. "I promised Mr. Emmett I would not take you away from your schoolwork."

Jane nodded. She rarely spoke, but she was a bright child who followed instructions accurately and worked efficiently.

"Let's go in the office," Lucy said. "Mr. Emmett has asked that we sort through the records in the two file cabinets against the wall and pull out the files for children who have moved on from St. Andrew's. I'm counting on you to help me recognize the names of the older children. Can you do that for me?"

The girl nodded again and followed Lucy down the hall. The brick structure of St. Andrew's had five stories, housed more than four hundred children, and contained its own school up through the eighth grade. After that, capable students went to a conventional high school, while others entered the working world—often in the employ of families like Lucy's or the growing number of factories around the city. The classrooms were in the front of the building on two floors. At the rear of the first story was a series of cramped offices for the director, assistant director, and volunteers. Just as Lucy approached the office, she was accosted around the hips. Laughing, she stooped to hug the child. "Benny, I'm happy to see you too," she told the six-year-old boy. "But shouldn't you be in class?"

"I told Teacher I had to see you," Benny said. "I told her I know you come on Fridays. She said I could go, but I have to come right back."

Lucy kissed the top of his head. "Then you'd better hurry back. You don't want to miss your arithmetic lesson. Ask permission to come find me again when school is out for the day."

Lucy continued to the office, squeezing past a desk in the hallway and a bookcase that made the narrow doorway almost impassable. *Will probably would have an idea to make this space more efficient*, she thought.

Lucy pulled open the top file drawer. "Okay, Miss Jane, let's get to work."

8

Then it's settled," Lucy said to her family at luncheon on Saturday. "Everyone plans to be engaged for the afternoon and evening."

"Are you sure you and Daniel don't want to join us at the Glessners'?" her mother asked.

"I'm afraid Daniel and I have other plans." *Just not together*, she did not add aloud.

Mentally she was leaping at the chance to be alone in the house with access to her father's library. The truth was Daniel would be busy all day and into the evening, wooing a new investor for the bank.

"Father, if no one is going to be home, why not give the staff the evening off?" Lucy suggested.

"I'll need Elsie when I get home," Flora protested.

"And Archie will have to see to the horses," Oliver added.

"Yes, but forgoing dinner preparation and serving would relieve the staff of considerable work for a few hours. Why not let them enjoy a half day on their own?" Lucy put her own dinner at risk with this suggestion, since no one would prepare her evening fare, but the midday meal had been filling enough to carry her until the next morning.

"I suppose there's no harm in it," Samuel said. With a

glance he authorized Penard to dismiss the staff for a few hours.

———◦◦◦———

Lucy thought they'd never leave! Now she sat in the brown leather armchair in her father's study, holding a book of replications of neoclassical paintings of a century ago with their hallmark order and clarity. The book had been on Samuel's shelf for years. This was Lucy's chance to study it without evoking questions about a sudden interest in art. She wondered if she dared take it upstairs to her room. Would her father even miss it? Considering that only two days ago he was flustered about a mislaid paperweight—which still hadn't turned up—Lucy decided it was wise to confine her exploration of the book to the study.

Lucy stared at an image meant to illustrate the tremendous strides Russian painters had made in technique and style during the Enlightenment, but she couldn't get Daniel out of her mind. Despite their quarrel at breakfast the day before, Daniel had arrived in an ornate carriage promptly at five-thirty in the afternoon and they took a leisurely ride to the lakefront. Lucy had suggested the outing because the lake was one of Daniel's favorite places to relax, and apparently the mere anticipation of it had soothed his nerves. He loved the shoreline at Lake Forest, but when it was not possible to go to the lake house, he feasted on the view of the lake in Chicago. By the time he had appeared at the Banning house, it was as if the morning never happened. Rather than badger her about setting a wedding date, he recounted humorous episodes at the bank—and Daniel could tell a good story. Lucy was glad to hear him laugh, and she laughed with him. Rather than disparage her work at the orphanage, he imagined how he would approach painting the October sky hanging over Lake Michigan with its multifaceted gray hues.

Daniel had a discerning eye for color and brushstrokes, though he had not lifted a paintbrush since before he went off to college. One of his last projects was to illustrate a children's chapter book as a gift to Lucy. He'd taken apart the binding, added a one-of-a-kind illustration for each chapter, and had the book rebound. She still had the book in the bottom drawer of a dresser in her suite. By the time it dawned on Lucy—still a girl at the time of the gift—that Daniel had given up art, he insisted he was not returning to a hobby of his youth. He was a banker, not a painter, he told Lucy, and he had to stay focused to succeed. Nevertheless, she enjoyed imagining with him on the rare occasion he let his artist self peek out.

He was Daniel at his finest on Friday evening. Lucy was reminded of all the reasons Daniel could be as appealing as he was to so many people, and how easy it would be to slip into life at his side, on his arm, as his wife.

But she wouldn't, of course.

Lucy turned a page in the art book and tried to refocus with a fresh image.

She and her brothers were planning a surprise anniversary party for her parents in a few weeks. Daniel and his parents already were wound up with pleasure just thinking about the event. After the party, Christmas would soon be upon them, and the two families always spent the holiday together. And of course the New Year's festivities would be grand. Daniel would have a list of balls they could choose from, and most likely they would drop in on several of them, saving their favorite for the stroke of midnight.

Could she really stay engaged to Daniel until after New Year's for the sake of a peaceful holiday season?

In the silence, Lucy easily heard the horse clip-clop to a stop on the brick outside the house. She lurched from the chair and craned her neck at the window to see Leo and Will stepping out of a carriage. *What are they doing here?* She couldn't be found in her father's study. Lucy slammed the art book shut, shoved it into its spot on the shelf, pushed her textbook under a cushion, and scampered down the hall to the parlor, where she picked up the far less conspicuous *Dictionary of Needlework*. She saw out the parlor window that the two men were headed for the front entrance.

Leo threw open the front door and glanced in the direction of the parlor. They all did that, Lucy knew. The family's first impulse when arriving home was to look and see if anyone else was home—even when no one was supposed to be there. Lucy found herself staring at both Leo and Will.

"Lucy!" Leo pulled off his calfskin gloves. "I thought you were out with Daniel."

"Not at the moment," Lucy responded.

"I can see that. Since you have time on your hands, you can entertain Will for a few minutes."

Will put his hands up. "Please, don't let me disturb you."

"It's no disturbance." Leo spoke for Lucy, a characteristic that had irritated her for as long as she could remember. In this instance, however, he was right.

"It's no trouble," Lucy agreed.

"I'll only be a few minutes. I just need to change. Will has never been boating on Lake Michigan, and I intend to rectify that." With that assurance, Leo took the marble steps two at a time, leaving Lucy and Will to stare at each other.

Lucy stood up rather belatedly. "I'm sorry. I'm being rude. Please do come in and sit down."

"Are you quite sure I'm not disturbing you?"

"Not in the least."

"What are you reading?" Will sat stiffly in a side chair.

Lucy laid the needlework book down on the side table, front cover down. "Nothing, really. Just something I picked up to pass the time."

Will glanced around the room. "Your mother has done a remarkable job in here."

Lucy chuckled. "Yes, she would like to think so, but as you can probably imagine, she had the help of an expensive decorator. Just like everyone else on Prairie Avenue."

"It's such a curious neighborhood," Will remarked.

Lucy raised an eyebrow. "How so?"

"Oh, I mean no offense, of course," Will said quickly. "It's just that I find the architecture fascinating. So many well-known architectural firms have taken commissions here—Burnham and Root, Treat and Foltz, Cobb and Frost. And one look at the Glessner home tells me that Henry Hobson Richardson was not afraid to distinguish himself, as he always did. He was based in Boston, but his influence is far-reaching, even after his death six years ago."

"It seems you're quite the student of Prairie Avenue," Lucy observed.

"No one with aspirations in architecture can ignore Prairie Avenue. One can easily imagine this neighborhood will be an attraction to visitors who come to Chicago for the World's Columbian Exposition next year."

Lucy leaned slightly toward Will. "Between you and me, it does seem a bit much sometimes. Every now and then I calculate how many orphans could be housed in one home on Prairie Avenue—probably without inconvenience to the families who live here."

"The orphanage is lucky to have you," Will said. "I mean that."

"It's the least I can do," Lucy said. "I have no home of

my own, no money of my own. I have very little control over anything, when you get right down to it. I'm holding out to call time my own and spend it as I choose—with the children who have so little."

"Perhaps when you're married you'll have other resources at your disposal as well."

I doubt it, Lucy thought. Aloud she said, "I'm so sorry not to offer you refreshment. I would ring for a tray, but we've given the staff the day off."

"No bother. Leo promised this would be a quick stop."

"He seems to be welcoming you to Chicago with gusto!"

"Leo does everything with gusto, but I'm sure you know that."

"Yes. As a little girl, I always wanted to be where Leo was, because it was sure to be more exciting than my needlework or lessons."

"Then you know well why I enjoy your brother and allow him to whisk me around."

Lucy laughed, and just then Leo appeared in the doorway. A straw boater hat topped off the striped blazer and flannel trousers that Leo, like all the young men of Prairie Avenue, wore on boating excursions. He cocked his hat on his head, showing off the silk hatband.

"While we're all here," Leo said, "let's sort out this art exhibit business. How about Tuesday evening?"

"It turns out I must be at the disposal of my employers that evening," Will said. "Some last-minute business before the fair dedication. How about Monday?"

"I have a department dinner at the university that night," Leo said. "It's sure to be full of boring speeches, but I'm told it's mandatory. Wednesday will be busy with fair preparations, and Thursday is sure to be crowded with the fair dedication on Friday." He paused thoughtfully. "Lucy, I know it was your idea to go, so why don't the two of you go on Monday without me?"

Lucy and Will spoke at the same time.

"Oh, I'm not sure—"

"I don't think—"

Leo interrupted them both. "I know. Lucy is an engaged woman, and even if she weren't, propriety demands you have an escort."

"Leo, it's not . . ." Lucy felt herself blushing against her will.

"I have the same mother you have," Leo said. "So here's what we'll do. I will escort you from the house on some pretext, and we'll meet up with Will at the gallery. Then I'll duck out to my boring dinner and meet up with you a few hours later and bring you home. In the meantime you and Will can gawk and gaze to your heart's content."

"Leo, might that be overly duplicitous?" Lucy's pulse beat faster at the thought.

"You could ask Mother to go with you," Leo teased.

"Don't you dare," Lucy snapped.

"Or Daniel." Leo's green eyes lit.

"Daniel has a wonderful eye for art," Lucy said, surprising even herself.

"He just doesn't find it practical," Leo said. "He won't go without protest. You'll never get out of the house on your own in the evening. If you genuinely want to look at these paintings, you're better off with Will."

"That's all true. However, a chaperone would be safer than your shenanigans," Lucy said. "Perhaps Aunt Violet?"

"Yes, possibly, if you feel you must have a chaperone. But Will is quite keen to go, you know."

"Do I get a vote in these arrangements?" Will asked.

Leo grinned and raised an eyebrow.

Will turned to Lucy. "Miss Banning, my friend has asked me to escort his sister and it would be my pleasure to do so. May I see you at seven on Monday evening? We will of course enjoy the company of your aunt."

"Good, then it's all arranged," Leo said. "I'll talk to Violet myself. Come on, Will, we have to get moving. The lake can get choppy in the afternoons this time of year." He tipped his hat to Lucy. "We're off to the new Columbia Yacht Club. I'm trying to persuade Father to join."

And before she could protest further, Lucy was once again alone. With a sigh of surrender, she returned to the study and pulled her book off the shelf to resume her study. As she turned the pages to find her place again, Will's features mingled in her view of every painting.

Will Edwards was simply her brother's friend. Leo had brought many young men home with him over the years, and none of them had ever made Lucy think twice about Daniel Jules. She had known she would marry Daniel as surely as spring gives way to summer. Her future with Daniel Jules was not imperiled because of Will Edwards. Lucy was certain of that. After all, she had met Will only three days ago, and she had been testing her feelings for Daniel for weeks.

Lucy's realization of how she felt about Daniel was indistinct. She didn't have a list of reasons not to marry him. She harbored no ill will toward him and in fact held cherished memories. Clearly he would be a successful banker and offered her a comfortable life. In time she was sure she could broker an agreement that allowed her some involvement with the orphanage. All she had to do was make it seem advantageous to Daniel, which she was confident she could do. Their families would continue flowing in and out of each other's lives.

Still, it would not work.

Lucy sighed again, this time in fatigue. The words and pictures in the book were not sinking in. Maybe a short but brisk walk would help. Lucy reached for the miniature tin hammered box where her father kept his business cards. She wanted one for a bookmark. He fastidiously had kept the box on the same corner of his desk for at least ten years.

But the box was not there. Not on the desk. Not on the credenza. Not on a bookshelf. Not in a drawer. Lucy was sure she had seen it on Thursday.

Was it possible Samuel Banning was not as forgetful as the family chided him for being? Or perhaps far more forgetful than any of them imagined?

Lucy put the book back on the shelf without a bookmark, picked up her textbook, walked down the hall to the foyer, and started up the steps for a cape to wear outside.

That's when she heard it. It stopped almost as soon as it started, a soft mewing, faint but earnest. Lucy froze on the stairs and cocked her head to listen. Nothing. Richard had been nagging to get a kitten, and Lucy wouldn't put it past him to sneak one into the house. Her skirts swished as she began to move again.

There it was. She stilled her skirts and held her breath.

And it came again.

It was no kitten. With countless hours at the orphanage, Lucy knew the cry of a newborn when she heard it. Deftly she moved through the dining room toward the sound, and once again it suddenly silenced.

By now she was sure the sound had come from the kitchen, beyond the butler's pantry that linked the dining room and kitchen. The staff was supposed to be out. No one should be in the kitchen. As a child, Lucy had not been allowed in the kitchen. Once, when she was eight and wandered into the but-ler's pantry out of curiosity about the smells wafting into the dining room, Penard had pounced on her, turned her around, and marched her out. Her mother sternly admonished her to stay out of the kitchen. Lucy hadn't been through those doors in years. In reality, she still was not allowed in there.

But that sound!

She would only know for sure if she did the unthinkable.

9

*L*ucy stood at the door to the butler's pantry, one hand clutching her textbook and the other tentatively raised to push the door open. She stood perfectly still, lest the rustle of her skirts mask the slightest noise from within those mysterious walls. But the sound had stopped and several minutes passed—long enough for her to think perhaps it was nothing after all. Lucy shifted the book, using both arms now to press it against her chest as she held her breath. No baby's cry reached her ears, but the more she listened, the more Lucy believed someone was in the kitchen. Mrs. Fletcher would make no effort to silence ordinary sounds, nor would Penard or Archie or Bessie or Elsie.

Charlotte.

The new maid was the unknown factor.

Muffled shuffling made Lucy lean into the door with one shoulder. Quickly she crossed the pantry and ducked through the shorter, broader door to the kitchen. She peered in—and gasped.

"Charlotte!" Lucy couldn't believe what she saw.

Charlotte sucked in her breath and clutched her bundle closer. She sprang out of her chair at the table where the servants ate. "Miss Lucy! Please, miss, I can explain—"

"You have a baby!" Disbelief and intrigue fused in Lucy's hushed voice. She moved toward the quilt in Charlotte's arms. The baby cooed.

Charlotte exhaled and offered no further resistance. Lucy saw the tear eking its way out of Charlotte's left eye. Charlotte could have been any number of young women who appeared at the orphanage, stricken, bereft of any option but to place their children in care because men had run off or died or never been husbands in the first place. Every week, Lucy saw them arrive, terrified and agonized at having reached their last option. She took their names and whatever false address or employment information they might leave and opened files on their offspring. The children might be newborns or toddlers or nearly ready for school.

The art book slithered out of Lucy's hands to the table as she reached out to fold back a quilt corner. "He's so young!" she marveled. The baby's startled blue eyes stared at her out of a serious plump face topped with brown feathery fuzz. "But how are you possibly managing a baby? Penard would never have taken you on if he knew."

"I know, miss. I didn't tell him. I couldn't. And Henry is so little trouble."

"Where have you kept him?"

"In a carpetbag in my closet."

"Charlotte, you must know you can't possibly keep him here."

"Yes, miss." Charlotte swallowed hard. "I had to start working before I can board him."

"You have no money?"

Charlotte shook her head.

"Have you arranged a place to board him?" Lucy probed.

"No, miss. I can hardly bring myself to think of it." Charlotte leaned forward and kissed the top of Henry's head.

"What about his father?"

Charlotte merely shook her head more vigorously. Rather than dissolving in tears, she composed herself and straightened her posture. "Henry and I are on our own."

"He can't be more than six weeks old."

"Three weeks and two days. He came early, but he's growing every day."

What an impossible situation, Lucy thought. Obviously Charlotte could not keep a baby in the household. Whatever situation made her abandon her previous home with a newborn and no job must have been dire. Under what circumstances could hiding a baby be the better option? Lucy had witnessed the wrenching hearts as mothers left their children at St. Andrew's. Many of them intended to visit regularly. Employment obligations, distance, lack of transportation, living on a pittance—these added up to notes meant to substitute temporarily for visits, and gradually lengthy lapses between notes, and finally the realization that children who did have a parent would nevertheless grow up in St. Andrew's along with children who did not. Lucy understood Charlotte's reluctance to leave her baby in the care of another woman, yet keeping him at the Banning house would never work. He would get older and bigger and louder and need more attention than a working maid could give. Neither Penard nor Mrs. Fletcher would stand for it, not to mention Samuel and Flora.

It simply wasn't done on Prairie Avenue.

"Charlotte, you look like you haven't slept," Lucy said softly.

"Four nights now, miss," Charlotte confessed. "Henry sleeps all day as long as I can sneak up and feed him, but he wants his mama at night."

"Of course he does." With gentle pressure on the maid's arm, Lucy guided her to sit with her at the table. The unpadded straight-back chairs felt narrow and unfamiliar. Lucy couldn't help but glance around the kitchen, soaking in details of food preparation mystery. Pots hung on hooks from the ceiling, and bins held flour, sugar, and potatoes. Knives on a butcher block awaited the next meal. Open shelves held the dishes she supposed the servants ate off, and a wide modern stove gleamed.

"I wanted some hot water to give him a bath," Charlotte explained. "I would not have brought him down with me if I had known you were home. I'm so sorry I disturbed you, miss."

"That's not important, Charlotte. The question is what are you going to do with Henry?"

Charlotte raised her eyes and fixed them on Lucy's face for the first time. "Are you going to tell Mr. Penard? Or your parents?"

Charlotte had every reason to ask, Lucy knew. One word from her and Charlotte would be out on the street without even the wages she had earned in the last two days. Penard never would have entertained hiring a maid with a baby, and Flora Banning never would have given approval. No one in the household was attached enough to the new maid to argue she should be kept on after such deception. A maid in Charlotte's position was up early, before the family, and worked long hours until well after dark. She might have a couple of hours in the afternoon when she could get off her feet and put her hands to work on mending or other needlework for the family. Her job was to take care of the family's needs, not look after a child who would grow in mobility, appetite, and demands.

"If it's all the same to you, miss," Charlotte said, "I'll just duck upstairs for my things. I can be gone before anyone else comes home." She stood and turned toward the stairs.

Lucy put a hand on Charlotte's arm. "No, please don't do that."

"But, Miss Lucy—"

"We'll figure something out." Lucy pressed her grip more firmly. "I'd like to help you."

Charlotte's gaze drifted around the kitchen, uncertain.

"Charlotte, please, let me help. I have connections. I can make some telephone calls. Perhaps you don't know of my volunteer work at St. Andrew's Orphanage."

"Henry is not an orphan!" A sob stole breath in Charlotte's protest.

"No, of course not," Lucy was quick to reassure. "He has you. Many of the children at St. Andrew's have one parent."

"I can't put him in a place like that. I won't."

"The children there are well cared for, I assure you." Lucy began to feel defensive. It wasn't as if Charlotte had other viable options. "They are fed, they sleep in warm beds, and they go to school. You can visit whenever you like."

"But it's such a big place, Miss Lucy, and so many children. How can they look after my little Henry?"

It was a good point, and Lucy didn't have to be a mother to understand. "Sometimes the director is able to place babies in homes with women who care for them," Lucy explained. "I don't know if any of these women are available right now, but please let me try."

"How will he eat?" Charlotte asked.

"A wet nurse," Lucy answered, "or Nestle infant formula, which would not cost you anything."

"Will I be able to see him on my afternoons off?"

"Any time you want. You can even take him on outings, if you like."

"They won't try to adopt him out?"

"Not if you don't want them to."

Charlotte pressed her lips together, then said, "You would really do this for me? Without saying anything?"

"Yes, Charlotte, I will—if you'll let me."

"When?"

"It might take a few days to arrange," Lucy admitted. "You could leave him at St. Andrew's until—"

"No! I don't want to take him there. It's bad enough to give him to another woman."

"Very well." Lucy backed off. "But it will still take a few days, and you're both at risk in the meantime. Are you sure you want to take that chance?"

Charlotte stroked her son's cheek. "I have to."

"I can't talk to the orphanage director until Monday," Lucy explained, "and then we'll have to wait to see what he can arrange. The fair dedication is on Friday, and I know things are going to be bustling around here getting ready for that. I can't make any promises about how quickly this can be done if you're not willing to leave him at St. Andrew's."

Charlotte shook her head. "No. I'd rather take my chances with Mr. Penard."

"Very well, then. One step at a time. I promise I will not say a word to anyone."

"I don't know how to thank you," Charlotte whispered, her eyes lowered.

Lucy held out her arms. "Let me hold your baby. That will be thanks enough."

Smiling with pride, Charlotte laid her son in Lucy's arms. He blinked his eyes twice, then closed them, seeming to settle in securely.

"He trusts you," Charlotte said.

"I hope to live up to his trust and yours," Lucy answered.

Charlotte's gaze settled on the forgotten art textbook on the table. "That book must weigh more than Henry," she said. "It looks like a fancy schoolbook."

Lucy glanced at the book, then back at Charlotte. "I have a secret of my own," she confessed. "It *is* a schoolbook. I'm enrolled in an art history course at the University of Chicago."

Charlotte's eyes widened. "And Mr. and Mrs. Banning don't know? Is that the secret?"

Lucy shook her head. "Only my Aunt Violet knows. Everyone else thinks I'm at the orphanage more than I am."

"But Mr. Daniel—"

"He would not understand."

"Your secret is safe with me, Miss Lucy. No one will hear any different. Are you going to earn a college degree like your brothers?"

Lucy shrugged. "One step at a time, just like you."

Charlotte smiled, looking at Lucy full on. "What a pair we are."

Lucy looked around the room once again. "If I'm caught in here, I'll be in as much hot water as you are. We should both be on our ways."

Charlotte laughed. "I'm not allowed in some rooms of the house, either."

Lucy was relieved the young woman could manage a laugh in her dilemma. Charlotte was only slightly younger than she was. Only the circumstances of birth separated them. How easily she could have been the troubled maid and Charlotte the privileged daughter.

"Have you had enough to eat? You would know better than I what's available, but please take something with you. Some cheese and meat, perhaps?"

"Yes, Miss Lucy." Charlotte took a napkin from a basket, opened it, and laid two biscuits and a chunk of cheese in it before knotting it securely.

"You'd better get Henry upstairs." Lucy handed the child back to his mother.

Lucy picked up her book. She still had plenty of time ahead of her to read and study. After opening the door that would take her back through the butler's pantry to her own world, she turned to watch as Charlotte moved toward the narrow stairs that led to hers.

"I promise, Charlotte," Lucy said, "I will figure something out and find a way to speak to you."

"Yes, Miss Lucy." Charlotte disappeared up the stairs.

Lucy reentered the dining room, crossed through the foyer, climbed the marble steps, and glided down the hall to her suite. Once again she was alone with her book and her secret, but this time keenly aware that another young woman was in a room above her with another secret. Her misgivings about Daniel and her clandestine class attendance seemed so much less risky than what Charlotte faced. Her life would have awkward moments but would not change drastically if her covert activities were discovered. Charlotte, however, had everything to lose—even her son.

◦─◦

Upstairs, Charlotte changed the baby, fed him, and hoped for a nap herself. As she dozed off, with her baby in the crook of her arm, she had the sensation that the scene in the kitchen had been a dream. Perhaps she had been napping all along. Was it truly possible she was not alone? That someone like Lucy Banning wanted to help her? That Henry could be safe and loved?

10

*L*ucy squirmed in the pew, and her mother glared at her as if she were a squirrelly six-year-old. She stilled her knees and transferred motion to her eyes. Arches and buttresses and high curved ceilings annoyed Lucy more every week, not to mention the elaborate casing around hundreds of organ pipes across the front of the church. Such impracticality. *What was so sacred about the Middle Ages that architects are still trying to re-create it?* she wondered. Prairie Avenue was full of homes built on a Gothic premise, and nearby Second Presbyterian Church fit right in. The twentieth century was less than ten years away. Perhaps the current Arts and Crafts movement in which Flora Banning dabbled would take hold and move architecture in a forward direction.

The Bannings' pew, for which Lucy's father duly gave a generous donation each year to the church, was situated toward the front to the right of the center aisle. Lucy had sat in this pew since she was a small child, when the current building opened in 1874. The Bannings had not yet moved to Prairie Avenue, but they joined the church as soon as it opened in a neighborhood that seemed to attract wealthy families. The Jules family had the pew behind them for many years, before they moved to Riverside and transferred their membership.

As Lucy blossomed and Daniel began to regard her more seriously as his future wife, he started sitting with the Bannings. Now on the weekends when he stayed in the city rather than take the eleven-mile Burlington-Northern train ride to Riverside, Daniel positioned himself at Lucy's left elbow in the Banning pew.

The balconies on three sides of the eight-hundred-seat sanctuary were full, even though there were plenty of available seats below. A quick scan revealed that, as usual, the seats above were filled with servants and working families who would never afford the donation required for the privilege of sitting on the main floor. The injustice made Lucy want to squirm again.

Lucy blinked twice to return her focus to the words coming from the man in the pulpit. The sermon text was from James, one of Lucy's favorite portions of the Bible. Her mind's eye could see the words of James 2 on the page of her own Bible on the cherrywood table next to her bed: "If a brother or sister be naked, and destitute of daily food, and one of you say unto them, Depart in peace, be ye warmed and filled; notwithstanding ye give them not those things which are needful to the body; what doth it profit? Even so faith, if it hath not works, is dead, being alone. Yea, a man may say, Thou hast faith, and I have works: shew me thy faith without thy works, and I will shew thee my faith by my works." She loved the confrontation to action that threaded its way through the entire book of James. In her mind, it was inescapable. Nevertheless the preacher seemed to be finding his way out of James's demands for compassion. *Does he even see the people in the balconies?* she wondered.

She glanced at Daniel, who caught her eye and leaned his head to whisper, "Wonderful sermon, don't you think?"

Lucy wanted to sigh. No, she wanted to get up and stomp out of church.

Of course Daniel would find the sermon wholly acceptable because it asked nothing of him. Was he even listening? Or was his mind already on the business deals of the week ahead? They were planning to spend the day together: dinner with her family—which Charlotte would have to help serve while her baby slept upstairs—followed by a long walk if the fine weather held, a private supper in the parlor, and a carriage ride.

It was going to be a long day.

Charlotte used to look forward to Sunday mornings. Brightness emblazoned her grandmother's face on Sunday mornings, and Charlotte wanted her face to know that brilliance someday. But then her grandmother had passed away, and no one cared whether Charlotte went to church. She had not been in years. Now no one there would understand what had become of her life.

But what would it be like to go to church in Chicago? Charlotte wondered. She had served the Bannings their eggs Benedict breakfast and watched them arrange themselves in the most spacious carriage for Archie, the footman and assistant coachman, to drive them to Second Presbyterian Church. No one coming to this part of town could miss the church. Even Charlotte had seen its Gothic tower before she found her way to the Banning house a few blocks away. It was the landmark everyone used to give directions to Prairie Avenue. The building could hold ten times as many people as filled the church of her childhood. Perhaps the voice would be different there. Perhaps someone would understand what had become of her life.

Of course Charlotte couldn't go to church. Even if Sunday morning responsibilities offered respite—which they did not—she could not be seen with Henry by anyone who might follow her trail back to the Banning home. She learned the hard way in a farming community, where the nearest neighbors were two miles away and nevertheless everyone seemed to know everyone else's business. And if she boarded Henry with a woman and ever had a Sunday morning off, she would use it to go see Henry, not God. She was pretty sure her grandmother had been wrong about God always being with her, and the truth was she was not inclined to go looking for him now. Her rare prayers were more like wishing hard than thinking anyone was listening.

On this particular morning, Charlotte wasn't seeing either Henry or God. Her baby was sleeping soundly upstairs.

After forming the chilled rice into small mounds for Mrs. Fletcher to fry into croquettes, Charlotte snatched twenty minutes to check on him. Her heart nearly stopped when she found him awake and thrashing against the side of the carpetbag. If he cried out, no one would hear him two floors below amid the kitchen clatter, but she hated to think he would feel for a moment that she was not attentive to his distress. Only repeated heavy exhaling had allowed her to leave him again and prepare to serve Sunday midday dinner.

The meal boasted cream of mushroom soup, baked halibut, roast duck, rice croquettes, stewed peas, Parisian salad, and baked apricot pudding. Mr. Penard selected gold-rimmed white china and instructed the maids to set the table with the gold linens to match. To Charlotte's mind, the family hardly noticed the preparations, which was no doubt Penard's goal. If someone commented on the table setting or the food, it would have meant something was amiss. While Penard served, she held her position at attention in the butler's pantry, peeking through the narrowest of cracks where the tall door was almost imperceptibly ajar. When she saw Penard's subtle signal for her assistance, she entered the dining room, then disappeared again as soon as she dispatched her task.

Charlotte could see Lucy's face, how she smiled politely at her fiance's chatter and caught the eye of Mr. Leo across the table in an unspoken secret language. She saw how Lucy tilted her head to listen deferentially to her father's analysis of the morning church service and reached to squeeze her mother's hand with affection that seemed genuine to Charlotte. And she saw how Lucy's gaze rose periodically to the door behind which Charlotte stood, subtly but expectantly, as if hoping Charlotte would appear. Charlotte, however, kept her eyes down whenever Penard summoned her. Only that morning, he had admonished her.

"Never look directly at any family members while serving."

"No, sir, of course not," Charlotte replied.

"And never speak unless spoken to."

"No, sir."

"Never offer an opinion. Answer questions as briefly as possible."

"I know my place, sir."

"See that you don't forget."

Charlotte would put her own composure at risk along with her employment if she allowed herself to look into the face of this woman who had held Henry twenty-four hours ago and promised to help.

As the meal came to an end with the pudding and coffee, family members gradually excused themselves for Sunday afternoon leisure in the parlor, leaving only Daniel and Lucy lingering at the table. When Daniel looked momentarily vexed at the presence of soiled dishes in front of him, Penard crooked a gloved finger at Charlotte. She stepped once again into the dining room and as unobtrusively as possible cleared space in front of Daniel and Lucy.

"My dear Lucy," Daniel was saying, "your hesitancy to talk about our wedding befuddles me. You may make every arrangement you wish. I only ask that you agree to a date so that we don't find ourselves without an appropriate venue."

"Venue?" Lucy asked. "Are we not to marry at Second Presbyterian?"

"Of course the ceremony will be there. We must reserve the sanctuary and be sure the pastor is not planning to be on leave. After the church ceremony we can adjourn to a hall elsewhere for the wedding meal and dancing."

Charlotte reached for Lucy's empty goblet.

"Thank you, Charlotte," Lucy said.

Charlotte's face burned with Lucy's glance as she picked up Daniel's goblet as well. Fortunately Penard had stepped into his pantry.

"Lucy!" Daniel said sharply. "I'm trying to have an important discussion with you and you're chitchatting with the kitchen maid."

Charlotte pressed her back to the wall and turned her eyes down, demure. Too late. Penard had heard Daniel's outburst and appeared in the dining room to glare.

Lucy idly fingered the beaded cuff of her dress, a garment Charlotte knew Lucy would give away without second thought if doing so would not distress Flora Banning.

"I was rather hoping for a simple affair. Perhaps we'll have the reception here at the house. Mother will have redone the place in anticipation. She might as well have an opportunity to show it off."

Daniel leaned back in his chair, amused, and chuckled.

"You can imagine how our mothers would respond to that suggestion."

"It's not their wedding—it's our wedding." Daniel laughed easily, which could be endearing and could diffuse tension in a business meeting, but at moments like this it made Lucy feel as if he saw her as a young, naïve child.

"I'm afraid I would have to side with the mothers." The smile was gone. "Our families are prominent, Lucy. You know as well as I do how important social connections are to business arrangements. We can't afford to offend people with a small wedding or a reception to which they are not invited."

"You said a moment ago I could make every arrangement as I wished," Lucy challenged.

"And you may—except that it must be the social occasion our families expect. Your parents long ago opted not to build a ballroom. There simply isn't space here for an appropriate occasion."

Charlotte held firm against the urge to wince on Lucy's behalf.

"I'll get my cape," Lucy said, "and we can have that walk you promised me." Lucy stood up, and Daniel politely pushed his chair back as well.

As Lucy and Daniel left the dining room, Charlotte let her breath out and went into the butler's pantry to rinse the dishes in the sink. Penard gripped her elbow. "Don't ever let that happen again," he muttered sternly.

Outside a few minutes later, Daniel offered his arm, and Lucy slipped hers through his elbow out of long habit. She knew full well he would mistake the gesture for affection, if not compliance to his point of view.

"This is much nicer than quarreling," Daniel said.

"Yes, it is," Lucy agreed. *Not talking is best of all.*

"I heard a rumor about George Glessner," Daniel said as they passed the Glessner house. "Reportedly, he is fascinated with fire. He even follows the fire trucks when there's a call. I wouldn't be surprised if he got himself sooty in the bucket brigade."

"If he did, I'm sure it would only be because he was trying to help," Lucy responded. "I've known George since he was a little boy. He's the same age I am. Our families lived near each other on Washington Street, before the Great Fire."

"They are an odd family."

"They're perfectly nice people." *If you agree with him, this will stop*, she told herself. *You can have your silence.*

Daniel laughed. "Have you heard what George Pullman said about their house? He wonders what he ever did that he should have to wake up every morning and look at it across the street."

Lucy glanced at the Pullman mansion positioned diagonally from the Glessner home on the intersection they shared. "George Pullman undoubtedly is a shrewd businessman, but perhaps he has little imagination when it comes to architecture. I rather like the Glessner house. It has personality and artistry."

Daniel was again amused. "I can assure you, we'll have none of the Glessner style of nonsense when we build our home."

"I suppose we'll have our own style of nonsense," Lucy quipped.

"Our home will make a statement," Daniel assured her, completely missing her tone. "It will reflect taste and success."

Lucy opened her mouth to respond, but the words did not come. Her thought was lost in the sight of Will Edwards striding toward them.

"Why, Lucy," Will said, "what a pleasant surprise to run into you."

Daniel patted Lucy's arm still tucked in his elbow.

Lucy took the cue. "Daniel, this is the young architect I was telling you about. Leo's friend, Mr. Will Edwards. Will, this is Daniel Jules."

"Ah, the fiance." Will smiled and extended his hand. "I'm delighted to meet you."

Daniel was forced to let go of Lucy to shake Will's hand. "And how do you know Leo?"

"It's not a very interesting story, I'm afraid," Will said, "but he has been very kind to me since I arrived in Chicago. I'm on my way to meet him right now."

Lucy laughed. "He's probably hoping for rescue from an afternoon in the parlor with Mother and Father. I'm sure the two of you can cook up something. I look forward"—she almost mentioned the art exhibit the next evening but caught herself—"to hearing what happens."

"It was nice to meet you, Mr. Jules," Will said. "I won't delay your stroll any longer." If plans for the art exhibit had crossed Will's mind, he didn't show it, to Lucy's relief.

Daniel looked over his shoulder as Will progressed toward the Banning house. "He seems likeable enough, though perhaps a bit overfamiliar."

"What do you mean?" Lucy asked.

"The two of you barely know each other and he addressed you by your first name. However, I am pleased to know he already understands you're an engaged woman."

"Don't be so old-fashioned." Lucy put her arm through Daniel's once again. "He's my brother's friend. Why should he not use my name?"

She mustered every ounce of self-restraint within her to keep from looking over her shoulder at Will's enthusiastic gait.

Will waited until he was sure Lucy would not be looking before he slowed his step and looked over his shoulder. Daniel had a firm grip on Lucy's arm as they turned the corner and were lost to Will's sight.

So this was Daniel.

She wasn't going to marry him. He could see it in her face. If she were going to marry Daniel, her face would not look as it did when she looked at Will.

11

"I will not have this ridiculous nonsense going on under my roof! Anyone who thinks I would tolerate it is a complete imbecile. I expect this situation will be rectified immediately."

Samuel Banning was on a rant. His voice boomed through the lower level and echoed up the stairs.

Henry! Lucy nearly tripped over her skirts trying to get down the stairs on Monday morning. Clatter startled her further. *What was that?*

In the dining room, Charlotte's bleached face greeted her. Lucy scanned the room and determined the clatter had been a hammered copper pot knocked off its display table. Leo was righting the table and replacing the pot.

"Father has discovered something that disturbs him." Leo stated the obvious.

Henry! Lucy's mind cried out. Standing behind her father, she raised her eyebrows at Charlotte and gestured as if she were holding a baby. Charlotte's response was in her eyes—and negative. It was not the baby that upset Samuel.

"I will not stand for this!" Samuel bellowed. "My study is my private sanctuary and no one, and I mean no one, is permitted to rearrange my things."

Lucy stepped forward and took Samuel's arm. "Father, I'm sure we can sort this out—"

He shrugged her off. "You and your mother say that to me every time I report one of these incidents. I'm telling you, something is going on."

"Father, please—"

"Save your breath, Lucy," Leo said. "He means it this time."

Lucy looked around for her youngest brother. "Isn't it time to take Richard to school?"

"I sent him alone in the carriage," Samuel responded. "I'm going to find out what's going on once and for all."

"What do you mean?"

"I mean, I intend to personally search this house from top to bottom. The paperweight never showed up. My tin-hammered box is missing, and now the pearl-handled letter opener disappeared. I know for a fact it was on my desk yesterday afternoon."

"Perhaps Mother borrowed it," Lucy suggested. "Have you looked in the parlor?"

"We've been married more than twenty-five years. Your mother knows better than to bother my things."

Leo smiled blandly and rolled his eyes. "I think I'll just head over to the university. The allure of the all-day department meeting has grown substantially in the last few minutes."

"Do you really have to go, Leo?" Lucy pleaded with her eyes as well as words.

"I'm afraid so. My presentation is the first one on the agenda. I'm sure you'll manage." Leo winked and left the room.

Lucy caught Charlotte's eye. "Charlotte, perhaps you could pour us some coffee. Father, let's sit down and think this through. You can try to remember every move you made yesterday afternoon. I'm sure the letter opener will turn up."

Samuel glared at his daughter. "Lucy, my dear, I know you mean well, but I did not lose the letter opener. I did not merely misplace it, and I am not being forgetful. So don't try to placate me or ply your silly distractions. I'm going to get to the bottom of this if I have to look under every pillow and behind every curtain in this entire house."

Charlotte began pouring coffee, but Samuel spun on his heel and left the room.

"Miss Lucy," Charlotte whispered, the sterling silver coffeepot still in her trembling hand.

"I know," Lucy responded. "But I don't think he'd really search the rooms."

"He sounds serious to me, miss." The color drained from Charlotte's face.

Lucy shook her head. "I doubt he's ever even been on the third floor. He rarely even goes to the second floor."

"He's the master of the house, and he's awfully angry."

"Charlotte!" Penard came from the butler's pantry. When he saw Lucy, he tempered his tone. "Might I have a word with you?"

"Penard, are you aware my father's letter opener is missing?" Lucy asked. "Perhaps you could have a look around his study. I believe he's in there. I'm sure he'd appreciate your assistance."

"Mr. Banning is still here?" Penard sounded startled.

"Yes, I suppose he's decided to go into the office late today."

"Miss Lucy, he has an important engagement this morning with a new client. Last night he was quite emphatic that he did not want to be detained overly long at breakfast."

"Thank you, Penard. I'll speak to him myself," Lucy said, already on her way out of the room with no telltale glance at Charlotte.

She rapped on the open study door. "Father, I'm sorry

you're having an upsetting morning. However, Penard tells me you have an important meeting. Perhaps you ought to be on your way to the office after all."

Samuel slapped the surface of his walnut partners desk. "Penard is correct, as usual." He waggled a finger at Lucy. "I'll grant you the appointment slipped my mind, and I do have to go, but I assure you I did not lose that letter opener—or the tin box. I'll be home for luncheon at 1:00 and will take up the search then." He pushed an annunciator button and said curtly, "I need a carriage immediately."

Lucy sat down on the opposite side of the partners desk. "Father, do you have time for a question while you wait for the carriage?"

"What is it, Lucy?" He picked up a stack of papers and slid them into his briefcase.

"These next few days are very full," Lucy said. "My social obligations related to the dedication of the fair on Friday are fairly demanding on top of my usual commitments. I will require frequent changes of clothing. I know Mother is going to need Elsie's help, and it will be unrealistic for Elsie to assist us both in this busy week. I'd like to have my own ladies' maid."

Samuel peered at his daughter. "It's rather short notice, don't you think? There's no time for Penard to hire staff before the dedication weekend."

"I was thinking about the new kitchen maid. I'll be out much of the time, but when I'm here, I'd like to have her at my disposal."

"What is her name again?"

"Charlotte. I might even ask her to sleep in the anteroom in my suite. I expect I'll need her late in the evenings and early in the mornings."

Samuel sighed. "I suppose it's a reasonable request, though

I doubt Mr. Penard and Mrs. Fletcher will see it that way." He reached toward the wall behind his desk and pressed an annunciator button.

Penard's voice crackled through the tubes. "Yes, sir, Mr. Banning?"

"Would you come in here, please? Bring Mrs. Fletcher with you, and the new maid."

"Yes, Mr. Banning."

Lucy reminded herself to breathe. This could work.

When Charlotte followed Mr. Penard and Mrs. Fletcher into the room, Lucy merely remained comfortably seated and allowed her father to do the talking. She did not look at any of the servants. In a matter of minutes, Charlotte was her ladies' maid for the foreseeable future. Charlotte would also continue some kitchen and serving duties with the condition that she be allowed a period of time to rest in the middle of the day because her role in assisting Lucy might keep her up quite late at night.

Samuel called for a carriage again and Penard went to see that it was properly dispatched, while Mrs. Fletcher muttered she'd better get started on luncheon. Lucy and Charlotte were left staring at each other across the study.

"Miss Lucy, I'm not sure I understand—"

"It's quite simple, Charlotte," Lucy said. "For the next few days at least, your primary responsibilities will be to me. This will require you to be in my suite much of the time. I suggest you plan to sleep in the anteroom."

Charlotte's eyes widened.

"We'll go upstairs now," Lucy said, "and you can become familiar with my rooms."

Lucy led the way down the hall, through the foyer, and up the marble staircase, talking authoritatively all the way.

Charlotte hesitated. "It's all right," Lucy said. "When you are with me, you may use these steps."

Charlotte followed, silent.

"I realize you've never been a ladies' maid before," Lucy said, "but I'm confident you can handle the responsibilities. My schedule this week is fuller than usual, and I won't have a great deal of time for changes of clothing. I'll rely on you to have my gowns and accessories laid out and ready for me. I am not given to elaborate hairstyles. I'm sure you can help me keep my hair pinned in place without too much trouble."

When they reached the door to Lucy's suite, she said, "Come in with me now and I'll show you how my things are organized."

Charlotte had not said a word all the way up the stairs and down the hall. Once behind a securely closed door, though, she let out a long breath.

"Do you think you and Henry can be comfortable here in the anteroom?"

Lucy watched the frightened maid survey the suite—the rich cherrywood of the matching furniture, the floral wallpaper, the delicate lampshades, the rugs. Every detail was in its place. That would have to change for the baby.

"Miss Lucy, how can I thank you?"

"I'm not looking for gratitude," Lucy answered. "I just want your baby to be safe. My father would not allow anyone to search my rooms. If he threatens to, I'll simply plead the same penchant for privacy he has. I'll tell Bessie that you can look after the cleaning in here. No one will have a reason to enter."

"I don't know anything about being a ladies' maid," Charlotte confessed.

Lucy laughed. "Oh, a bit of corset-tightening, a bit of

gown-pressing, a bit of companionship. The main thing is you can spend much of your time in here and have Henry with you."

"Mrs. Fletcher is not going to like this," Charlotte said. "I've only just started working for her and now she'll be shorthanded during a busy week."

"One step at a time, Charlotte. Now go get your things—and your son."

With Charlotte gone, Lucy pondered the question of accommodating an infant. She did not want Henry hidden away in a carpetbag, but neither could he be openly visible—just in case. The large chest of drawers in her anteroom was stuffed with linen sleeping shifts, papers, and favorite childhood books. Lucy pulled out the bottom drawer, which was the deepest. She arranged the books it held on top of the chest, pausing for a moment over the book Daniel had illustrated for her so long ago. *No time for nostalgia.* She then went into her bedroom for a large pillow, wrapped it in a clean linen shift, and positioned it snugly in the bottom of the drawer. A baby deserved much more, but it was the best she could do.

Charlotte was back quickly with two ordinary-looking carpetbags. She dropped one and set the other gently on the floor, then bent to open it. Soon Henry and his quilt filled her arms.

"I've made him a bed," Lucy said. "We can move the chaise lounge over here and the dresser will be less visible but you can still see him." Together they repositioned the lounge and adjusted a side table.

"You've thought of everything," Charlotte said. "I wish I could do something for you."

"You can get my brown lightweight cloak from the closet and find me a sensible hat. Obviously this can't wait until

Friday. I'm going to the orphanage this morning, but it's not my usual day, so no one must know."

"Right away, miss." Charlotte laid Henry in his new bed and stepped into the bedroom to find the closet.

Lucy examined herself in the full-length mirror. She had chosen a day dress of copper color with black lace accents. The sleeves swelled from the bodice in an ostentatious manner that irked Lucy but pleased her mother. At least they narrowed over the forearm and cuffed at the wrist, offering some practicality. Lucy glanced at a clock on the side table. If she didn't get out of the house soon, she risked having to explain to her mother where she was going.

"Will this do?" Charlotte held a demure beige hat featuring black lace with two silk ribbons falling down one side.

"Very nicely. The hat pins are on the vanity table." Lucy sat and allowed Charlotte to pin the hat in place not because she could not do it herself but because she knew Charlotte wanted to be useful. "I'm not sure how long this will take. Mr. Emmett does not know I'm coming and may be engaged. I promise you I'll wait as long as it takes to talk to him, and I won't leave until he has promised to help."

"What shall I do while you're gone?" Charlotte asked.

Lucy thought quickly. "I'm going out this evening to an art exhibit with Aunt Violet and . . . a friend. I think I'll want to wear the ivory damask gown embroidered with glass beads. It's there on a hook at the end of the closet. I believe some of the beads may be loose. Perhaps you can inspect the gown and stitch down anything you find out of place."

"Yes, Miss Lucy. I'm very good with a needle. My grandmother taught me."

Lucy glanced into the drawer at Henry, who was quiet but alert. "Did she make Henry's quilt?"

"Yes, ma'am. It was my baby quilt."

"How lovely that your son can use it."

"I'll get started on the gown right away."

Lucy knew no beads were loose. The gown was brand new. But the task of examining the gown would keep Charlotte in the suite with her son for a legitimate purpose, at least until Lucy returned.

12

I wish you would go with me," Lucy said on Thursday morning. "This parade is a once-in-a-lifetime opportunity. No one would think twice about my asking my ladies' maid to accompany me." Lucy wondered when the last time was that Charlotte had done anything fun. She suspected it was long before Henry came along.

Charlotte shook her head vigorously. "I'm a farm girl. I wouldn't know what to do in a crowd like that." She pulled the brush through Lucy's hair one last time before twisting the hair in the back to pin it up. "Henry and I will be just fine, thanks to you."

"Bessie and Elsie will wonder why you're not going. Penard gave them a few hours off so they can be in the crowd."

"I'm afraid I feel a headache coming on," Charlotte said. Lucy saw her maid's sly smile in the mirror. It was the first time she'd seen Charlotte smile, and she hoped it wouldn't be the last.

"That's what you told them yesterday when you were supposed to have your first afternoon off."

"I'll just say it's the same headache. After I've 'rested' a bit, if Henry is sleeping, I'll see if I can help Mrs. Fletcher with dinner." Charlotte pushed a pin firmly in Lucy's hair. "What about your class this afternoon?"

"It's canceled, fortunately. My professor is marching in the parade as a representative of the fair's fine arts building."

Charlotte put the brush down and opened a jewelry box. "Would you like the silver brooch for your collar? Or perhaps the opal fan pin?"

"The pin. I want a festive look." Lucy picked up the pin and held it to one shoulder briefly before fastening it on. "I wish I had some word for you from Mr. Emmett. I can't imagine how hard it is for you waiting to know if he can find a place for Henry. It's been three days, and I can barely stand it myself."

"Yes, miss, but I feel so much safer now. I'm with Henry most of the day, and no one bothers us here." Charlotte smiled at the baby who studied her from his drawer-bed nearby.

"Once Father put Penard in charge of searching the servants' rooms, I knew we'd done the right thing moving you here," Lucy said. "Of course he didn't find anything."

"What do you suppose has really happened to your father's things?" Charlotte asked.

Lucy shrugged. "I have no idea. I have to admit, he is meticulous by nature. It would be odd for him to suddenly become so forgetful. It's a good thing he's had a busy week getting ready for the fair dedication tomorrow. He seems to have put his distress out of his mind for now."

"I hope the items turn up soon," Charlotte said.

Lucy sighed. "Tomorrow and Saturday will be busy. After the weekend's obligations are over, though, I may not be able to persuade anyone I need my own maid. Mother and I always got along with just one before. I'm worried for you."

"Please don't worry for me so much, miss. This is a big day for your family, what with your father and Mr. Daniel meeting the vice president and all of you in the review stands."

Lucy glanced at the clock Charlotte had wound just that morning. "Aunt Violet will be here with her carriage any moment for Mother and me," she said. She stood up and smoothed the skirt of her dress. Soft flutes of sky blue silk were smocked at the waist and sleeves. Daniel had chosen the fabric, and the dressmaker had created the garment especially for this occasion. Ironically, Lucy was not likely to see Daniel except from a distance in the stands, and by dinnertime she would have changed into another gown. Anyway, the October cool required at least a cape covering the dress. Lucy had dressed to keep her mother's eyebrows from arching too high.

"Here's your hat." Charlotte offered a hat made of fabric that matched the dress.

Lucy took the hat and arranged it on her head. *Lucy Banning, you put up a good front.*

"That friend of Leo's seems like such a nice young man," Aunt Violet remarked as soon as the three women were settled in the reviewing stands in front of the Federal Building toward the end of the parade route.

"What friend?" Flora asked, adjusting her hat.

"Will Edwards, of course."

Lucy's heart lurched. Will and Violet had seemed to get along nicely when the three of them attended the art exhibit Monday night, but she was certain her aunt understood that Lucy was not advertising the outing to her family.

"Oh yes, Mr. Edwards." Flora smoothed her dress absently. "Leo brought him to dinner last week. I didn't realize you'd met him."

Lucy's eyes widened, but Violet took it all in stride.

"Leo brought him around to have tea yesterday," Violet said. "We had a lovely chat. I think Lucy would like him quite well."

"Lucy is not looking to meet a young man," Flora huffed with finality.

Lucy turned her attention to the barricaded street awaiting the parade and tried not to smile at Violet's smoothness. The truth was Lucy had liked Will quite well on Monday evening. They spoke freely of what they saw in the art while Aunt Violet discreetly managed to absorb herself with a painting on another wall. If they moved, she moved. Will's observations and their interaction were a great help in organizing her thoughts for her paper. She felt confident she would turn in work she could be proud of after she made a few changes and wrote it out one more time before Tuesday.

They stayed until the gallery closed, then went to a nearby shop for coffee to round out the evening. On their way home, Violet's driver dropped Will off at the building where he had taken rooms—far more humble than Prairie Avenue, Lucy was painfully aware. Continuing on to Prairie Avenue, Violet prodded Lucy to express her opinion of Will, but Lucy guarded her words. Even Violet did not know the truth of her doubts about Daniel, and she could not risk sounding effusive about a man she barely knew.

But it *had* been an exquisite evening that replayed itself in her mind over the next two days.

"Wouldn't you agree, Lucy, that Mr. Edwards is a likeable young man?" Violet leaned forward to catch Lucy's eye.

Lucy looked at the two sisters sitting to her left. Other than their physical features, they couldn't be less alike. Was Aunt Violet truly set on having this conversation in the presence of Flora?

"At dinner last week he seemed well spoken." Lucy chose

her words carefully. "I sense he has an inquisitive mind."
Really, Lucy, is that the best you can do?

Violet chortled. "From what I saw, there is a great deal to admire before one gets to his inquisitive mind."

"Violet!" Flora screeched.

"He's the most handsome thing to darken my door in decades," Violet said. "There's no harm in appreciating that Mr. Edwards is a handsome young man. Isn't that right, Lucy?"

"Violet, please!" Flora shifted in her seat and sighed. "I don't know what scandal you're trying to provoke. I'm a married woman. Lucy is engaged to Daniel. And you're far too mature to be entertaining unseemly thoughts about a friend of Leo's—especially in public."

"I do admit my thoughts are quite entertaining!" Violet said, her green eyes twinkling. "Perhaps I'll risk unseemly."

Lucy could no longer hold in the laughter. "Yes, Aunt Violet, Leo's friend does have some appealing attributes. Perhaps I'll have the opportunity to get to know him better—if Leo will bring him around again."

"You'll have no time for friends of Leo's," Flora said. "I understand that Mr. Edwards is new to Chicago and Leo wanted to give him a good meal, but I don't expect we'll be seeing more of him."

"Leo seems to like him a lot," Violet observed. "You might be surprised how much he pops up."

"That's ridiculous. We know nothing of his family. And while I value the talents of an architect when needed, that hardly puts him in the circle of friends we move among."

"The marvelous feature of a circle," Violet said, "is that it's easy enough to make it bigger."

"Daniel says there will be almost a hundred thousand marchers in the parade." Lucy's bright tone turned the conversation back to the event before them. "And they have eighty thousand seats set up for the dedication ceremony tomorrow."

"If we can believe the newspaper reports," Violet said, "Chicago will have to put on quite a pageant to match what New York did. Their parade went on and on, and the fair is not even happening in their city."

"We are fortunate to have the fair in our own city," Flora said. "Samuel has been working tirelessly for months to make sure it's a success."

"I'm sure all the directors have," Violet said, "but now it comes down to public spirit."

"Surely no one can accuse Chicago of not having public spirit," Lucy said. She gestured to the street in front of them. "Just look at the flags and streamers on the houses and shops. There's no telling how many people will be out to see the parade." The streets of the parade route were cleared of traffic, but the crowd of onlookers grew deeper by the moment.

"I do hope Samuel is well," Flora said. "He gets more tired than he likes to admit. I wish we could have been seated with them instead of way up here."

"Be grateful you have a seat," Violet said. "Look at all the people just standing along the street."

"Samuel would never leave me standing in the street," Flora responded.

"I'm sure Daniel will look after Father," Lucy said. "He's so excited to meet Vice President Levi Morton."

"Psht!" Violet said. "In a hundred years, no one will know who Levi Morton is. He couldn't even get his party's nomination for the election next month. Rutherford B. Hayes—now there's a president to remember. He put everything he had into rebuilding the South after the war, and he fights for education and giving prisoners a second chance. He's here today too. Daniel should be trying to shake his hand if he's going to pander to anyone."

"Daniel never mentioned former President Hayes was going to be here today." Lucy craned her neck to try to get a better look at the dignitaries sitting closer to the parade route.

"No, I suppose he wouldn't," Violet said. "Morton is a banker, and Daniel understands that world. Hayes cares more for people."

"Violet Newcomb, I must insist you control your tongue!" Flora said. "I will not have you disparaging the son of my dear friends and the man Lucy is going to marry."

So much for a safe topic of conversation. Aloud Lucy said, "Let's leave politics for the men who will vote in next month's presidential election. Today is about Chicago. I'm proud of our city, and I'm proud that our family has had some small part in bringing the Expo here."

"We can all be proud," Flora agreed.

"Mr. Edwards mentioned yesterday that he was to be in the crowd today," Violet said. "Not marching, of course. He's too new to the city for that. But because his company has designed some of the smaller fair buildings, all the employees were given two hours off to watch part of the parade."

"I don't suppose we'll see him," Flora said blandly. "Keep your heart in your chest." Her words were aimed at her sister, but her eyes were fixed on her daughter.

"No, I don't suppose we'll see him in this crowd," Lucy agreed softly. *But it would be so good if we did.* "Oh look, here come the girls!"

"What girls?" her mother asked.

"Open your eyes, Flora," Violet said. "How can you miss them?"

A thousand little girls—literally—swarmed into position

before the reviewing stands. Dressed in red, white, and blue, they lined up to form the American flag.

"How clever!" Flora exclaimed.

"Some of the girls are from St. Andrew's," Lucy commented. "Mr. Emmett was so pleased they could participate." She peered into the mass of girls, hoping to spot one she knew. Thinking of the girls from the orphanage, however, only made her worry even more intensely about Charlotte. Ever since Saturday's discovery in the kitchen, Lucy felt responsible for Charlotte. At home she was vigilant about the whereabouts of both family and servants and made frequent excuses to spend time in her room, providing good reason for Charlotte to be there and assist her. But she could not be there every moment of the day.

"I'm going to go say hello to the girls." Lucy suddenly stood up, ready to push her way through the seated crowd.

"Oh, Lucy, it's such a lot of trouble," her mother said.

Lucy ignored her. She would enjoy greeting some of the girls from the orphanage if she could find them in the crowd, but her true thought was that perhaps Mr. Emmett was nearby to oversee his charges.

Once she was down to street level, Lucy scanned every face within sight. She had never seen so many people in one place in her entire life and could only imagine the throngs that filled Wabash as the parade moved north and then west on Lake to State Street, where it turned south again before circling the Federal Building.

Finally Lucy found a child she knew, draped in red and standing in position at the end of a stripe on the flag.

"Jane!" she called.

The girl turned, then broke into a rare grin. "Miss Lucy!"

Lucy gave Jane a congratulatory hug, then asked, "Is Mr. Emmett nearby to watch your big moment?"

Jane shook her head. "He didn't come. Mrs. Baker brought us down. Mr. Emmett said there were too many children to manage and they would all stay at St. Andrew's. He said he would never forgive himself if one of the little ones got lost or hurt in the crowd."

Lucy nodded. "That's probably wise. I'm so glad you're here, though."

"They were supposed to get here a long time ago." Jane twisted a corner of red fabric between two fingers. "I'm getting tired of standing around."

A voice rose from the crowd. "Here they come! It's starting!"

Lucy joined the applause as the first rank of mounted police appeared in view.

13

*D*aniel snapped his pocket watch shut. "It's 1:20. The ceremony should start in precisely ten minutes with a march composed especially for the occasion."

Lucy sat beside Daniel in the front row of the second rank of seating inside the massive Manufactures and Liberal Arts Building on the grounds of the World's Columbian Exposition. They had arrived more than an hour early to claim seats with a center view of the enormous platform.

"I wonder where Leo and Oliver are," Lucy said. "You agreed to meet here, right?"

"That was the plan," Daniel replied, "but you know Leo. If he's involved, anything could happen."

Lucy chuckled in agreement. "Maybe they just haven't spotted us yet."

"If they don't show up soon, someone else will want their seats, tickets or no tickets."

Lucy scanned the vast sea of seats around them. Ribbons of color in women's dresses splashed against the dark backdrop of men's formal wear. Heads bobbed under a wave of one extravagant hat after another. Her parents and Aunt Violet were somewhere in the crowd, seated closer to the main stage. Lucy took Daniel's word for it that eighty thousand people could be seated, and untold thousands more would be standing for a chance to glimpse this epic event. Five thousand chairs filled the red-carpeted platform alone to accommodate dignitaries from around the globe. The mammoth hall stood more than two hundred feet high and spanned forty-four acres. Sunlight streamed through a greenhouse-like ceiling and diffused through steel arch trusses filled with glass, setting the colossal structure alive with energy.

Lucy glanced at the program in her hand. "From the looks of this, we're going to be here a few hours."

Daniel nodded. "Believe it or not, it was supposed to be five hours. The planning committee cut it down to four, but we'll see if they stick to it."

"They can't possibly keep a crowd this size quiet and still that long!"

"My guess is they're not even going to try," Daniel said. "We'll have to leave it to the historians to record the importance of this day."

"Over here, Leo," Will said. "I just spotted them."

Will pointed, and Leo followed the invisible line from his friend's finger to his sister's hat. Together they nudged their way through the burgeoning crowd to the empty seats awaiting. Leo entered the row first, squeezed past Daniel and Lucy, and left the seat next to Lucy for Will.

"I hope you don't mind my bringing Will," Leo said. "At the last minute, Oliver said he had a better offer. I think it has something to do with Pamela Troutman."

Lucy smiled. "Mother would approve."

"Anyway, Will's office closed for the day so I thought he may as well have a seat with us rather than stand in the back by himself."

"I'm delighted to share the occasion with you, Will," Lucy said.

"The pleasure is mine," Will said, "with gratitude." He glanced at Daniel, but something told him not to bother offering his hand. "Nice to see you again, Mr. Jules."

Daniel nodded ever so slightly.

"I understand you met the vice president yesterday," Will said.

"That's correct." Daniel was watching the band prepare to play and did not turn to look at Will.

"Do you have any political ambitions for yourself, Mr. Jules?" Will was nothing if not persistent.

"Not at present," came the curt reply.

"Perhaps in the future?"

Leo leaned in to the conversation. "Daniel's a popular man. He could run for any office he likes. A real man for the people."

"Is that so?" Will asked. From his two brief encounters with Daniel Jules, he would not have judged him to be much interested in people.

Daniel picked up Lucy's gloved hand from her lap, tucked it into his elbow, then patted it. "I believe the ceremony is about to begin."

The band struck the first chord of the "Columbus March," and Will settled back in his chair. He knew Daniel's reputation from Leo's stories. Leo always spoke of Daniel with the affection of a brother. *So why is he giving me the cold shoulder?*

❧

Lucy sat for more than an hour with her arm laced with Daniel's, constantly resisting the impulse to withdraw it. Why had he treated Will so rudely? One moment she would tell herself to save her questions for a private setting later and enjoy the ceremonies, but the next she seethed with impatience, both with Daniel and the proceedings. After the opening musical march came a lengthy prayer by a California bishop and an introductory address by the director general of the exposition. By the time Mayor Washburne formally welcomed guests from around the world to the proud city of Chicago, Lucy was getting restless. She wasn't the only one. People seemed to leave their seats and move freely around the enormous hall and even launch conversations audible from several rows away. Nevertheless, Daniel was enthralled with the proceedings, occasionally tightening his grip on Lucy's fingers during a particularly rousing oration.

Foremost on Lucy's mind, though, was Charlotte. After Thursday's unsuccessful attempt to see Phillip Emmett along the parade route, Lucy had determined to leave the house early that morning and go to the orphanage to find him. She had spoken to him on Monday morning. Surely he was making inquiries. Did he really have nothing encouraging to report? Did he not understand the urgency of the situation? Lucy wanted to find out in person. Flora Banning, however, had other plans for the morning. She insisted the family begin the day by sitting down to a formal breakfast together. Flora reasoned the day would be a long one, and it would be hours before anyone could eat properly again. At her instructions, Mrs. Fletcher had prepared a particularly hearty breakfast of compote of dried fruits, poached eggs, bacon, and bread pudding. Lucy had little choice but to sit and eat just enough to ease her mother's mind. By then it was too late to go out before Daniel was due to arrive to escort her to the ceremonies.

A Miss Harriet Monroe stood on the platform to recite a dedicatory ode. Lucy eyed the door.

"Daniel," she whispered, "I need some air. I think I'll step outside."

"I don't want to miss anything," he whispered back.

"I'm not asking you to go. I'll just get some air and come back in a little while. There are still plenty of speeches to hear."

She extracted her arm from Daniel's grasp and stood up. Will was immediately on his feet. "Is everything all right?" he asked.

"I just need some air," Lucy said.

"Shall I accompany you?" Will glanced at Daniel.

"No, that's not necessary, thank you. I'll be back soon."

As Lucy made her away across the huge hall toward the outside light, a guest musician began his performance. The walkways were bursting with onlookers, some moving, some standing still. Getting out of the building was no small feat. Finally, though, she breathed outside air just as another ceremonial reading began.

Leo leaned over and spoke to Will. "Where is Lucy going?"

Will shrugged. "She just said she wanted some air. She wanted to go by herself."

"She'll be all right," Leo said. "When you get to know Lucy, you'll see she takes care of herself pretty well."

Unsettled, Will watched as Lucy threaded her way through the crowd. The bright crimson gown she'd chosen for the occasion made her progress easy to follow. When she reached the door, his unease got the best of him, and Will left his seat as well.

Outside, Will saw Lucy leaning against an electric light post. When the fair opened in May, thousands of electric lights would illuminate the grounds. For now, this was the only post that mattered, because Lucy Banning was leaning against it looking distracted. Her family had been involved in planning and financing the fair for at least the last two years. Why would she now excuse herself from the ceremonies that culminated their labors?

He decided to find out. Just as he began to move toward her—sure that she hadn't spotted him yet—Lucy stepped away from the light post and walked with determined steps.

Where is she going?

He followed her.

She quickened her pace. He quickened his, all the while contemplating whether he should intentionally close the gap between them—which he could do easily with his long stride. Not once did Lucy look back. After a couple of minutes, it was clear she was heading for the rank of carriage cabs whose drivers were trying to take advantage of the history-making day.

"Lucy!" Will called.

If she heard him above the crowd she gave no indication. Will watched as Lucy touched the elbows of people in her way, politely urging them to step aside. Many of the women's gowns did not permit easy movement. Lucy's own stride grew less and less ladylike.

She had to find out if Mr. Emmett knew anything! Charlotte had hidden a baby in the Banning home for eight days now. Even with Lucy's help, her luck could run out at any moment. Henry was getting bigger by the day, and his cries louder. Flora might send a servant into Lucy's room looking for a piece of jewelry, or Bessie might bring up a bundle of laundry and forget the instructions to leave it in the hall. Anything could happen. It was urgent that Mr. Emmett find a place for Henry to board—soon.

Lucy paused for the fourth time to look at the watch hanging from a gold chain around her neck. Almost half an hour had passed since she left her seat. How long would it take before Daniel wondered where she was? The notion that he might come looking for her was far-fetched, though, and after a while, Lucy no longer cared what Daniel might be thinking. She had to get through this crowd and find a carriage driver who would take her to the orphanage, or at least to a train stop. The silence of the last four days was enough to persuade Lucy she ought to pay to have a telephone installed in the orphanage office, but that did little to solve the immediate problem. The only way to talk to Mr. Emmett was to go to the orphanage.

Although the ceremonies were well under way, people still swarmed toward the Manufactures Building. Trying to go the opposite direction, toward the empty cabs, was like swimming against the ocean current. Lucy made little headway and generally was swept off course to the side. Even on a late October day, she was beginning to perspire from the effort. From a distance, she saw cabs coming and going, but none was within her reach.

Lucy sank onto a bench and sighed. The errand she proposed would take far too long. It was hopeless. She would just have to go back inside and sit with Daniel, Will, and Leo and ponder how she might carve an opportunity to go to the orphanage out of the busy weekend schedule.

***

Will watched her compose herself sitting on the bench for another ten minutes. She took a handkerchief out of the small embroidered lace bag she carried and dabbed at her hairline. Clearly she had tried to leave—but why? And what made her give up? Lucy looked at her watch several times and glanced over her shoulder at the jostling cabs. Eventually, though, she stood up and began to retrace her steps toward the building. Will waited for her at the light post.

Finally, she was close enough and he made his presence known.

"Lucy." Will stepped into her path.

Lucy sucked in her breath. "Will! You startled me."

He looked into her green eyes, judging how hard to push. Finally he shrugged and said, "I didn't mean to frighten you. I was worried."

"Why on earth would you worry about me?"

"I had the sense something was amiss when you left the hall."

"I just needed some air. I realize it's been quite awhile, but I'm sure there's still a couple of hours left. I can't have missed much of importance."

"I suppose not," Will said.

"I walked around for a bit—a preview tour of sorts," she explained.

Will nodded. *You did more than walk. You tried to leave.*

"I should go back in," Lucy said. "By now Daniel will be getting worried."

"I'm sure he's wondering if you're all right."

"I'm perfectly fine, I assure you. Shall we go in?"

She seemed to have brightened up, but Will wasn't convinced. "I think I'll catch a bit more air," he said. "Can you find your way back to your seat?"

"Of course. I found my way out, didn't I?"

Will nodded. "Then I'll see you inside." Daniel would not be pleased if he saw Will escorting Lucy back to her seat. For Lucy's sake, he chose not to cause a stir. No doubt she would have enough explaining to do already.

But something was wrong. He was sure of it.

Lucy hated deceiving Will. Technically she hadn't said anything grossly untrue. But she hadn't said everything there was to say, either.

No one could know about Charlotte. No one. She couldn't even risk sending a messenger with a note.

She made her way back to Daniel, experiencing firsthand that the crowd had grown even thicker during her absence. An enormous choir was singing Handel's "Hallelujah" chorus, and the audience was on its feet in traditional deference to the masterpiece. Lucy reached her seat at the peak of the music.

"Where have you been?" Daniel asked.

"I told you I needed some air."

"You were gone a long time."

"I know. It's an awfully long time to sit and listen to speeches."

"Where's your friend?"

"What do you mean?"

"That friend of Leo's. Edwards. He went out right after you did."

"Thousands of people are coming and going. Why would I know where Mr. Edwards is?"

The music ended, and the audience broke into applause. As Lucy brought her hands together, she spotted Will slowly working his way back to his seat. She glanced at Leo and realized he had followed her gaze and was watching Will also. Curiosity lit his eyes, and Lucy quickly looked away.

A dignitary from Kentucky rose to give the next speech. Lucy settled in to at least look as if she were listening.

14

$\mathcal{P}$enard set the receiver down and turned from the telephone in the foyer.

"Charlotte, please let Miss Lucy know she has a telephone call."

"Yes, sir. She'll want to know who's calling, sir."

"The caller seems reluctant to give his name," Penard said flatly. "Perhaps it's orphanage business. Just go upstairs and ask her if she'd like to take the call."

Orphanage? Charlotte raced across the foyer, through the dining room, into the butler's pantry, and across the kitchen. She clumped up the narrow wooden stairs as rapidly as she could. This could be the word they were waiting for. She knocked quickly, then entered Lucy's suite.

"Shh!" Lucy whispered. "Henry just dropped off again."

"The telephone! You have a telephone call."

Lucy jumped to her feet. "Do we know who it is? Are you sure it's not just Daniel?"

Charlotte shook her head. "Mr. Penard would have said if it were Mr. Daniel."

"I'll go down immediately."

Lucy burst into the hallway and scampered down the hall to the top of the stairs. Behind her, Charlotte closed the door quietly and watched as Lucy composed herself before descending the marble steps with grace and poise. Charlotte turned in the other direction and went down the back stairs with as much serenity as she could muster. By the time she arrived in the foyer, Lucy was in the midst of guarded conversation.

"That's lovely news. . . . I would be delighted to handle that for you. . . . Yes, I quite understand. . . . Yes, that is correct. . . . Good-bye."

Charlotte thought her heart might stop. She couldn't tell anything from what Lucy was saying! Of course, the phone was in the foyer and anyone could walk by, so Lucy would choose her words carefully.

Finally, Lucy hung up the phone. "Charlotte," she said loudly, "may I have a word with you in the dining room?"

Shoulders erect and head up, Lucy walked into the dining room. Charlotte followed meekly behind. In the dining room, Charlotte glanced around. Lucy pointed at the butler's pantry, and Charlotte gently pushed the door open to see if anyone was there. Empty. Charlotte turned to Lucy expectantly.

"He's found someone!" Lucy's voice was barely above a whisper. "He knew it was urgent so he asked to use the telephone of a neighbor and called me immediately with the address. We can take Henry there today."

"Today?" Charlotte echoed.

"Now. We can go now! Go get Henry ready. I'll be up in a few minutes. I'll take care of everything."

Lucy turned and walked out of the dining room, leaving Charlotte stunned, her eyes stinging. *Henry.* She would have to leave him. She would have to take her baby to another woman and leave him there. She would have to kiss his sweet face and walk out the door. Her chest heaved just at the thought of it. Gasping for breath, she moved through the kitchen and up the back stairs once again.

Lucy breezed into the parlor with far more calm than she actually felt. Her mother had her needlework on her lap, and Aunt Violet was flipping through a magazine.

"Mother," Lucy said, "I'm going to go out for a few minutes. I have to go to Lenae's shop."

"The dressmaker? But she'll come here if you ask her to."

"I prefer to go to her today." *Don't say more than you have to.*

"Lucy, dear, can't this wait a few days? Your father is at the ceremony dedicating some of the individual fair buildings. Daniel is coming for you, and you haven't begun to dress suitably."

Lucy hadn't expected to leave the house for several more hours. It was true she was dressed in a plain yellow day dress from two years ago and had never intended to go out in it. Under the circumstances, though, plain garb might be the best thing.

"Daniel has given me several lengths of fabric for holiday gowns," Lucy said. "I'd like Lenae to look at them and make some sketches as soon as possible. The holidays will be here before we know it. I'm sure Daniel has a full calendar planned."

Daniel was the magic word, and Lucy knew it. If Daniel wanted it, then Flora was more likely to concede.

"Are you sure this can't wait until Monday?" Flora said.

Violet looked up from her magazine. "Let her go, Flora."

"It will be a quick errand," Lucy said, "and I know the shop is open today."

"But your father and your brothers have taken the carriages," Flora pointed out. "How will you get there?"

Lucy's heart lurched into her throat. She hadn't thought about the unavailability of transportation. The address Mr. Emmett gave her was too far south to walk, and she couldn't infer to her mother that she would ride the streetcar.

"I can get a cab on Michigan Avenue," Lucy said, which was true enough.

"Nonsense." Aunt Violet inserted herself again. "The cabs will be busy with all the extra people in Chicago. Take my carriage. Paddy is outside with nothing to do. Your mother and I are not going down to Jackson Park until this evening for the fireworks."

Lucy met her aunt's eyes evenly. Paddy sometimes took her to class at the university. She could trust him to take her anywhere, and Aunt Violet knew that.

Gratefully, Lucy smiled. "That's a wonderful idea, Aunt Violet. We won't be gone long."

"We?" Flora asked.

"I'm taking Charlotte with me," Lucy explained. "The fabric is rather a lot to manage without assistance. Daniel was generous in the quantities."

"How long will you be gone?"

"No longer than necessary." *But perhaps longer than you think.*

Violet stood up. "Go get your fabric, Lucy. I'll tell Paddy to get ready for you."

Charlotte clutched Henry to her chest. She couldn't bear the thought of leaving him! But what choice did she have? Going home was not an option, and Henry couldn't stay in Miss Lucy's bottom drawer forever. A growing child needed fresh air, and soon he would start being wakeful for more and more of the day. Already Bessie and Elsie were muttering that Charlotte was not carrying her weight with the work of the household during this busy week. It wasn't fair to expect Miss Lucy to protect her indefinitely.

Charlotte laid her son on her grandmother's quilt spread

out on Lucy's bed and began to bundle him up. She didn't try to stop the tears that moistened her cheeks. Even though she was in Lucy's suite, the sound of the door opening made her jump.

Lucy closed the door behind her.

"What if I don't like her, Miss Lucy?" Charlotte choked on the thought. "How can I be sure she'll take good care of him?"

Lucy put an arm around Charlotte's shoulders. "You're his mother. Of course you're worried. But the name Mr. Emmett gave me is someone who has cared for several infants in the past. I haven't met her, but I've seen the children when they're old enough to come to the orphanage. They're happy and healthy."

Charlotte stroked the baby's cheek. "I knew this was going to happen, and I know it's the best thing I can do for Henry right now, but it's so soon! He's barely five weeks old. All of a sudden I have to give him to a stranger."

"You can see him," Lucy assured her. "Has Penard settled on your regular day off?"

"Thursday." Charlotte's throat thickened. "As soon as luncheon is prepared, I'm free to go."

"Then you can see him every Thursday and every other Sunday afternoon when you're off. I'll make sure Mrs. Given understands that Henry has a mother who loves him."

"That's her name? Mrs. Given? Her real name?"

Lucy nodded. "Mary Given."

Charlotte picked up her bundled baby and sat on the edge of the bed with him. Lucy opened an armoire and removed several folded flats of fabric from the center shelf.

"This is our excuse," Lucy said. "Daniel brought these back from his last trip to New York. I told Mother I want you to help me take them to the dressmaker." From the bottom of the armoire, Lucy took a basket. "You can make Henry comfortable in here, then we'll cover him with fabric while we go downstairs. You can carry him. Aunt Violet's carriage is outside."

"Do we have to go now?" Charlotte asked. "A few more minutes—"

"I'm sorry, Charlotte," Lucy said softly. "I can only imagine how hard this is for you. But we must go now or I won't be able to help you."

Charlotte's reply was hoarse. "I can't do it by myself."

"You don't have to. But we must go."

15

*P*addy asked no questions. With his assistance, Char- lotte stepped into the silk-covered interior of a sleek carriage fancier than anything she had ever imagined. Lucy sat across from her, and Paddy closed the beveled glass door that shielded them from the outside world. Charlotte's fam- ily rarely traveled, and when they did they rode in a simple farm wagon older than Charlotte. Since arriving in Chicago, Charlotte had walked everywhere. In fact, this was the first time she had left the Banning household since beginning her employment. She had followed careful instructions to find the Banning house and had little reason to try to navigate an intimidating city beyond its walls.

Charlotte had eyes only for Henry. Once inside the car- riage, she cleared the fabrics away from his face and lifted him out of the basket to kiss his eyelids, his cheeks, his tiny curled fingers. Clear blue eyes returned her gaze, trusting eyes, secure eyes. That could all change in a few minutes.

Lucy pushed up the silk window shade. "Charlotte, you must watch where we're going if you're ever going to find your way here on your own."

Charlotte forced her stare away from her son and out the window. Miss Lucy was right, of course. Charlotte would go see Henry at every opportunity. She couldn't afford to lose her way and waste precious minutes.

"I'll give you the address," Lucy said. "It looks like it should be simple to use the streetcar down Michigan Avenue and then walk just a few blocks to the west."

"Yes, Miss Lucy." Charlotte choked back a sob. "I've never even been on a streetcar."

"It's not difficult. Perhaps I'll be able to go with you the first time."

"Would you really do that for me?"

Lucy reached forward and put her hand on Charlotte's knee. "I'll do whatever I can to make sure you see your baby."

For a long time, they didn't speak. Charlotte looked out the window, trying to soak up landmarks that would reassure her when she made this trip on her own—shops and signs and railings and homes. The opulence of the Prairie Avenue neighborhood yielded to a more commonplace existence, and finally to a row of diminutive houses set snugly up against each other and close to the road. With an almost physical pain, Charlotte realized this was not a neighborhood used to seeing the likes of a Banning.

"Perhaps you should just let me out here," Charlotte said.

"Nonsense," Lucy answered. "I'm going to be sure Henry is properly settled."

Finally Paddy tightened the reins, and the speckled mare obediently slowed and stopped.

"This is it," Lucy said.

Charlotte assessed the structure that would be her son's home. The house was narrow across the front and clad in large gray shingles. Three wooden steps led up to a small porch. On each side of the unpainted door was a square unshuttered window. Below the porch, the browned remains of a flower bed now past its season recalled a splash of beauty, a whisper of hope.

Charlotte followed Lucy out of the carriage, aware that movement in the immediate vicinity had slowed with their arrival. It was Miss Lucy they were gawking at, she was sure, or the handcrafted wood and iron carriage with a uniformed driver. Charlotte glanced at Lucy, who smiled at a couple of people and never let on that she was out of place here.

———

Inside, the house lived up to its outside promise. Four simple rooms were sparse but clean.

Charlotte judged Mrs. Given to be about forty.

As if reading her thoughts, Mrs. Given explained, "I'm a widow. I was married for twelve years, but my husband died several years ago in an accident at work. He worked for Mr. Pullman, who is not always as careful about his employees as he should be."

Charlotte threw Lucy a glance. George Pullman lived in the next block from the Bannings. The families went to each other's parties. Lucy, however, gave no indication that the barb affected her one way or the other.

"I'm sorry for your loss," Lucy said quietly.

Mrs. Given continued. "We never had children of our own, so it gives me pleasure to look after little ones. I have a sitting room, two bedrooms, and a kitchen. The children stay together in the second bedroom."

"You have other children?" Charlotte had not pictured Henry with other children.

"Don't worry. I don't have any other babies just now," Mrs. Given said. "I'll be able to feed and care for your son. I do have two toddlers—twins, actually—who have been with me since they were very small. They'll soon be ready to go to the orphanage or be adopted. The neighbor is looking after them so we can talk."

Charlotte was still standing, clutching Henry to her chest.

"Why don't you sit down," Mrs. Given said, "and I'll answer any questions you have."

Charlotte chose the overstuffed red armchair. The fabric was worn, but the seat felt solid. Lucy sat across from her on the dark green settee, next to Mrs. Given, and smiled encouragingly. In the corner of the room, Charlotte saw a small oak table with three mismatched chairs. A cross-stitched sampler of the Lord's Prayer hung on the wall above the table, and a half-finished quilt draped over one chair. Striped curtains on the windows gave the front wall a splash of color. All in all, the room was not unlike the home she'd left behind less than two weeks ago—small but functional and clean.

"We don't have electricity in this neighborhood," Mrs. Given said, "but I have plenty of gas lamps."

Charlotte nodded. She'd never had electricity, either, until arriving at the Banning house. On the farm they still used kerosene lamps.

"Charlotte, what questions would you like to ask Mrs. Given?" Lucy prompted.

Charlotte roused herself to sound like a competent mother. "You have clean water?"

Mrs. Given nodded. "Yes. It comes right into the kitchen, though I have to heat it for baths. And you won't see a rat in my home."

A rat! Charlotte hadn't thought about that.

"An icebox to keep food fresh?" Charlotte asked.

Mrs. Given nodded. "The iceman comes on a regular schedule. I don't abide spoiled food."

"I don't mean for Henry to be adopted out."

"Mr. Emmett has explained your situation," Mrs. Given said. "I know you love your little boy."

"I'm going to come and see him."

"Any time you like."

"I'm off on Thursdays and every other Sunday afternoon."

"I shall expect you, then."

"Can I see his bed?" Charlotte asked.

"Of course."

Mrs. Given led the few steps to a small bedroom that opened off the sitting room. "The twins have outgrown their crib," she explained. "I've put them in their own little beds just recently, so you can see I have room for a baby."

Charlotte ran her hand along the top rail of the wooden crib. So far her son had slept in a carpetbag and a dresser drawer. Here he would have a real bed! And he wouldn't be a dark secret.

"I've brought his quilt," Charlotte said, her voice catching. "It's what he's used to. It was my quilt when I was a baby."

"Then I'll be sure to take good care of it." Mrs. Given held out her arms. "May I see the baby?"

Charlotte flashed a look at Lucy, who nodded. The moment had come. She had to give her son to another woman to care for. No longer could she steal away from her work and sneak up the stairs to breathe his sweetness, to comfort herself with the feel of him in her arms, to stroke his smooth cheek or feathery head. She would have to survive on the anticipation of his nearness on a rigorous schedule.

Exhaling slowly, Charlotte laid her son, quilt and all, in the arms of Mrs. Given. She couldn't help but smile as the older woman cooed and Henry waved his arms and kicked against the blanket in response. With all her heart she wanted to believe Henry would be all right here.

Lucy touched her arm and spoke softly. "I hate that we can't stay longer, Charlotte, but—"

"I know," Charlotte said, nodding. "Mrs. Banning thinks we've gone to the dressmaker's shop."

"We'll still have to go there. We can't take all that fabric back into the house. Mother is sure to ask Lenae about it the next time she sees her."

Charlotte continued to nod, but she could no longer speak. When she left the simple house and climbed back into the ornate carriage, her arms and heart were empty.

Will first recognized the horse, then the carriage, then the driver feeding the mare an apple. "Hello, Paddy," he said.

Paddy tipped his hat. "Good day, Mr. Edwards. What brings you downtown today?"

"Just taking a stroll to enjoy the decorations. Chicago is certainly proud of the fair," Will answered. He glanced around the street of shops. "Is Miss Newcomb shopping today? I thought she would be at her sister's getting ready for tonight's festivities."

"She is," Paddy answered. "It's Miss Lucy who got a sudden bug to see the dressmaker."

"Miss Lucy?" Will scanned the nearby shops for the dressmaker's sign. "It seems like a busy day to have a dress made."

Just then Lucy and Charlotte emerged from the shop. Lucy's shoulders drooped, and Charlotte looked trampled. Both of them kept their eyes on the sidewalk, their hats nearly perpendicular to the ground. Will wondered what could possibly have happened in the dress shop to make them look the way they did.

"Hello, Lucy," Will said.

Lucy's head lifted, but her smile seemed strained. "Oh, hello, Will."

In her soft acknowledgment, she seemed neither surprised

nor pleased to run into him. Charlotte stood discreetly behind her.

"Paddy tells me you've been to the dressmaker's shop," Will said guardedly.

Lucy nodded. "Daniel brought me some imported European silks from James McCreery and Company in New York City. I'd like Lenae to do something with them for the holidays."

"I see you're thinking ahead as usual."

Lucy did not return his grin, nor seem inclined to converse or banter. Will looked from Lucy's face to Charlotte's and back again. "I don't mean to pry, but is everything all right?"

"Yes, of course," Lucy said quickly. "It's just been rather a hectic time. We've been anticipating the fair dedication for so long, but I admit I've found the hustle and bustle a bit exhausting."

Will nodded. "Yes, I suppose so. Your family is quite invested in the affair. Will you attend the fireworks tonight?"

"Yes, Daniel wants to go very much. I begged off from hearing any more speeches today, but I did promise to go to the fireworks."

"I'm sure they'll be spectacular." Will examined Lucy's face for any sign of sincerity.

"No doubt," she said. "But I'm not suitably dressed, and Daniel will be arriving soon. Charlotte will have her hands full trying to make me presentable."

"Then I won't detain you further." Will stepped aside. "It was lovely to run into you again."

"Lovely to see you as well," Lucy said, but her voice was flat.

Paddy held the door open, and Lucy and Charlotte climbed into the carriage. Will stood firmly on the sidewalk and watched Paddy secure the door, climb to his own seat, and click his tongue to get the horse moving. As the carriage pulled away, Will shook his head. Whatever was wrong was getting worse by the day. Yesterday, Lucy had seemed anxious. Today she was stricken. And now he was convinced Charlotte knew Lucy's secret as well.

16

*L*ucy kissed both of Irene Jules's cheeks a week later. "It's so good to see you," she said. "Thank you for inviting me to dinner."

"You know you don't have to wait for an invitation," Daniel's mother responded. "You're always welcome. The one drawback to living in Riverside is that we don't see the Bannings nearly enough. I always mean to get into the city more, but somehow it doesn't happen."

Lucy scanned the room. "I see you've redone the parlor since I was here last. It looks delightful."

"We're still waiting for some handcrafted cabinetry, but that's coming soon."

Daniel touched Lucy's elbow and gestured toward the baby grand piano at the far end of the room. "I insisted they have a Steinway so you can play whenever you come."

"Oh yes," Irene said. "Daniel says you've gotten very good with your private studies."

Lucy smiled. "I admit I enjoy it. I've had to let the lessons go, though. Lately, there doesn't seem to be enough time in the week for a lesson, much less sufficient practice to please my teacher."

"How is the work coming on the women's building?"

Howard Jules asked. "I suppose that's one of the things taking up your time."

"It's fascinating! It's one of the most rewarding experiences I've ever had. I'm working alongside some amazing women."

"Your mother tells me you're also spending quite a bit of time at St. Andrew's these days," Irene commented.

Lucy was modest—and truthful. "I'm doing what I can. I wish I could spend even more time."

"Ah, but you have a wedding to plan," Irene said. "It does make for a busy life."

"We took the train out tonight," Daniel informed his parents. "It was Lucy's idea."

"How modern of you," Irene said. "We go everywhere by carriage."

"I've taken the train to New York and Boston several times, of course, and to Lake Forest," Lucy said. "I thought it might be fun to get a flavor of what it's like for shorter distances. I find it more efficient than a carriage."

"If you miss the last train back, you're welcome to stay the night," Irene said. "Goodness knows Daniel stays at your house often enough."

Lucy returned Irene's smile. Irene was like a second mother to her, and Lucy guarded many fond memories over the years. However, she had no intention of missing the last train back to the city.

"Do you think your parents have any idea about the surprise anniversary party?" Howard asked.

Lucy grinned genuinely. "Not an iota. Leo and Oliver have covered every contingency. We just have to wait until November 12 and spring it on them."

"I can't wait to see the looks on their faces."

The Jules's butler appeared and announced that dinner was served. Irene took Lucy's arm.

"I asked for all your favorites tonight," Irene said. "Our cook's red velvet cake is heavenly! Save room for a nice thick slice."

Lucy was doing her best. When she had dressed for the occasion, she let Charlotte select extravagant accessories and experiment with a new hairstyle. In a favorite gown, she hoped the evening would brighten her spirits. Howard and Irene Jules were gentle, well-meaning people, and Lucy was sincerely fond of them. However, the conversation over dinner made her progressively more restless. Predictably, discussion drifted toward wedding plans—Irene suggested a September date, after the heat of summer had passed—and the details of choosing an architect and planning the layout of a home. An innocent enough remark from Irene was the final undoing for Lucy.

"Just think," Irene said, "a year from now you could be ordering furniture for a nursery in your new home."

Lucy turned up the corners of her mouth wanly and avoided Daniel's glance. She had no thought of a baby of her own, but she couldn't help thinking of Henry and the ashen color of Charlotte's face during the last week. For days Charlotte's body had reminded her every few hours that it was time to feed her child, and she couldn't. Lucy knew her maid was physically uncomfortable as well as emotionally distraught and had made every excuse she could think of for Charlotte to seek shelter in Lucy's suite. But the excuses were running thin, and they both accepted it was time for Charlotte to make more of an effort in the kitchen again.

Finally the red velvet cake arrived. Lucy's piece was far bigger than she could manage, even though she'd barely picked at each course as it was served. She was relieved to see Daniel looking at his watch. Predictably, in the next breath he said it was time for them to catch the train for the eleven-mile trip back to Chicago.

Daniel supported Lucy's elbow as she climbed the steps at the rear of the train car, then opened the wooden door for her to enter.

"Sit anywhere you like," he said.

Lucy chose a seat in the middle of the car and arranged herself gracefully. She was a striking woman, Daniel thought, as he often did. While Lucy was not beautiful in a classical sense, nevertheless her presence turned heads—even on a train late at night where no one knew she was a Banning and a resident of Prairie Avenue.

Daniel settled in next to Lucy. Few other passengers boarded, but he knew from experience that as the train neared the city, riders would increase.

"I do wish they would build a proper train station in Riverside," Daniel said. "The railroad has been stopping here for twenty years or more."

"I suppose it's part of the city planning and they'll get to it in time," Lucy responded.

"In spite of that, it was a nice evening, wouldn't you agree?"

Lucy nodded absently. "I always enjoy seeing your parents. What they've done to the house is lovely."

"Mother loves having trees all around—and her own pond in the back lawn. If the weather is mild enough in September, I rather suspect she'd like to give us an outdoor party around the time of the wedding."

"So it's to be September, then?"

Daniel turned his head to look at Lucy, who suddenly seemed small as she leaned against the window.

"Do you not find September acceptable?" he asked. "That is almost a year away. I could still make an argument for July, if you don't want to wait until September." He reached over and squeezed her hand on her lap, but she didn't respond.

"What I think," Lucy said, "is that our mothers have settled the matter between themselves."

Daniel chuckled and patted her hand. "September it is, then. Perhaps after church tomorrow we can have a word with the pastor and formally get the wedding on the church calendar."

Finally Lucy turned to look at him. "That might be premature."

"Why is that?" Daniel had in mind clearing up one problem between them, but it would be cleared up long before September. Tonight, in fact.

Lucy shrugged. "As you pointed out, September is nearly a year away. There's plenty of time to start making specific plans after New Year's."

"It can't hurt to get a date on the calendar." Daniel studied Lucy, who had once again turned her gaze to the darkness outside. He surrendered to the sway of the train as he wondered what was really on Lucy's mind and contemplated when he would ask the question weighing on his.

Back in Chicago, at a proper train station, Daniel hailed a carriage cab that took them home to Prairie Avenue. He used his key to let them into the house, and out of habit they moved to the empty parlor.

"I guess everyone else has retired for the evening," Daniel said.

"It looks that way," Lucy said. "If you like, I can ring for Charlotte and she can bring us some refreshment."

Daniel shook his head. "Not for me, thank you. That meal will carry me far past breakfast."

"Yes, I agree. Perhaps we should just turn in as well."

"Are you too tired for a bit more conversation?" Daniel asked. He was not going to sleep one more night without knowing the truth.

She looked at him directly for the first time all evening. "What is it, Daniel?"

"Perhaps we should sit down."

"This sounds serious." Lucy sat in an armchair. Daniel sat where he could look directly at her.

"A business acquaintance made a curious remark to me," he said. "He claims to have seen you on the university grounds more than once in recent weeks. I recall you initially had orphanage business there, but I can't help wondering what would take you there repeatedly."

Lucy hardly knew what to say. She was tired and worried. This was not how she had imagined this conversation might take place. However, she always knew the moment would come. She looked him in the eye and didn't blink.

"I've enrolled in an art history class." Lucy opted to stick to the facts. "It meets on Tuesday and Thursday afternoons from one until three."

Involuntarily, she was holding her breath, waiting to see what he would do.

"So you're not working at the orphanage?" he finally asked.

"I used to go three afternoons a week. Now I go all day on Friday."

"I see."

"Do you, Daniel? Can you really understand? Because I would like to take more classes."

Daniel stood up and waved one hand dismissively. "It seems you have more time on your hands than I realized. You're engaging in the idleness of an unmarried woman, and I won't have it."

"Daniel!" Lucy was on her feet now.

He began to pace with heavy steps. "Perhaps rather than

wait until September, we should marry in the spring. I had hoped we could move into a completed home, but in view of these circumstances, we can live somewhere temporarily while we build. Perhaps we should even have a Christmas wedding."

"Christmas!"

"Yes, Christmas. Or New Year's at the latest. Our mothers would be thrilled and easily forgive us for the short notice."

Lucy knew the fiery look she saw in Daniel's eye. His mind was made up, and the time for subtle persuasions was past.

"Daniel, I don't think that's going to happen," she said.

"It will be a challenge, I grant you, but entirely possible. My experience is that anything can be done. It simply costs more to make arrangements on short notice. We can still have the wedding we want."

Lucy took a deep breath. "But I don't want a wedding, Daniel."

He spun around and stared at her. "What did you say?" His face reddened rapidly.

Mindful that her parents were just down the hall, Lucy moved swiftly to close the pocket doors under the parlor's arched woodwork. She turned back to Daniel, trembling.

"I don't want a wedding, Daniel. I'm fond of your parents, and I'm fond of you. But not in that way. Our families have a unique relationship, but that is not sufficient basis for a marriage."

"It would seem you've given this a great deal of thought."

Lucy nodded. "I have."

"How dare you humiliate me!"

"Daniel, please, I'm not trying to hurt you."

"If I understand you correctly, you are breaking our engagement. How on earth would that not hurt me?"

"Please forgive me, Daniel." Lucy gulped air, hardy able

to speak. Whenever she had imagined this moment, she felt relief. But its reality shook her nerves.

"It's that foolish class," Daniel said. "It has filled your head with silly notions. Your parents don't know about your class, do they?"

She shook her head.

"And you don't want them to know."

"They wouldn't understand."

"With good reason!" he bellowed.

She stepped forward and put a hand on his arm. "Please, Daniel, we can work this out. Let's try to talk calmly."

He threw off her touch. "Surely under the circumstances you don't expect me to keep this secret."

"If you have any affection for me at all, you will," Lucy said. "I will bear the blame for breaking the engagement."

"As well you should—you are the one who broke it, after all."

"I promise I will say nothing disparaging about you. I've made this choice, and I'm prepared to bear the consequence. But please, just let me finish this term."

He put out his hand. "My mother will want her stone back."

"I wouldn't think of keeping it." Lucy slipped the sapphire off her finger and handed it to him.

"I'm going to bed now."

Daniel shoved open the parlor doors and tromped up the marble steps, while Lucy sank into the settee. She had almost granted herself permission to surrender to tears when her mother came down the hall in her nightdress and robe.

"What in the Sam Hill is going on in here?" Flora demanded.

17

"Aren't we a pair?" Charlotte slowly brushed Lucy's hair out a morning two weeks later.

Lucy lifted her eyes to the mirror and her own strained reflection below Charlotte's sallow skin. She wore a muted coral Liberty tea dress. Somehow the fashionable tight-waisted clothing in bold colors had little appeal for her in recent days. Lucy was grateful for the gentler lines of the chiffon seersucker gown. Wistfully she wondered what it would be like to get dressed in the morning and be ready for the day, rather than constantly planning around the occasions—as simple as a meal—that required elaborate changes of clothing. But this would not be the day for a fashion revolt. The green silk gown she would wear that evening, with its froth of lace at the neckline, was already pressed and waiting on her bed.

"I suppose Mrs. Fletcher has laid out a heavy breakfast," Lucy said.

"That she has. Your mother gave specific instructions that breakfast must be the same menu your parents had on the day they married."

"Mother does this every year on their anniversary. Kippers, compotes of every variety, hot rolls, sweet rolls, three kinds of sausages. And I haven't got any appetite at all."

"You have to eat, Miss Lucy."

"You're one to talk. You look thinner every day, ever since . . ." Lucy couldn't bring herself to finish the sentence.

"Since I put my baby out to board," Charlotte whispered. She rallied and brushed with vigor. "But I've seen Henry three times. Mrs. Given has experimented to find what he likes mixed with his milk. My little boy likes only a little sugar mixed in."

Lucy blinked twice. "I thought Mr. Emmett was going to provide Nestle infant formula."

"Oh, what Mrs. Given makes is so much more economical and Henry seems to like it."

Lucy sighed, put one elbow on the vanity, and leaned on her hand. "A mother ought to be able to feed her own baby."

In the mirror, Lucy saw that Charlotte turned her back and pretended to plump the cushion on the chaise lounge. After leaving Henry with Mrs. Given—and in the reality that the busyness of the fair's dedication was over—Charlotte had moved back to her room on the third floor and resumed most of her duties in the kitchen. Lucy, though, continued to make frequent requests for Charlotte's services, if only to give Charlotte a moment to collapse on the lounge where she had last suckled her son.

Lucy's own dilemma seemed inconsequential compared to Charlotte being bereft of her son. Two weeks had passed since she revealed two secrets to Daniel—that she did not want to marry him and that she did want to take college classes. Obviously the broken engagement rumbled through the family. Flora and Samuel were flabbergasted, Oliver was scolding, Leo was silent, and Richard asked the question on all their minds—was Daniel still going to be their friend? So far, Daniel kept the second secret, and Lucy repeatedly insisted to her family that the breakup was all her doing and they should find no fault in Daniel.

Daniel took the intractable route. Lucy's decision was not going to change his routines.

"Did Daniel spend the night again?" Lucy asked Charlotte.

"Yes, miss. He came in late. He's in the dining room having his breakfast right now."

"I suppose I'll have to face him. Will you help me put my hair up?"

Lucy entered the dining room a few minutes later to find Daniel picking at the remains of his meal and reading a *Wall Street Journal*. She squared her shoulders and took her usual seat next to him.

"Good morning, Daniel."

"Mmm." He made no effort even to glance up from his paper.

Charlotte slipped in from the butler's pantry and silently picked up the sterling coffeepot to fill Lucy's cup. Daniel gestured that Charlotte should clear his dishes, and she complied.

Lucy picked up the society page of the *Chicago Tribune*, scanning to see with relief that so far her broken engagement was not gossip fodder. "Daniel," Lucy said, "can we talk for a moment?"

He shrugged. Charlotte put a lone hot roll on Lucy's plate, which Lucy pulled apart with no intention of eating.

"Daniel, I wonder if it's wise for you to spend so much time here," Lucy said.

"Why would that be?"

"Under the circumstances."

"What circumstances do you speak of?"

Lucy swallowed and pressed her lips together. Daniel's obstinacy only served to confirm her decision.

He finally turned and looked at her. "Your parents are

my parents' oldest and dearest friends. I was quite attached to them long before you were even born. They have kindly opened their home to me for my convenience."

"Yes, but Daniel, it might be easier on everyone if there were some distance just now. For a while."

"Perhaps you are thinking only of yourself. I had not thought you capable of that until recently."

Lucy sighed. "I'd like to think I have everyone's best interests at heart. Can't we discuss this in a civil manner?"

Daniel picked up his newspaper and folded it to a new section. "Here is a civil reality. Oliver and Leo are my best friends—once again, since before you were born."

"Are you really going to make this so difficult?" Lucy said through gritted teeth.

"I don't know what you're talking about."

"You make me an outcast in my own home."

Daniel threw his head back and laughed.

"Daniel, please." Heat shot through Lucy's chest.

"Don't be silly, Lucy. Did you not think through your decision before you announced it?"

"I know I've hurt you, and I'm sorry."

He shook his head. "I doubt that."

"You've been my friend too, you know. All my life, you were there."

Daniel stood up. "It was my intention to be there for the rest of your life as well. You have chosen to throw that away for a frivolous university class and a motley bunch of orphans. I can't stop you, but you can't seriously expect that you would pay no price for your decision."

"Of course I'm paying a price, but—"

"I don't intend to change a thing, Lucy. Get used to it."

Daniel picked up his newspaper, dipped his head politely, and left the room.

Lucy glanced up to see Charlotte standing nearby, eyes deep in her face.

～

Oliver and Leo contrived to get their parents out of the house so final preparations for the surprise party could proceed. Under Penard's faultless and unforgiving instructions, the household staff laid two long tables with the finest linens, china, and crystal the Bannings owned. Footmen and serving maids were on loan from the Glessners, Pullmans, and Kimballs to ensure every thought was fulfilled before it was fully formed. Knowing that Flora Banning would never intrude in the kitchen, Mrs. Fletcher had been rolling pastries, chopping vegetables, and seasoning meats for days. The dinner menu included seven full courses to serve twenty-four seated guests plus the family. Lucy played the hostess with Richard's help, and by seven-thirty that evening, guests buzzed around the parlor, broad foyer, and festive dining room waiting for the guests of honor. Expecting her usual eight o'clock dinner, Flora had come through the front door and gasped at the scene—then nearly squealed.

Charlotte, Bessie, and Elsie, in their crispest black dresses and new white aprons Mrs. Fletcher had wrangled out of Penard's household budget, moved among the guests with trays of dried prunes wrapped in bacon, tea cakes, and finger sandwiches. Borrowed footmen offered drinks, while Penard double-checked every arrangement of the exquisite meal.

Leo nudged Lucy from behind. She smiled and offered her cheek for a kiss.

"Well, it's not a Pullman dinner for eighty," Leo said, "but I think we've pulled off a successful party."

"Mother and Father seem pleased," Lucy said.

"Irene and Howard are tickled pink."

"I wouldn't know," Lucy said. "They haven't really spoken to me all evening. I don't know what to say to them, either."

"It will get better," Leo said. "They love you."

"But can they forgive me?"

The doorbell rang, and Lucy raised an eyebrow. "Are we missing someone?"

Leo intercepted Penard on his way to the front door. "I'll get it. I invited Will."

"Will? You invited Will?" Lucy followed Leo to the front door. "To a party for our parents?"

Leo pulled the door open and extended a handshake. "I'm glad you could come."

"I'm sorry to be late." Will grinned. "I suppose I've missed the dramatic moment."

"I'm afraid so. But no harm done. Dinner hasn't been served yet."

Flora drifted from the parlor to the foyer. "Leo, you rascal," she said. "What a wonderful job you did keeping a secret while you carried us around town jabbering on about horseless carriages and all that nonsense." She paused and ran her eyes down the front of Will's dark suit. "Is this your friend Mr. Edwards?"

"You remember him! I'm glad," Leo said.

"I look forward to continuing our acquaintance tonight," Will said.

"Are you staying to dinner, Mr. Edwards?" Flora asked, confused.

"Of course he's staying to dinner, Mother," Leo answered. "I invited him. They've been working him like a slave at that office. Will needs some fun."

"How thoughtful of you to look after him," Flora said blandly. She turned to Lucy. "Your brother seems to have found himself a project."

"Mother, please," Lucy said, her voice low.

Unflapped, Leo offered an arm. "Come along, Mother. I wonder if you realize John Glessner is here with his wife. She'd probably like to see the new ink drawing you hung in the parlor."

Lucy was left standing with Will, silence hanging between them.

"Leo tells me you're going through a difficult time," Will said. "If I can be of any assistance, I hope you'll call on me."

"Ah, so he told you I've broken my engagement. It's quite scandalous. I've embarrassed my parents no end."

"I'm sure you did what you thought was wise," Will said. "Your parents will come around."

"You seem optimistic."

"They want you to be happy, I have no doubt."

Lucy forced a smile. "Wait until they see the gift we've come up with. We commissioned a ewer from a glass factory in Venice. It's been months in the making. It's painted in a Renaissance-style floral design in the loveliest shade of green. The gold vermicelli background is magnificent—I can't wait till they open it."

"It's sure to be a stellar moment."

Lucy smiled and felt herself relax for the first time in days. "I'm going on like a ninny about a piece of glass. Never mind me."

"Don't apologize," Will said. "You have an eye for fine art, that's all."

Daniel sauntered out of the dining room. Looking past Lucy, he locked eyes with Will.

"Good evening, Mr. Jules," Will said. "It's nice to see you again."

"You do seem to keep popping up," Daniel said.

"Daniel, there's no need to be rude," Lucy admonished.

"Every time I turn around, there's Will Edwards. For instance, at the fair dedication. You need some air, and suddenly he needs some air." The timbre of his voice rang sharp, and his face flashed shades of fury. Lucy glanced around, smiling awkwardly at the wife of one of her father's partners who seemed disconcerted by the rising voices.

"Daniel, are you sure you feel all right?" she asked, taking his elbow and trying to steer him toward the stairs. "Perhaps you need to sit down."

Daniel was unmoved. "Are you trying to get rid of me?" He lowered the volume of his voice, but his words carried a distinct growl.

"Of course not," Lucy said quickly. "I'm just concerned for you."

"It's a bit late for that, I'm sure you would agree. How convenient that you've relieved yourself of the baggage of Daniel Jules, and in steps Will Edwards."

"Daniel, please!" Lucy spoke sharply, though quietly. "This is not the time or place."

"Oh, so now you have become concerned about social expectations. You deceive and disappoint your parents, you toss me aside without regard for the feelings of the people who care for you, and now—"

Will stepped forward and put his arm on Daniel's shoulder. "Mr. Jules, I must insist that you stop this tirade. This is an ungentlemanly outburst I'm confident you will regret in the morning. I will not stand by and listen to you treat Lucy this way."

Daniel glared at Will, and Will was unyielding. Finally Daniel broke his stare and drifted toward the parlor.

Shaken, Lucy whispered, "I've hurt him so deeply."

Penard stepped into the foyer and announced dinner was served.

18

"Miss Lucy, your book!" Charlotte pulled the art history textbook out of its hiding place in the bookcase and handed it to Lucy.

"I don't know where my brain is." Lucy sighed. "This class is almost finished. I can't go batty now. Where did I leave my satchel?"

"The closet, behind the green gown." Charlotte stepped quickly across the room and opened the closet door.

Lucy smoothed the skirt of her beige dress. The placket in the bodice had a subtle yellow check and the buttons were brown, but otherwise the dress had no ornamentation and only modest drape, nothing extravagant. Charlotte had styled her hair in the plainest manner possible under a tan hat featuring only a simple ribbon. Nothing about her appearance should attract attention, which was just the effect she hoped for.

Charlotte handed her the satchel and hung a wool cape around Lucy's shoulders. "Paddy will be around the corner with the carriage by now."

"I know, I'm late." Lucy blew out her breath. "I'll see you in a few hours."

Outside Lucy's suite, Charlotte turned to the narrow back

stairs, and Lucy continued down the marble front stairs. Lucy resisted the impulse of habit to glance in the parlor on her way out—why invite conversation if her mother should be in the room? She stepped out the front door, closed it securely behind her, walked down the steps, and turned to the right. Paddy would be waiting for her around the next corner, parked headed toward Michigan Avenue, as he was on most Tuesday afternoons.

Finding Aunt Violet sitting inside the carriage was a pleasant surprise.

"Step right up!" Aunt Violet said.

Lucy chuckled as Paddy closed the carriage door behind her. "Where are you off to?"

"Ladies auxiliary at the church," Violet answered. "Paddy's going to drop me there, then take you to school. I hope that won't make you late."

"I'll manage." She would have to move swiftly when she got to campus, but it was worth a few minutes with Violet.

"Have you recovered from Daniel's outrageous behavior at the party?" Violet asked.

Lucy smiled. "Leave it to you to get right to the point."

"It's only a few blocks to the church. I don't have time to dillydally."

Lucy sighed heavily. "I'm glad neither my parents nor his parents witnessed that scene. It would have spoiled the whole evening for them."

"Is he still insisting on using his room at the house?"

"Yes, but less frequently. In the last two weeks, he's only been there for dinner twice. In the mornings, if I know he's there I have a tray brought up to my rooms so I don't see him."

"Wise solution. Sooner or later he's going to have to accept how you feel."

"I'm sorry to have hurt him."

"Daniel is a likeable enough young man when he wants to be," Violet observed. "He's doing well at the bank. Many young women would welcome his attention, as I'm sure he will discover soon enough."

"I know. Just not me."

"No, not you. Will's the one for you."

"Aunt Violet!"

"Don't be coy with me, Lucy Banning."

"Will is Leo's friend. I assure you, he has nothing to do with what happened with Daniel."

"I believe that. But you still have a heart, and he deserves it, in my opinion."

Lucy rolled her eyes and looked out the window.

⁓⁓

Daniel leaned forward in the carriage cab and signaled the driver. Even inside the carriage, it was cold enough to see his breath. The driver—hired for the day and well paid to brace the frigid air up top—kept a discreet distance behind Violet's carriage. Daniel's own carriage would have been far more comfortable, and he kept a wool blanket there, but it also would have been far more recognizable. The anonymous-looking cab, with mismatched wheels and cracked roof, was indistinguishable on Michigan Avenue among the dozens that flowed north and south all day long.

Lucy had deceived him for months. Her conniving to enroll at the university had begun even before his proposal in July. He could see that now. What could she have been thinking, accepting his proposal one month and registering for a class the next? He paid her every attention, offered her every luxury, yet she was not satisfied.

The more he thought about it, the more he became convinced she had help. He wanted to know who. Now he did.

The horse pulling Violet Newcomb's carriage stopped in front of the church, and after its owner was discharged, resumed a trot. It seemed to Daniel that the driver was overly comfortable with the route toward the university.

⁓

The minutes immediately after class were the most disorienting for Lucy. She was used to meeting Daniel for tea in the late afternoons, and a month after the breakup, she still found herself wondering if he would get to the teahouse before she did. As she stepped out of the stone building into the December cold, she shivered with the habitual nearness of the man who had waited his life for her. Had she not broken their engagement, he would have been keeping vigil with a pot of tea. Kissing her cheek in welcome. Offering aid as he put her in a carriage.

Lucy squeezed her eyes shut for just a moment to banish the image. She walked toward the street, then down two blocks where Paddy was waiting for her, and stepped into the carriage. Inside, she closed her eyes and surrendered to the clip-clop of the mare and the sway of the carriage.

⁓

Daniel sat in the glacial carriage for more than two hours while Lucy was inside the university building. Now he signaled the driver once more.

⁓

Lucy signaled to Paddy to stop along Michigan Avenue. He complied but greeted her with puzzlement.

"We're still six blocks from your home, Miss Lucy," Paddy said as he dutifully held the door open.

Lucy wrapped her cloak around her. "I feel like walking. I

know Aunt Violet will be waiting for you at the church. Go on and get her. I'll get home on my own."

Paddy shrugged, which made Lucy smile. Clearly he had learned it was futile to dispute her choices, just as he reasoned in vain with her aunt.

Lucy stood in front of the brand-new Lexington Hotel at Michigan and Twentieth. Made of brick and terra-cotta, the building had been erected hastily in order to be ready for the onslaught of visitors to the fair in a few months. Rising ten stories from the sidewalk, it boasted luxury suites for residents who would be at home in the Prairie Avenue neighborhood two blocks away, as well as rooms whose occupants would change every few days during the fair. If she walked far enough north on Michigan, Lucy would encounter the armory building finished the previous year—a building she wished had never come to existence. Following labor unrest that led to riots and violence several years earlier, the wealthy residents of Prairie Avenue lobbied for an armory in their neighborhood. Its decorative exterior was deceptive. Though designed by a well-known architectural firm—Burnham and Root, the driving force behind the coming fair—the building served not beauty but fear. Lucy's wealthy neighbors insured protection of their property should the working class around them once again roil. The thought of it made Lucy's stomach churn, and she decided in that moment she would turn east to Prairie Avenue before the armory, perhaps at the Calumet Club at Eighteenth, where her father enjoyed his leisure hours.

———— ❧ ————

Daniel's cab slowed, but traffic on busy Michigan Avenue would never permit a carriage to crawl at Lucy's speed on foot. Daniel knew the route she was likely to take. It would simply be the reverse of a stroll they often took on Sunday afternoons when they left the Banning home and ambled along the row houses on Michigan Avenue. Confident, he gave the driver instructions to proceed at a normal speed. As he passed Second Presbyterian, Daniel saw Violet Newcomb entering her carriage. She would go to her own row house now, he knew. At the Calumet Club, Daniel gave the order to stop.

He got out.

—◦—

Lucy's pace was hardly a saunter. It was more like a bolt for home. Walking dispelled anxiety for her, but it was undeniably cold in the waning late afternoon, and darkness came early to Chicago in December. By the time she reached the church, the ladies' carriages had dispersed, for which Lucy was grateful. She would not have wanted to stop and be polite, but neither would she have wanted to be coaxed into a carriage. Keeping her cloak from flapping in the wind off the unsettled Lake Michigan, she put her head down and persevered.

"Hello, Lucy."

Lucy gasped as Daniel stepped out from the shadowy wall of the Calumet Club. Recovery came swiftly.

"Hello, Daniel."

"It's rather brisk for most people, but I know how much you enjoy an invigorating walk."

She nodded. "You know me well." She moved to go around him and continue.

Daniel blocked her effort and offered his arm. "May I walk you home?"

"That's not necessary, thank you."

He did not move his arm. "It would be my pleasure. Please?"

Stifling a sigh, Lucy took Daniel's arm.

"I should apologize for my behavior at the party," he said. Daniel had never been a man of apologies. Perhaps his fury toward her was dissipating. "Thank you, Daniel. That means a great deal to me."

He put his fingers over her hand tucked into his elbow. A harmless gesture, yet it seemed overly familiar. When she twitched in response, though, he increased the pressure, as if to say there could be no thought of removing her hand.

They moved along Eighteenth Street toward Prairie Avenue. *In two short blocks, I'll be home*, she thought.

"I hope we can be friends, Lucy," Daniel said.

She glanced up at him and answered tentatively, "I hope so too."

"We're adults, reasonable people."

"Yes, we are."

"There's no reason to distress our parents any more than we have—or more precisely, more than *you* already have."

Lucy was silent as they walked the next block. She had promised to accept full responsibility, so she couldn't argue with his choice of words.

"Leo's friend, for instance," Daniel said.

"Will Edwards?"

"Yes, Mr. Edwards. I shouldn't get too close to him if I were you."

What is he getting at?

"I would be careful about becoming involved with Mr. Edwards," Daniel reiterated.

"I'm not 'involved' with Will Edwards."

"That's good, because if you were, people would be hurt, and I'm sure you don't want that to happen."

Lucy was counting the steps to her house now—and hoping Daniel was not planning to stay for dinner. At the front door, finally, he let go of her hand.

"I'm glad we had this little talk," he said. "I have a train to catch. Good-bye, Lucy."

Lucy watched his disappearing form, unbending and proud. At least a full minute passed before she breathed normally again. The door opened behind her and Penard spoke.

"Are you all right, Miss Lucy?"

I don't know. Am I?

19

"Such a busy season it's been," Flora said as Archie, the footman, set her soup in front of her. "I can't tell you all how happy I am to have a normal family dinner tonight and not be rushing off to a party."

"How is it that we have everyone home tonight a mere five days before Christmas?" Leo asked as he picked up his roll.

"Thank goodness the major parties are behind us now," Flora said. "The Kimballs had a lovely gathering, and I was honored to be invited, but the Pullmans were a bit too extravagant, in my opinion. When on earth will they stop adding on to that house? My goodness, have you seen the new conservatory?"

Richard spooned his soup. "Is it true the Fields once spent seventy-five thousand dollars on a birthday party for their son?"

"Don't slurp, Richard," Flora admonished. "Yes, that's true, a Mikado ball when he turned eighteen. But it's poor taste to discuss it."

"Francis Glessner gave a nice dinner," Lucy said. "I was served in the library, and it was delicious to feast my eyes on their book collection along with the dinner."

"Would you believe Mrs. Pullman is having another party?"

Flora said. "On Thursday she is having a group of ladies in for a midafternoon Christmas tea. I promised Charlotte would help serve."

Lucy's eyes flashed at Charlotte for a fraction of a second. She was likely the only one to notice the maid's breath catch among the clatter and clinking of the soup course.

"What do you mean, Mother?" Lucy made sure to keep her tone even.

"There's nothing mysterious about it," Flora answered. "The Pullmans' housekeeper asked for some assistance for the affair, and when Penard approached me with the question, I saw no reason not to oblige. After all, their servants were here for the anniversary party last month."

Lucy sipped a spoonful of soup in a manner that appeared far more casual than she felt. "I believe Thursday is Charlotte's day off," she said.

"Oh, she'll be paid nicely, I'm sure," Flora said, unaffected. "It will be well worth her time, if I know Mrs. Pullman."

Lucy set her spoon down and laid both hands on her lap. Charlotte stepped forward to remove her soup bowl.

"Charlotte," Lucy said, "I wonder if anyone mentioned this arrangement to you."

"No, Miss Lucy." Charlotte's soft response came as she stepped away from the table again.

"Mother, perhaps Mrs. Pullman doesn't really need Charlotte after all," Lucy said. "It's only an afternoon tea. Surely one less maid won't be the end of things."

"I don't know what you're making such a fuss about," Flora said. "It's the holidays. It's a busy time. It comes as no surprise to any of the staff that they may be asked to serve in extra capacities."

"My point is simply that I think Charlotte should have been asked," Lucy said. "Perhaps she has plans for her day off."

"I'm sure she'll appreciate the extra pay. Won't you, Charlotte? You could use a few extra coins, isn't that right?"

Charlotte's eyes were demurely aimed at the floor. "Yes, ma'am."

"She'll want you early in the morning, I'm sure."

Lucy let her shoulders slump. What else could Charlotte say under the circumstances? She could hardly explain she was planning to see her baby son on Thursday and would have to wait a full week if she didn't go on schedule.

"I believe I have some gifts to get tomorrow," Lucy said. "I'm afraid I've rather left things to the last minute. Perhaps I'll take Charlotte with me to help with packages. I'm sure Mrs. Fletcher can spare her for a few hours." *Two can play that game*, she thought.

Charlotte discreetly disappeared into the butler's pantry.

"But you know I'm going to my needlework group tomorrow," Flora protested, "and your father and brothers have to be downtown. I'm afraid you won't have a carriage."

"No mind," Lucy said lightly. "We'll catch a cab on Michigan Avenue."

"As long as I don't hear any nonsense about using the streetcar," Flora said.

"I promise."

Two hours later, Lucy pushed the annunciator button and called for Charlotte to help her undress. When the maid arrived, Lucy was already out of her gown and in a sleeping shift.

"I'm sorry my mother did that," Lucy said immediately. "I should have warned you about how much the neighborhood shares servants during the holidays."

"We're not really going shopping tomorrow, are we?" Charlotte asked.

"Well, I'll have to come home with some packages or face

an inquisition," Lucy said. "But I'll put you on a streetcar going south as soon as we're out of the neighborhood and we'll meet up to come home together."

"Thank you, Miss Lucy." Charlotte's gratitude was sincere. "But Mrs. Given will not be expecting me."

"She looks after two toddlers and an infant," Lucy reasoned. "I'm sure she must venture out from time to time, but she can't be gone long. I promise, you are going to see Henry tomorrow."

"Thank you, Miss Lucy," Charlotte said again. She rearranged items on the vanity table for no particular reason. "Mr. Daniel was not waiting for you today, was he?"

Lucy rolled her eyes. "No, thank goodness. He was only there that one time two weeks ago. I've learned my lesson about walking alone."

"But why shouldn't you walk alone?" Charlotte wanted to know. "If the weather is fine and you love to walk, why shouldn't you?"

Lucy shrugged one shoulder. "Perhaps in time. But I don't want to invite a reoccurrence."

"Mr. Penard insists that we continue to lay a place for Mr. Daniel at every meal," Charlotte said.

"I know. I realize my brothers miss him. But I'm grateful that if he stays the night, he comes in late and leaves early at least some of the time."

Charlotte left a few minutes later, and Lucy brushed her own hair. *This is going to change*, she promised herself. *Charlotte and I are both going to have some control over our own lives. Somehow. Soon.*

Lucy was already registered for the next term. She had scoured the course offerings carefully to find a class that met on the same schedule as her current class. Any change in routine would arouse questions she didn't want to answer.

The days bustled by, and Christmas Eve was upon Prairie Avenue. Candles, outdated for daily use by gas lamps and then electric lights, came out of the closets and sprang up in the windowsills in nostalgic arrangements. Greenery adorned mantels and railings. Towering trees rose in foyers and parlors, where they awaited ribbons and ornaments. Dinner at the Banning house, Lucy knew, would be shamelessly profligate and Flora would crave even more celebration. Samuel would ceremonially press a few coins into the hands of each member of the household staff. It would be a fraction of a fraction of what Lucy knew he could easily afford. For the members of the staff who had been working in the household for the entire year, envelopes awaited in the butler's pantry with a bonus month's wages. There was no question of Lucy not being present for these traditions, but she was determined to spend a few hours at St. Andrew's. She made no particular secret of her intentions—daring her parents to object to offering a morsel of cheerfulness to orphans on Christmas Eve. She took the larger carriage, laden with packages wrapped in paper and tied in string.

Children were singing carols when she entered the gray dining hall—dozens of soprano voices fighting to be heard, each one seemingly more enthusiastic than the next. They seemed oblivious to the drear around them. Lucy made a mental note to arrange to have the dining room painted. Some of the boys could do the work if they had proper supervision. In another corner, a group of older children were stringing popcorn in winding lengths. Mr. Emmett had mentioned to Lucy that someone had kindly donated the tree, but still most of the children would finish the holiday with little or nothing more than they had when it began. The lucky ones might get a sweet treat or a note from a parent. A few very,

very lucky ones would spend Christmas somewhere other than St. Andrew's. Lucy intended to make sure every single child had a fat, juicy orange that didn't have to be shared and that the bookshelves and modest toy cupboards were filled to overflowing.

"Miss Lucy!" Little Benny barreled toward her from across the hall, and Lucy barely freed her arms of packages in time to receive him. Benny threw his arms around her neck and squealed, "Merry Christmas."

"Merry Christmas," Lucy responded.

"I have a new friend." Benny dragged Lucy by the hand.

She followed him between the wooden tables and benches, where the children ate their meals in two shifts three times a day, toward the Christmas tree.

"Here's my new friend," Benny said. "His name is Mr. Will."

Lucy's eyes lifted and widened. "Will! My goodness!" She glanced down at Benny. "Mr. Will is my friend too."

"I meant what I said when I offered to help," Will said. "You kindly passed my offer on to Mr. Emmett and he just as kindly sent me a note inviting me to stop by."

"You might have told me," Lucy said. But she was pleased to see him, and the shine in his eyes told her he was glad she had come.

"Mr. Will brought us a tree." Benny's round face glowed. "And he's going to come back soon and build proper offices. He promised!"

"Then I'm sure he'll do just that," Lucy assured the boy, "because Mr. Will strikes me as a man of his word." She turned to Will. "I have a carriage full of packages outside. Perhaps you'd like to help me fetch them."

Will glanced at the progress on the tree. Benny leaned over one of the older girls with great interest in what her fingers were doing with needle and popcorn and cranberries.

"The crew seems to have this well in hand," Will said. He offered his arm and she took it.

"So you're going to be coming round to St. Andrew's to build offices," Lucy said.

"I've already given Mr. Emmett some rough sketches. I think we've settled on a plan. You'll be pleased to know he wants to make the volunteer office considerably larger."

"That is good news. When do you expect to begin?"

"Right after New Year's. I'll work in the evenings and on Saturday afternoons when my firm's offices are closed. Mr. Emmett feels several of the older boys would do well with the experience, so I have a built-in work crew."

"It's a wonderful idea." Lucy stopped short of the carriage. She didn't want the driver to overhear, but Will was sure to find out soon enough. "Will, I've got a confession to make."

He turned and looked at her square on. "You're not really here three days a week."

"How did you know?"

"I've met Benny a time or two before," Will explained. "He's adamant Friday is the day Miss Lucy comes."

"He keeps track of a calendar amazingly well for a six-year-old." Lucy's tone sounded nervous even to her own ears.

"Don't worry, Lucy. I'm not going to run and tattle on you."

"Aren't you even curious where I really do go on Tuesdays and Thursdays?"

"Of course," he answered, "but only because I find you interesting in many ways. It's really none of my business, though."

Lucy worked her lips, but the words would not form.

"We'd better get the packages," Will said.

Lucy resumed progress toward the carriage. "Will, I don't know what to say."

"Don't say anything. Let's just make a bunch of children very happy this afternoon."

Will opened the carriage door and leaned in for a stack of boxes. Lucy swallowed the knot in her throat and wished one of the packages were for Will.

⁓◈⁓

Lucy ate the succulent roast turkey with the savory apple-walnut dressing Mrs. Fletcher only prepared for Christmas Eve. She ate wild rice, sweet potatoes, red beets, and green salad. She even ate pecan pie. But she wondered all the while what Will was eating for dinner, and with whom. And where would he spend Christmas Day? Secretly she hoped Leo would invite Will to the Banning celebration, but the family traditions were rutted deep and never varied. Their only guests from year to year were the Juleses.

Daniel and his parents would arrive for a late Christmas morning breakfast, as they did every year. Flora went to great pains to be sure Lucy understood certain long-standing traditions would not be disrupted for her convenience. The truth was Lucy did not want to disrupt traditions. It was awkward for her to encounter Daniel personally, but she wanted everyone to continue sharing their affections freely. While she was sure to decline an invitation to stroll if Daniel offered, it was imperative they learn to be comfortable with their families around them.

As Lucy sipped her after-dinner coffee, she realized she knew virtually nothing about Will's family other than their humble station. Why had he not taken a train to New Jersey for Christmas? If Leo knew the details of Will's family, he never mentioned them.

⁓◈⁓

After the sumptuous meal and the family's exchange of gifts, it was time for the Bannings to prepare for the late night Christmas Eve service at Second Presbyterian.

"Why don't you come?" Lucy coaxed Charlotte as the maid fastened the gold chain Richard had given his sister around her neck. "The other maids always go."

"I'm sure there's still work to do here for tomorrow." Mr. Penard always had a list of details to confirm or improve. Charlotte supposed Christmas would be even more taxing than the usual Banning dinner.

"It can wait," Lucy countered. "Even Mrs. Fletcher goes to church on Christmas Eve. Surely she can't begrudge you the same opportunity."

"What would I wear? I haven't got any church clothes."

Lucy waved a hand. "There must be something in my closet that would fit you. Choose anything you like—and keep it as a gift."

Charlotte protested further, but in the end, Lucy wore her down. Now she sat in the balcony at Second Presbyterian between Elsie and Archie and wore Lucy's gray flannel suit. The skirt was a little big at the waist, but the length of the jacket hid the pins that held the skirt in place.

Second Presbyterian was as far from her grandmother's small clapboard church as Charlotte could imagine possible. For almost three months Charlotte had considered the towering Gothic structure from the outside, and now she absorbed the experience from the inside. The stained glass windows under the arches were dim in the midnight moonlight, but she could imagine their brilliance with morning sun pouring through them. Hundreds of organ pipes glittered in the light of the candelabras standing in front of them. Just the greenery adorning the sanctuary must have cost a small fortune—by

Charlotte's standards, though a pittance by Prairie Avenue standards, she knew.

She had no voice for the carols, though. Words about a baby boy in his mother's arms choked in her throat. Looking down from the balcony, she soaked up the families gathered in the pews below, grandchildren visiting for the holiday and three generations sitting together in many pews. Even in the pew behind her, a boy not yet old enough for school wriggled with Christmas delight well past his bedtime. Her own loss stabbed her. All her dreams of what her family might be already were dashed, and she was only twenty. If only her grandmother had lived to meet Henry.

Tomorrow was Sunday, but none of the staff would have the day off because it was Christmas and a day full of feast and extravagance for the Bannings. Charlotte was used to working on Christmas. On the farm, the animals still hungered and gave milk on holidays.

Henry's first Christmas. It was little comfort to tell herself Henry was too young to know his mother was not with him on Christmas, or even that it was Christmas. Charlotte sniffed and blinked back tears she had not expected.

Beside her, Archie offered to share his hymnal and quietly took her hand. Charlotte knew she should not allow Archie to hold her hand. It wasn't fair to him. He was a thoughtful enough young man, but nothing could ever come of his attentions. Just for that moment, though, just for a few seconds, Charlotte yearned for the kindness of a man's touch.

At the start of the next stanza, she withdrew her hand.

20

*I*s it a month in spring?"

"No, it is not 'May.'"

"Does it come after the night?"

"No, it is not 'day.'"

"Will I get somewhere if I take it?"

"No, it is not 'way.'"

"Will I spend some coins?"

"No, it is not 'pay.'"

"Is it the color of your Aunt Violet's mare?" Will was getting desperate.

Lucy laughed. "No, it is not 'gray.'"

"Will I find some in a barn?"

"No, it is not 'hay.'"

"Do we do this in church?"

"No, it is not 'pray.'"

"Mmm." He thought harder. "Can I ride it through the snow?"

"No, it is not 'sleigh.' But that's clever!"

Will shrugged. "I give up. I'm sure you're sorry you asked me to play."

"That's it!" Lucy fell back in the settee in laughter.

"'Play'? That's the word?" Will asked.

Leo clapped him on the back. "You're better at Crambo than you confessed."

"I assure you, I truly was ready to admit defeat," Will insisted. "My mind just doesn't make the right connections for some of these parlor games."

"You did very well," Lucy said. "Your clue was 'ray,' and you came up with a lot of rhyming words."

"Until I stumbled on the right one quite by accident."

Leo stood up. "Who needs a fresh glass of holiday punch?"

While Leo carried glasses to the crystal punch bowl on the round table in the foyer, Will assessed the group. When Leo invited him to spend New Year's Eve at the Bannings', he hadn't known what to expect, but he had thought it would be more formal than a group of Leo's friends usurping the use of the parlor. He supposed both Leo and Lucy would have been invited to balls, and in fact some of the guests seemed as if they were dressed with the intention of going to a ball later. George Glessner was there with a young woman named Phyllida whom neither Leo nor Lucy had met before, but George wore a tuxedo complete with cummerbund, and Phyllida wore an ivory satin gown with generous drapes in the skirt. A colleague from Leo's department at the university was there with his bride, married only two weeks so not yet disengaged from the unattached band of friends who had gone through school together. They were dressed nicely, but not for the ballroom circuit. Harry, David, Amelia, and Cynthia came as a group without particular pairings. Will met all these friends of Leo's for the first time that night.

The rest of the Bannings had dispersed around the neighborhood to various parties. Even Richard had an invitation and was going to be allowed to stay out until midnight before a coachman would go fetch him.

Will picked up his empty glass and sauntered out to the

foyer to the table encumbered with platters of food that seemed to rotate periodically but never disappear. Charlotte stood by attentively refilling punch glasses and offering delectable finger foods on small plates.

"Ah, Will, my good friend." Leo spoke with holiday satisfaction. "I hope you're enjoying the evening so far."

"It's a nice party, Leo. Not too stuffy."

"You couldn't seriously think I would invite you to a stuffy party." Leo took Will's glass and handed it to Charlotte to refill.

"Thank you, Charlotte." Will took the glass back. The maid dipped her head slightly in acknowledgment of being spoken to but showed no further reaction. Will could read no emotion in her flat expression. Was it the result of unrelenting training about what it meant to be in service, or did she really feel no hint of excitement even on New Year's Eve? The image of her ashen face the day he had encountered Lucy and Charlotte in the street in mid-October hung before his eyes now.

"Will, I hope you'll take advantage of this opportunity to chat with Cynthia Sterling," Leo suggested. "I've known her for years, and I'm certain you'd enjoy her company. As a matter of fact, she went to school with Lucy."

"Which one is she?" Will's eyes followed Lucy's movement across the foyer and into the dining room and the way she glanced back toward Charlotte in a gracious sweep.

Leo playfully punched his arm. "Pay attention! In the green dress."

Will looked across the foyer into the parlor. "Oh yes." Cynthia was a striking woman, but nothing compared to Lucy. His eyes moved back to Lucy.

"Perhaps we'll pair you with Cynthia for the next game," Leo suggested. His eyes twinkled. "If you're lucky, you'll be next to her at the stroke of midnight."

Will had no intention of kissing anyone at the stroke of midnight. Already he had decided to step outside for some air to clear his head shortly before, conveniently "forgetting" what time it was.

⁓⁓⁓

Charlotte carried an empty tray into the kitchen and prepared to refill it with tiny sausages wrapped in pastry, which she removed from the oven. Penard had given Mrs. Fletcher the evening off, while he himself stayed to supervise service at the party. Most of the work was left to Charlotte and Archie, the footman and assistant coachman who would be sent to fetch Richard at twelve-thirty. However, Mrs. Fletcher had prepared for two days and left an assortment of finger foods, desserts, and beverages that would see the parlor group into the New Year. Charlotte simply had to warm some of them periodically and make sure the supply was never-ending.

Charlotte glanced at the clock. Nine-thirty. She was already dead on her feet. How would she last another three hours—or more?

Archie came in from the coach house, stomping snow off his feet. "Even the horses are restless tonight. They know it's time for a party."

"It's all the lights, I suppose," Charlotte said. "Everything lit and everyone dressed up."

"How about you?"

Charlotte looked at him and raised an eyebrow.

"Aren't you the least bit in a party mood?" Archie asked.

Charlotte moved to the icebox for the cucumber sandwiches she had made that afternoon. "I hadn't much thought of it," she answered. "I'm serving and cleaning up, just like any other evening."

"But it's New Year's Eve! Are you at least looking forward to the new year?"

Charlotte sighed. "I guess I am."

The new year could hardly be worse than the one it replaced. Last year at this time she hadn't even known she would have a baby and could not have imagined that experience would transfigure her existence. Last year there had been no Henry. This year he was all she thought about. Last year she had never lived anywhere but the farm, her life an open book to everyone who knew her. This year a crowded city was her safety. No, the coming year could not be worse than this one.

Archie winked. "I hope you'll find yourself in the kitchen at the stroke of midnight."

Ignoring him, Charlotte picked up the trays of sausages and sandwiches and headed for the foyer.

———

He brooded outside. With a party inside, no one thought to close the drapes, and he could sit comfortably in his carriage and observe everything that happened in the parlor's glow. Two people. They were the only ones who mattered, and each time they shifted toward each other, his heart pitched anew.

He was the reason she had done it. Daniel could see that now. She had thrown him off for this architect from New Jersey who offered her nothing.

She was across the room from Will, but Daniel saw how her eyes lifted in the direction of his laugh.

How his glance returned to her as predictably as a ticking clock.

How she smiled across the room to him.

How he made space for her on the settee.

The way she didn't want to move from that spot until he offered his hand to assist her.

The cards they took up together at the game table.

Daniel saw.

She was his. What was she doing in there? She was his!

~

Lucy almost stayed upstairs in her suite for the evening. She certainly had not wanted to go to a ball, and she doubted she would be missed at any of the extravaganzas to which she had been invited. Leo was the life of any party, and even though the group was small, it was sure to be the best gathering in the neighborhood. She just hadn't felt like a party of any sort. She knew Charlotte was on duty and she could have rung for food if she wanted any, but mostly she would have been grateful for a quiet evening with a couple of books. Then Leo pleaded. He offered Harry and David for her amusement, and even tried to induce guilt by claiming to have goaded his friends into coming with the promise of her presence—as if anyone had to be goaded into coming to a party Leo Banning was hosting. However, when he revealed he had invited her old schoolmate Cynthia for Will, Lucy changed her mind and thought seriously about what to wear. The ribbon-striped fabric was lined with red silk, and a diaphanous chiffon frill cascaded around her neck and shoulders.

Lucy laid her last card facedown on the game pile and called out, "Seven."

Harry responded by saying, "Cheat!"

Lucy smiled and revealed the card she had played. "I know the rules of 'Cheat,'" she said. "I can claim my card is anything I like unless I'm challenged. In this case, though, it really was a seven."

"And you really are out of cards," Will said. "Congratulations. You win!"

Harry groaned. "I only had two cards left to get rid of."

"I think I'll reward myself with a piece of cake," Lucy announced.

Will was on his feet instantly to pull her chair out. "I could use a bit of refreshment myself."

He offered his arm and she took it. *How completely natural this feels*, she thought. They walked together to the refreshment table. Charlotte smiled vaguely and nodded at them.

"Cake, Miss Lucy?" Charlotte asked. "Mrs. Fletcher made the red velvet."

Lucy had not indulged in red velvet cake since the last time she had dinner at the Jules house—the night she broke her engagement. Her eyes flickered at what else the table offered but soon returned to the cake. *I am not going to give up my favorite cake for the rest of my life.*

"Yes, Charlotte, a piece of red velvet cake, please," Lucy said. She picked up a fork, already feeling sweetness melt on her tongue.

Cake in hand, Will lightly took her elbow and together they stepped away from the table.

"Are you all right, Lucy?"

"Why do you ask?"

"A moment ago you said you wanted cake, then you almost turned it down."

How could he possibly have noticed so brief a hesitation?

"The last time I had this cake was the night I broke my engagement," she admitted simply and softly.

They ate a few bites without speaking.

"And have you now redeemed your favorite cake?" Will asked.

"I'm working at it." Lucy took another bite. "Mmm."

"Do you think of him often?"

"It's as if he's always here," Lucy said, "which of course is frequently true. He still stays the night sometimes during the week. The rest of my family welcomes him. His scent is in every room and does not abate. I sometimes feel that he has me under his thumb somehow, even though I know that's ridiculous. I feel him near even when I know he is not."

"Yours is a complicated relationship," Will observed. "Your families have been entwined for decades."

Lucy forced a smile. "We must not get too dismal at Leo's party. We'll never hear the end of it."

"Let's find a game where we can be partners," Will suggested.

Leo poked his head out of the parlor. "Lucy, perhaps you would favor us with the results of your long years of study at the piano."

"I'm not sure I know anything gamey enough for your gang," she answered.

"Let us be the judge. Get in here and tickle the ivories."

21

*J*anuary blustered in as it always did in Chicago—icy temperatures, frigid winds, the menace of snow perpetually in the air.

It was Tuesday. Lucy fastidiously stuck to her routine of being out of the house on Tuesday afternoons, and January 17 was no different. Having pored over the course offerings seeking a class offered on Tuesday and Thursday afternoons for the next term, Lucy settled on an Introduction to Philosophy class. Certainly riskier than art history and no doubt unseemly for a woman, it nevertheless appealed. She now held in her hand the confirmation that she had reserved a seat in the lecture hall of a prestigious professor for the term that would start soon. How much longer Daniel would keep her secret she could not know, but she would welcome every class session she could manage.

The coming months would be busy. In addition to the class and her usual Fridays at St. Andrew's, Mondays largely would be consumed with committee work for the women's exhibit at the fair. Just the day before, the group she worked with had agreed to meet every Monday until opening day to review thoroughly every detail.

Successfully registered, Lucy turned her attention to

her wardrobe. When winter finally relinquished its hold to spring, she would need some lightweight dresses to serve both for classes and the orphanage. Marshall Field's store was just the place. Choosing something from the rack seemed so much simpler to Lucy than selecting fabric and looking at sketches and going to fittings and acting like every dress was a wedding gown. No, a few ready-made simple suits and dresses would suffice for looking inconspicuous.

Lucy had sent Paddy on his way as soon as he dropped her at the university. Relieved of worrying about Daniel's disapproval, she had taken to making her way around the city on public transportation more frequently, at least when she felt fairly sure she would not encounter family members. Chicago seemed to be adding streetcar and train lines constantly. The pressure of the world's fair spurred construction and infrastructure in every direction, which Lucy was eager to take advantage of. Now she wrapped her woolen cloak more tightly around her and hopped on an elevated train to head to the shopping district.

She heard her name almost as soon as she stepped off the train a few minutes later. Turning her head, she adjusted the angle of her hat's brim to respond.

"Will! Once again our paths cross in a delightful surprise."

"I've just come from presenting a proposal to a new client. I think I've got the job!"

"That's wonderful!"

"Come celebrate with me," Will said. "Let's have tea."

She agreed immediately, and they ducked into the lobby of a hotel well known for its afternoon offering. Lucy was thrilled to be seated close to the heat of the onyx fireplace dominating the room. Will helped Lucy remove her cloak and they slid into their chairs. As soon as they ordered, he launched into an explanation of the project he had just proposed, a new office building.

"It's the first commission I've brought to the firm on my own," he explained. "They loved my concept of openness and light. I'll be the one to lead the design team and present every stage to the client. I've never supervised a project of this scope before."

"It's a wonderful opportunity for you, Will. I'm so pleased."

"I'm babbling like a little boy."

He's blushing! Lucy realized. "I've never seen you look so happy."

"You were the first person I wanted to tell, Lucy. I can't believe you were right there, getting off a train."

Lucy grimaced. "Don't tell my mother I ride trains. They're as bad as streetcars in her estimation."

"Your secret's safe with me," he assured her. "All your secrets will always be safe with me."

Her breath caught. What other secrets did he know?

When Lucy left Will, she took a streetcar, deliberately going south past her neighborhood. If she hailed a carriage cab on Michigan Avenue and rode north, she would arrive home from the direction of the orphanage, where supposedly she had spent the afternoon. At five-thirty, Michigan Avenue bustled and cabs were plentiful. She had no trouble finding one and giving brief directions to go north and then cut east to Prairie Avenue.

She could see the tower of Second Presbyterian from several blocks away, but it seemed strangely lit for the hour. The sky around it hung thick and eerie in the late afternoon shadows.

A fire! The church had already burned once at its original location, before rebuilding at Michigan and Twentieth. Lucy leaned forward and to the side, trying to make sense of the scene in front of her and trying to remember if Aunt Violet or her mother were supposed to be at the church today. Two blocks short of the church, the carriage stopped, stymied in standstill traffic. Drivers quarreled over street space as they attempted to turn around and seek another route. Both sides of the street began to fill with pedestrians.

Lucy pulled on the handle and got out of the cab. The driver jumped down to attend to her.

"I'm sorry, ma'am, the road is blocked. We can't go any further."

"That's all right." Lucy handed the man a coin. Her eyes stung with the scene raging in front of her—literally. Smoke draped across the sky above an orange inferno.

"The Calumet Club!" a voice shouted. "It's on fire!"

Lucy gasped. Panic immediately subsumed relief that the church was not burning. Her father belonged to the Calumet Club, across the street from the church, and often dropped in for an hour or two after leaving his office before coming home to dinner. She pressed northward on foot, weaving between the stranded horses and carriages, until she was enmeshed in a growing throng of spectators.

The Calumet Club, one of Chicago's most exclusive establishments, was a proud structure, an architectural hallmark of Burnham and Root—the same firm responsible for several homes on Prairie Avenue. Barely ten years old, it was supposed to endure for decades, boasting twelve stories and turreted corners. Yet it was crumbling before Lucy's eyes. Jagged brick walls caved in heaving piles to the sidewalk below. Flames blazed in every direction as the fire crew abandoned their effort to contain the inferno.

Lucy hastened her step, foraging the mob for anyone she knew who might answer questions. Between the darkness and the smoke, she could discern nothing useful. Finally, she resorted to grabbing the sleeve of a stranger and begging for information.

"Is anyone hurt?" she asked. "Did everyone get out?"

One person after another shrugged. It was just too hard to see, too hard to hear, too hard to know. She would have to get closer.

Lucy pressed forward, aching to know if her father had been in the club that afternoon. She squeezed through the smallest openings in the crowd, feeling the heat rise with every step closer to the blaze. And then she saw a form she knew. "George!" Lucy called. "George Glessner!"

His shoulders turned, and she saw his soot-covered face.

"Oh, George, are you all right? Were you inside?"

George shook his head. "The call came through on the telegraph in my old schoolroom," he said. "I found it printed out on the signal repeater tape and came right over."

"Is everyone out?"

"A few of the men are trying to save some of the artwork, but I think they're giving up. It's burning too fast."

"Is anyone hurt?"

"One of the maids was taken to the hospital, and another one is missing. They fear she didn't make it down the stairs."

"How awful. My father—"

George shook his head, emphatically this time. "No, he wasn't there today. I saw him get out of his carriage in front of your house with my own eyes, not forty minutes ago. He's fine."

Lucy nearly collapsed in relief. "Thank you, George, thank you. I was frantic with worry."

"He's fine," George repeated. "Shall I walk you home?"

Lucy shook her head. "No, that's not necessary."

A crash made her jump, and a cry went up from the throng

as yet another tower of bricks surrendered to the lack of structure to hold them in place.

"If you don't feel you need me, I'm going to go see if I can do anything closer in," George said, and Lucy lost him to the blackness.

Half an hour after the fire started, nothing remained of the Calumet Club but a heap of smoking ruins. Lucy clenched grit in her teeth and coughed against the ashes settled in the weave of her cloak. Tears she had not realized she was producing streaked through the soot on her face and smeared across the back of her hand as she wiped them away.

"It's a shame about the artwork," a voice behind her said. "It was quite valuable, you know."

Lucy wheeled in the darkness. "Daniel?"

"Yes, it's me. Are you all right?"

"I'm fine," she insisted. "I was afraid . . . my father . . . but . . . he's safe."

Daniel reached out and took her hand. "Let me take you home. We're just in the way here."

Lucy nodded and let him thread through the crowd ahead of her, holding her hand tightly. They did not speak again until they were well past the worst of the chaos.

"It was foolish of those men to try to save the artwork at the possible expense of their own lives," Daniel said. "I can't imagine what they were thinking."

"I suppose no one expected a building like that to come down within thirty minutes." Lucy suddenly realized she was shaking.

"Architects are not the gods they think they are. You would think a brick building would withstand fire more admirably than that."

Lucy tried to withdraw her hand from Daniel's, but he tightened his grip.

"Architects are wrong about a great many things. Take your friend Mr. Edwards, for instance. His understanding is quite limited."

"Daniel, what are you talking about?" Lucy finally managed to ask.

He gave no indication of hearing her. "Mr. Edwards believes he is on the brink of a defining career, and I imagine you find that attractive. However, the truth is it's unlikely. He doesn't understand how these things are done."

Lucy tried again to pull her hand out of his. "Daniel, let me go," she said softly.

"He doesn't understand the truth about you, either," Daniel continued. "When are you going to tell him about your educational shenanigans?"

Lucy stopped abruptly and pulled hard. Her hand came free at last. Plunging both hands into the pockets of her cloak, she looked him full in the face under the radiance of a streetlight. "Daniel, let me go," she repeated. "Let me go."

His brown eyes glimmered, and one side of his mouth turned up. "I would have expected more of you, Lucy." Then he turned and left.

Lucy was still a block away from home, and she could hardly make her feet move below her trembling knees. In horror, she wondered if Daniel had anything to do with the destruction of the Calumet Club. Surely not.

Surely not.

22

$\mathscr{A}$ccording to the newspapers, the Calumet Club fire was traced to shavings left by carpenters doing repair work in room twelve. Lucy absolved herself of believing Daniel capable of such a deed as quickly as she had allowed the thought into her mind.

Nevertheless, a month later, Daniel's behavior was still unnerving. Lucy was wearying of avoiding him in her own home, and he seemed to turn up at odd, unexpected moments in the neighborhood or downtown. Most recently he had accosted her as she left the university. Lucy sat in church remembering the encounter a few days earlier.

The day had of course been glacial because it was the first week of February, and Lucy was looking forward to the quilts that awaited her in Aunt Violet's carriage. She jostled her way through an unusual glut of students on the first floor—all hesitant to brace the cold, she supposed—and finally she was out the front doors of the building. On the frozen path, she walked as quickly as reasonably possible in her uncomfortable shoes with her lungs rebelling against the onslaught of frosty air. Paddy had promised to park as close as possible. Aunt Violet would be in the carriage because it was Thursday and she was coming for her weekly dinner at the Bannings'.

Lucy was bursting to talk about her new philosophy class in the privacy of the carriage.

She rounded the corner and there he was—leaning into the carriage and talking to Aunt Violet. Paddy stood by looking none too pleased, his gloved hands clenched and ready if the situation should call for action. This small detail bolstered Lucy as she approached the carriage.

"Excuse me, Daniel," she said, "I believe my aunt is here for me."

"So I gathered," Daniel said. He turned and gave her a beguiling smile, the one he used to charm the wives of his most important clients, and one that seemed so sinister to her now. "I surmised quite some time ago that your capricious aunt was in cahoots with your university escapades."

"I am not in 'cahoots' with anything," Violet protested. "I am merely supporting my niece's ambitions, something apparently you were unwilling to do. If you had, perhaps things would stand differently between you."

"Aunt Violet . . ." Lucy said.

"Never mind your aunt's rudeness," Daniel said evenly. "It's clear where the source of your misguidance lies. Perhaps I'll have occasion to mention to your mother that I ran into her lovely sister today. No doubt she'll want to know where."

"We have an agreement, Daniel," Lucy said. "I hold you blameless in our breakup, and you keep my secret."

"Ah, but I truly am blameless in our breakup, so our so-called agreement really doesn't ask anything of you, now does it? Perhaps we should renegotiate the terms."

Aunt Violet had enough. "Daniel Jules, I have been fond enough of you over the years for my sister's sake, but you have tested the limits of my tolerance. Kindly step aside."

With this cue, Paddy stepped forward to assist Lucy into the carriage. Lucy heard nothing more from Daniel in the next two days, and it was unlikely he would show up at church now.

The organ pipes swelled with the opening chords of the closing hymn and the congregation stood. Lucy knew her mother, beside her, would not tolerate an open examination of the balconies, but Lucy couldn't resist a more subtle effort in the moments of preparation to sing. Clearly many of the families of Prairie Avenue and nearby streets held pews in the church as much—if not more—for social standing as devotion. This certainty frustrated her no end. But what drew the ranks that filled the balconies? Did they come out of piety? Seeking refuge? Crying for some sort of relief? Merely a warm place to sit on a cold day?

How had she not seen him earlier in the service?

He was there in a gray suit with a splash of blue silk handkerchief in the front pocket, plain as day, in the third row of the balcony, in the forward section to the left of the altar. Lucy supposed the wide brim of her hat had obscured her view to this point.

Will.

Will had come to Second Presbyterian Church for the first time.

She smiled, glad now for the wide brim that hid her face. He was there for her, she was sure. What other explanation could there be? Normally he went to a church closer to the neighborhood where his rooms were.

Lucy peeked again as she opened her mouth and sang. Will wasn't alone—Benny stood in front of him, intent on a hymnal he did not yet know how to read. It wasn't logically possible to bring four hundred children to church. Mr. Emmett was constantly recruiting ministers to visit St. Andrew's and hold services for the children. It must have been a treat for Benny to come to Second Presbyterian. Lucy had seen Will with Benny enough times at St. Andrew's to know Will would do anything for that little boy. Perhaps it was Benny who had asked to go to church and Will had merely obliged, but that thought did not diminish Lucy's pleasure at seeing Will there. What kind of man would alter his arrangements to make a small boy happy? Will was that kind of man.

Will caught her eye from the balcony at the start of the second hymn stanza, and Lucy blushed under her hat—once again grateful for the protection it offered. The last time Leo brought Will home for dinner, Charlotte caught Lucy's hands shaking as she pinned a brooch to her neckline and the maid discerned the truth. Charlotte smiled and said little, but Lucy could see she recognized that just the thought of Will's presence downstairs stirred Lucy.

In the foyer after the service, Lucy lingered with her parents and Leo. Flora had insisted Richard stay in bed with his sore throat, and Oliver was regularly escorting Pamela Troutman these days. As Lucy chatted politely with friends of her parents, Benny got loose from Will and charged at her, burying his face in the drapes of her green silk skirt.

Flora raised an eyebrow and said, "Lucy, it seems you have an admirer."

Lucy stooped and gave the boy a proper hug. Will appeared, looking apologetic.

"I'm sorry," he said, "he slipped right through the crowd on the stairs, but I had to wait my turn."

"It's no problem," Lucy said.

"This boy is with you?" Leo asked.

"Yes, he is," Will said, laying a hand on Benny's shoulder.

"Mr. Will is building offices," Benny announced. "He's going to give Miss Lucy a proper desk and a bookcase and everything."

Leo grinned. "You're building offices at the orphanage? That's great!"

Will shrugged. "I thought I might help."

"So you and Lucy have been seeing each other there?" Leo probed.

Benny jumped right in. "He comes on Friday afternoons. Miss Lucy tells him what she likes, and he promises to do it. He comes again on Saturday, but Miss Lucy doesn't. She only comes on Friday."

Lucy froze. *She only comes on Friday.*

"I'd better get Benny home," Will said. "They'll be serving lunch soon."

Lucy flashed him a grateful look and jumped at the change of subject. "Yes, Mrs. Fletcher will be ready to serve luncheon promptly at one o'clock. We should all be on our way."

***

The moment had come. By the time luncheon was over, Lucy had decided. Aunt Violet knew. Charlotte knew. Daniel knew. Will knew something, though he still had not asked for a full explanation of where she actually spent her afternoons. Benny was innocently telling the truth, but the incident after church persuaded Lucy that a casual remark could unravel everything.

She only comes on Friday.

Her parents might not have paid attention to the rambling comment of a tattered orphan, but if Daniel were to make such a remark, they would sit up straight and listen. The truth should come from her, not from Daniel's determination to hurt her.

It was time. When the meal was over, Lucy followed her parents into the parlor and asked Leo to come as well. She waited for Penard to finish serving the coffee, then pulled the pocket doors closed.

Flora gasped at the notion, first that her daughter should be taking university classes and second that she had hid the truth from her parents. Samuel grunted that her broken engagement was evidence that her studies had proven too great a distraction. Leo didn't say much, but he managed to stand behind his parents, out of their line of sight, where he was free to grin at his sister, especially when she revealed Aunt Violet's part in the plot. Lucy knew her mother would be full of questions, and she was not disappointed. Why was Lucy so unhappy with the life they had worked so hard to give her? Why must she be so obstinate? Didn't she know that Daniel would take her back in a heartbeat if she gave up these modern notions? Of course Lucy could not provide satisfactory answers, so she did not even try, and in the end Flora wore herself out and ceased her verbal objections. Lucy did not gain her father's overt approval, but at least he did not forbid her, either. She would go to class on Tuesday afternoon as usual, but without the shroud of secrecy.

A palpable mass lifted from her. She felt it. Daniel no longer held power over her. Lucy was certain it was only a matter of hours before he would learn that she had revealed herself to her parents.

She didn't tell them everything, of course.

There was still the matter of Will. Clearly Daniel had his suspicions, but Lucy could honestly say her relationship with Will was not what he supposed it to be. At least not yet. And if Leo knew anything of the burgeoning relationship between his friend and his sister, he gave no indication. It was for Leo's good that he did not know. It wouldn't be fair to draw him into the secrecy until Lucy herself knew what the relationship might hold. In the meantime, Lucy needed to reach Will as soon as possible and tell the truth about where she spent Tuesday and Thursday afternoons. She hated that he would be the last to know, but her course was already set.

And then there was Charlotte and Henry. Even Will couldn't know that secret. No one could know.

23

Charlotte counted the weeks—eighteen since she first laid her son in Mrs. Given's arms. She'd only had him to herself for four and a half weeks, and it saddened her to think he would never remember those days. But she would. Charlotte thought of Henry every moment of every day.

She served the Saturday afternoon tea in the parlor. Only Mr. and Mrs. Banning were in the room, though she suspected Lucy would come downstairs for a few minutes of refreshment, taking a break from her philosophy readings. Mrs. Fletcher had prepared small fruitcakes to go with the tea. Charlotte dropped a sugar cube in a cup of steaming liquid and handed the cup and saucer to Mrs. Banning.

"I'll have a fruitcake as well, please," the lady of the house instructed. Charlotte laid a fork alongside the cake and set it on the table beside Mrs. Banning's favorite chair.

The front door opened with a gust of frosty air, and Leo blew in. He stomped immediately into the parlor, yanked off his overcoat, and threw it onto a chair.

"This is about the most ridiculous discombobulation I've encountered since I left grammar school!" he said, dropping himself ungraciously into a chair.

"Whatever it is, Leo, I'm sure a cup of tea will help," Flora Banning said. "Charlotte, please pour Leo some tea."

"Yes, ma'am." Charlotte reached for a fresh cup.

"Don't trouble yourself, Charlotte." Leo waved her away. "A cup of tea is not going to fix this."

"Have you seen my fountain pen?" Samuel Banning asked Leo. "You know the one I mean, the silver one with blue ink."

"I haven't seen it, Father," Leo said. "I have a much bigger problem than a lost pen."

"It's not just a lost pen," Samuel protested. "That pen was given to me by a prestigious client whose fees provided for your college education."

"I'm sorry, Father. My mind is on another problem. My friend Will might lose his employment."

"I understand this young man is your friend, but have you no compassion for me? I have had my limit with things going missing. I shall have to institute another whole-house search."

"I'll help you look for it later. Just let me think for a few minutes what to do for Will."

Charlotte struggled not to appear too interested.

"Perhaps you'd better start at the beginning," Flora suggested. "Are you sure you wouldn't like a cup of tea?"

"Perhaps I will after all," Leo said.

Charlotte reached again for the fresh cup and filled it, then handed it to Leo.

"Will got his first real commission a few weeks ago, and now it looks as if the arrangement is falling apart."

"If it will make you feel better, tell us what happened," Flora prompted.

Leo turned up a palm. "I don't know what happened. Will sent some drawings by messenger days ago, and they never arrived at the client's offices. They insisted Will was being negligent and used some clause in the contract to pull out and begin interviewing architects again."

Flora Banning put her cup and saucer down on the table and picked up her pie plate. She turned to Charlotte. "Why don't you come back in a few minutes to clear?"

"Yes, ma'am." Charlotte was pleased to be excused. She scurried to the kitchen, promised Mrs. Fletcher she would be right back, and conquered the stairs in record time. She barely knocked before bursting into Lucy's room.

Lucy was on the chaise lounge with a philosophy book in her lap. "My goodness, Charlotte, what is it?"

"Mr. Leo has come home." Charlotte's words fired rapidly. "Mr. Will has lost his commission, and he might lose his position at the firm."

Lucy let the book drop to the floor as she swung her feet around and sat up straight. "What! I have to go to him. I have to find out what happened."

"I was sure you would want to, miss. Shall I have Archie bring the carriage around?"

"It's risky for anyone to know where I'm going," Lucy said, "but I can't waste time. Yes, have Archie bring the carriage around. Where's my warm cloak with the hood? My good shoes?"

As Lucy slid her feet into her shoes and Charlotte stooped to fasten them quickly, Lucy said, "I can't imagine what happened. Unless . . ." She hated to complete the thought.

Charlotte lifted her eyes. "Miss?"

"Unless this is Daniel's doing." Lucy spoke breathily. "He has suspicions about Will and me. Could he really do this?"

Within minutes Lucy was downstairs in the foyer, ready to go in search of Will. Her fingers were on the doorknob when her name rang through the foyer.

"Where are you off to?" Flora asked.

"Just a quick errand," Lucy answered lightly. "I won't be gone long."

From the top of the stairs, Charlotte cringed at the scene.

"Have you seen my fountain pen?" Samuel called from the parlor.

"No, I'm sorry, I haven't." Lucy gripped the knob. "Perhaps you left it on your dresser."

"I've looked everywhere," Samuel insisted. "It's further evidence that someone has been disturbing my things for months."

"I promise to help you look for it when I return." Lucy pulled the door open and descended the outside steps before anyone could detain her further.

⸙

Relief whistled out of Charlotte when she saw the door close behind Lucy. She had promised Mrs. Fletcher she would be right back, and if she didn't return to the kitchen, the cook might mention her absence to Mr. Penard. On the way down the narrow staircase, Charlotte passed Bessie on her way up with an armful of clean laundry.

After washing the pots Mrs. Fletcher left in the sink, Charlotte returned to the parlor to retrieve the tea cart. She washed up the tea things in the butler's pantry and carefully put the dishes away on a shelf.

"Go find out what happened to Bessie," Mrs. Fletcher instructed Charlotte. "I sent her upstairs, but she should have been back long ago."

Charlotte nodded, lifted her skirt, and went up the stairs. The door to Lucy's room was wide open. Charlotte stepped across the hall and looked in.

"Bessie! Mrs. Fletcher is looking for you. She—" With a gasp, Charlotte saw what Bessie held in her hands. "Those are Mr. Banning's things. He tore the house up looking for that letter opener months ago, and I heard him asking about the pen not an hour ago."

"I just found them," Bessie said.

"What? In here?"

Bessie nodded. "I was putting her delicates away in the drawer, like I always do. And there they were. There's a paperweight too, and a tin box, and a silver picture frame."

Charlotte grasped at the drawer, pulling it wide open. Everything Bessie named was there. "Where did you get these things?"

"I told you, I found them. They were there when I opened the drawer."

"When Miss Lucy dresses, I lay out her things myself," Charlotte said. "I would know if these were in the drawer. You must have brought them in."

Bessie drew back her shoulders. "I did no such thing. I found them, just like I said." She lifted her apron and started wrapping the items in a bundle. "I'm going to march right down to Mr. Penard and show him what I've found. You're a witness."

"The only thing I can witness to is seeing you holding Mr. Banning's things."

"I'm going to find Mr. Penard right now!" Bessie pushed past Charlotte and started down the hall.

Charlotte was right on Bessie's heels. "Think what you're doing, Bessie."

"You're just afraid suspicion will fall on you. And perhaps it should. Everyone knows you've had freedom in Miss Lucy's room for months, ever since you first got here. How do we know what happens in there?"

"Nothing happens in there! I lay out her gowns and fix her hair. I had nothing to do with those things you found, and you know it."

"Do I?" Bessie clutched her apron more tightly as she took the last turn in the staircase. "Perhaps you're covering for Miss Lucy herself."

"Are you mad? Can you possibly be accusing Miss Lucy of taking her father's things?"

"I only know I didn't do it," Bessie insisted, "and I'm not going to be caught red-handed for something I didn't do."

The two maids burst into the kitchen. Mrs. Fletcher looked up and scowled.

"What in tarnation is going on with you two?"

"Where is Mr. Penard?" Bessie demanded. "We need him immediately." She spilled her apron and the items clattered onto the kitchen table.

Mrs. Fletcher's eyes widened, and in one swift motion she pushed open the door to the butler's pantry. "You'll want to see this, Mr. Penard."

When he saw the collection on the table, he looked sternly from Bessie to Charlotte. "I presume one of you has an explanation."

Charlotte's head pounded as she listened to Bessie's explanation. Bessie had been in the Banning household far longer than she had. If there were a question of trust, Charlotte had little to stand on.

"Bessie, are you certain this is the first time you've seen these items?"

"Yes, sir. I know how unhappy Mr. Banning has been. I never would have kept this to myself if I had any idea."

"And Charlotte, you deny knowledge as well?"

"Yes, sir. I am in Miss Lucy's room regularly and I never found anything in that drawer that didn't belong there—until I saw Bessie today."

"I am *not* a thief!" Bessie's voice rose.

"Neither am I!" Charlotte matched Bessie pitch for pitch.

Penard exhaled. "If I am to believe both of you, then you would have me suspect Miss Lucy."

"Perhaps she was hiding the things somewhere else," Bessie suggested. "Perhaps she just moved them this afternoon while she was alone."

"Miss Lucy is innocent!" Charlotte protested. "I am sure of it."

"And what is your explanation?" Penard asked.

Charlotte had no response.

"I will return these items to Mr. Banning immediately," Penard said, arranging the items on a tray lined with a linen napkin. "I can make no guarantee as to his reaction, but it would be unconscionable to withhold information for a moment longer."

Charlotte put her face in her hands as he left the room.

"There's still dinner to serve," Mrs. Fletcher reminded her. "You both know what you should be doing."

Charlotte scrubbed pots and sliced vegetables and laid the table, listening with every motion for the sound of a carriage and the opening of the front door. When the door finally opened, Lucy glanced into the dining room without focusing on anything and said loudly, "Charlotte, please come and help me change for dinner." Charlotte quickly folded the last of the napkins, then ran up the back stairs.

Lucy sank onto the bed. "Will is in serious trouble, Charlotte, and I can't think of anything I can do to help."

"I'm sure he's comforted just knowing how concerned you are," Charlotte responded.

"The owner of the property where the office building is to be constructed is furious. The plans are nearly a week late, and he didn't believe Will when he said he sent them by special messenger days ago. Will handed them to a boy on a bicycle, the same boy who always comes to his firm, but the message company has no record of it, and the plans have completely disappeared. Will's employer is livid! Will doesn't know if he even has a position to go back to on Monday. I have to find out if Daniel had something to do with this."

"I'm so sorry, Miss Lucy."

Lucy sat up straight. "Archie won't tell anyone, will he? I went to Will's rooms looking for him. If my parents find out—"

"I'll speak to Archie," Charlotte said. "I'm so sorry about Mr. Will, and I'm sorry to add to your burden."

"What are you talking about?"

"It's your father's things." Charlotte quickly recounted Bessie's claim to have found the items in the drawer.

Lucy's face reddened. "Penard can't seriously be accusing you."

"Not directly, miss."

Realization crossed Lucy's face. "Not me! He doesn't think I took my own father's things!"

"I don't know, miss."

"Bessie has been here almost two years and has never given him cause to raise his voice," Lucy said. "What does he think is the explanation?"

"He spoke to your father, miss. I don't know what he said. Your father hasn't come out of his study this whole time."

Lucy pushed out her breath and put a hand over her eyes. "Dinner is sure to be eventful tonight."

24

"I'm not much in the mood for a dinner party," Lucy said as Charlotte fastened pearls around her neck a week later. "I don't know why I ever agreed to this."

Charlotte chuckled. "I don't recall that Mrs. Banning gave you much choice."

"I don't want to meet men!" Lucy dropped a fist on her vanity table. "She still thinks I might change my mind about Daniel, but if she opened her eyes at how odd he has become, she would give up. Or perhaps she has, and that's why she insists on giving dinner parties for my benefit." The shoulder seams in her gown made Lucy itch, and she could tell already that she would be stepping on the hem all night. In Lucy's mood, the pearls felt like rough street stones against her skin.

Charlotte began to pin up Lucy's hair. "Mrs. Banning doesn't understand about Mr. Edwards."

"And she never will. I don't understand why she thinks a banker is a fine catch, but an architect—a talented one—is humdrum. After all, she hired an architect to design this house and paid him well. But when I suggested inviting Will tonight, I thought she would pass out from the shock."

"Sometimes a person just gets something in her head."

"I wish she'd get it out! I'm worried sick about Will, and I have to go downstairs and bat my eyes at men I've never met and have no interest in."

"Has Will heard anything new?" Charlotte gave Lucy's hair a firm tug and twist.

"The firm's owner said they are going to be watching him closely. He's been working around the clock to replace the plans, but the client may not accept them."

"Maybe he'll hear good news on Monday."

Lucy sighed. "And then there's my father. He's hardly spoken to me all week after Penard went to him with the missing things."

"Do you think he believes Bessie—that she found those things in your drawer?"

"He doesn't know what to make of the way they turned up, but he's not letting any of us off the hook yet. He doesn't dare publicly say he believes Bessie over me, but she insists everything happened just the way she told it."

"And that leaves me."

Lucy shook her head vigorously. "I refuse to let him think that. If he tries to have you dismissed, I will insist that I want you for my ladies' maid."

"I did not take your father's things."

Charlotte's deliberate cadence was not lost on Lucy.

"I know that," Lucy said, "and his lawyer's mind knows that some of those things were missing before you got here. Perhaps it will be enough that he has everything back as long as nothing else disappears." Lucy pinched her cheeks pink. "Let's talk about something else. How's Henry?"

Charlotte smiled. "He can almost sit up by himself. Mrs. Given says he's the sweetest baby she's ever taken in. Tomorrow's my half Sunday off. I'll see him again."

"He must be so big," Lucy said. "I'm glad to hear he seems happy and well." She paused to examine her reflection. "I suppose I'm as ready as I'll ever be. It's time to turn on the finishing school charm!"

"And Mrs. Fletcher will be wondering what became of me. She's expecting me to help serve."

───⌒───

Lucy descended the marble stairs with shoulders back and chin up, gracefully, at a restrained pace. As she heard voices wafting from the parlor, she mentally reviewed the names of the dinner guests. Leo had invited a woman named Tamara Davies. Old friends of her parents, Patricia and Thomas Truman. Louis Stewart, the son of her father's law partner. Louis's friend Graham something or other. And Aunt Violet. Her aunt would be the saving grace of the evening. Lucy hadn't seen Louis Stewart in seven or eight years. Their fathers' partnership had brought them together occasionally during childhood, but he was older than she was—closer to Oliver's age—and she never paid too much attention to him, because of course she was going to marry Daniel Jules. However, she remembered Louis as companionable with a good sense of humor. As she hit the last step, she convinced herself it would be possible to pass a pleasant evening.

"Here she is now," Flora said as Lucy entered the parlor, "my daughter, Lucy. Come and greet our guests, dear. You remember Louis, I'm sure, and this is his friend Graham Pryor. Mr. Pryor's family is heavily invested in railroads."

Why do I need to know that? Lucy thought.

She offered her hand and said aloud, "It's a pleasure to meet you, Mr. Pryor."

"The pleasure is mine."

Lucy turned to Louis and smiled broadly. "How lovely to see you, Louis." She offered a cheek, which he kissed. He did cut an attractive figure. Louis had grown into his adolescent gangly limbs after all—quite tall, but considerably more filled out than the last time she'd seen him and sporting a handsome dark beard.

"Louis is getting ready to join our firm," Samuel explained. "He has prepared himself well, and we're delighted to take him in."

"How wonderful for you, Louis."

Flora steered Lucy to the Trumans and Tamara Davies. Lucy exchanged pleasantries, waiting for the opportunity to enthusiastically greet Aunt Violet.

"Do you think we have the makings of a party here?" Violet asked.

Lucy laughed. "As I recall, Louis has a story for every occasion."

Penard appeared then and announced dinner was served.

~~~

Will walked up Prairie Avenue toward the Banning house. Leo had mentioned he was having dinner at home, which was peculiar for Leo on a Saturday night. An impulse had moved Will's feet toward the streetcar that would take him up Michigan Avenue and into the Bannings' neighborhood. He was wrung out from a week of trying to prove himself to the firm's president and sleeping three hours a night while he re-created the valuable plans that had gone missing.

Bile rose through his chest as he thought of the moment a week ago when he realized the plans had disappeared. He held them to the last minute on Tuesday to make sure they were perfect, checking and rechecking every line and letter. Then he rolled them up and gave the tube to the messenger boy, Jacob, making sure Jacob knew the address where they were to be delivered. He saw the boy hang the bag around his neck and get on his bicycle headed in the right direction. Will shouted the name of the building after him for good measure. For the next three days he busied himself with other projects, trying not to become anxious about how the client felt about the drawings. They were to meet on Saturday morning to review them together, and Will would answer any questions.

On Friday afternoon the letter came. The irate client no longer wished to do business with Will's firm because the plans had not been delivered in the manner and at the time of their agreement.

From the office, Will telephoned the messenger company and inquired about the delivery. The clerk reported no entry in their log for that delivery, no record that it had been picked up, much less delivered. When Will asked about Jacob, the boy who had been serving them well for months, he learned only that Jacob had decided to take a position in a factory. No, they did not know which of the many Chicago factories it was. No, they could not give Will a home address for the boy. He had not even come around to collect his final pay packet.

Although he could not account for what happened to the first set of drawings, Will pleaded with the clients for the opportunity to redraw them, hoping that when the businessmen saw the fastidious attention to detail and everything they wished for in their new building, what they considered to be a breach of contract would become inconsequential. If he did not successfully redeem the situation, his future with his own firm was bleak. He had personally delivered the new plans to the client four hours ago and would no doubt be restless and in need of distraction while waiting for a response to come on Monday.

In the meantime, Will intuitively went to the Bannings', a house where he was not particularly welcomed by Flora and Samuel, but a home that sheltered the two people who mattered most to him, Lucy and Leo. If he could just have a few minutes with either of them, he was sure he'd feel more settled.

He walked past a line of carriages, vaguely thinking that someone on the block must be entertaining, and ascended the steps to the Banning front door. When the footman opened the door, surprised to see him, Will realized what he had done.

Leo was having dinner at home—that much was true— but he hadn't mentioned it was a formal dinner party with a guest list. Looking through the foyer to the dining room, Will saw the way Leo looked at the young woman seated at his side and smiled slightly. He'd have to rib Leo about that later. Then his gaze went to Lucy.

Smiling—laughing, in fact. Touching the arm of a man Will did not recognize seated next to her. Nodding at Charlotte as the maid removed a soup bowl. Turning to speak to another man on the other side of her. Gracefully lifting her face to speak to someone across the table. At ease.

And the table—laid densely with every china dish, sterling cutlery, and crystal vessel the mind could imagine in the course of a meal. As Charlotte removed bowls, Penard followed her around the table to serve heaping portions of meat. Will could only imagine what was to follow— potatoes, three kinds of vegetables, salads, desserts. He could eat for a month on what would be placed on that table for one meal.

Lucy looked happy. She looked as if she fit. This was how she and Leo had grown up. She didn't have to think twice about how to behave at such a sumptuous feast. When Will was with Lucy, she seemed restless, unsettled, as if she didn't want to fit in an extravagant dining room, as if she would rather move into a room at St. Andrew's. She had broken an engagement that would have assured her of a life of ease. When she came running to him a week ago as soon as she heard about the vanishing plans, he had taken her into his arms and received her comfort.

Could this be the same woman who appeared so well matched to her surroundings in the dining room?

Perhaps she did belong there. Most certainly he did not. Lucy deserved a carriage. He could barely offer a streetcar.

"Did you wish to speak to Mr. Banning?" the footman asked.

"I can see I've come at an inconvenient time," Will muttered. "No message."

Will turned and trod slowly back toward Michigan Avenue.

Charlotte unfastened the fifteen pearl buttons down the back of Lucy's silver gown and helped her step out of its billowing mounds of silk. She handed Lucy a robe and carried the gown to the closet to put it on its hook.

"I'm exhausted," Lucy said. "I think I'm too tired to wash my face."

"I'll help you," Charlotte offered, moving toward the small bathroom off the anteroom.

"No, please, Charlotte, you've done enough. Just sit and talk to me."

"Yes, miss." Charlotte sat erect on the edge of the chaise lounge and Lucy relaxed in an armchair.

"How did I do tonight?" Lucy asked. "You were there most of the time."

"Anyone looking in would think you were happy."

"Then my mother should be pleased," Lucy said, "and perhaps I'll have some peace tomorrow."

"Won't she want to know what you thought of the gentlemen?"

"Oh, probably." Lucy waved a hand. "I'll think of something

to say without committing myself. The truth is, the only thing I could think about all evening was Will. I wish he had a telephone. I want to know if he got the plans finished. I want to know if he's going to be able to sleep properly tonight. I want to know if he's hopeful. I want to know everything he's thinking."

"And I'm sure he wants to tell you."

Lucy smiled. "That was the perfect thing to say, Charlotte. Have you ever felt that way about a man?"

"No, miss, I haven't." Charlotte's answer was barely audible.

Lucy held her breath for a beat then asked, "Not even Henry's father?" In all these months of what Lucy hoped was a growing friendship, Charlotte never once mentioned Henry's father.

Charlotte stood up. "I'm weary myself. If you don't need anything else tonight, I think I'd like to turn in."

She was gone before Lucy could apologize. *Now you've gone and done it. She'll never trust you again.* Lucy turned off the lamp on the table next to her chair and sat in the darkness.

25

ucy stood outside the gallery, dreaming of spring. The winter had been bitter harsh—even for Chicago—but at last the first week in March arrived, the time of year when whimsical memories of spring emerged from shadow and feet began to believe warmth still existed.

Free of her engagement to Daniel, Lucy had eagerly agreed to visit a new art gallery with Will on this Tuesday afternoon. They made the decision to celebrate sending off the drawings of Will's first commission before everything had gone so wrong. Standing outside the gallery, braced against the wind, Lucy wasn't sure Will was even coming—but she wanted to be there if he did. She had not heard from him all weekend, despite her anxiety on his behalf on Saturday night and all day Sunday.

Monday was consumed with meetings and work related to the women's exhibit for the fair. It hardly seemed possible that the World's Columbian Exposition would open to the public in less than two months. The women's building was finished, while many others were not, and the committee was busy arranging exhibit items Lucy had carefully catalogued. Every week closer to opening day seemed more demanding than the last, but Lucy was confident the exhibit would be ready.

The weekend was agonizing and Monday exhausting, but now it was Tuesday and she hoped to see Will.

Lucy nodded politely at people who passed her on the sidewalk. She tried strolling nonchalantly up and down the block, always careful to keep the gallery within a glance. She loitered on a corner and monitored the direction from which she thought Will might come—if he were coming from his office, if he were still employed. Nearly an hour passed, and Lucy reluctantly surrendered to the reality that Will was not coming.

And then he was there. His lanky form threaded down the block toward her—from the direction of his office. Lucy planted her feet and waited for him at the gallery entrance.

"I'm sorry I'm so late," Will said after they greeted each other. "I had to take care of some things unexpectedly."

"At the office?" she said hopefully. "Is everything all right at the office?" She wanted to reach out and take his hand, but she did not dare.

"Is everything all right?" he echoed. "That's a bit difficult to discern at the moment."

"Please tell me about it," Lucy coaxed. "I want to know. Everything."

"It's not very interesting."

"Let's go inside. You can tell me about it while we see the exhibit."

He shook his head. "I'm sorry, Lucy, I can't stay."

"Will, what's wrong? Talk to me!"

He shook his head again. "I can't. I have to go right back to the office."

"More work?"

"Something like that."

"Will I see you Friday at St. Andrew's?"

"I'm not sure. It's difficult to plan very far in advance just now."

"I'll be there all day enjoying my new office. Please come and find me if you can."

He didn't nod. He didn't shake his head. He merely said, "I'm sorry about the exhibit, Lucy, but I do have to go."

"I understand," she said. But she didn't.

⌐

Will walked to the end of the block before he permitted himself a glance back at the gallery. Lucy was not there. She might have gone inside without him, or she might have gone home. He couldn't know.

He'd told her the truth: he was going back to the office. Monday had come and gone with no word from the client about whether they would consider the replacement drawings. Tuesday had largely passed as well. Will could think of nothing more he could do other than be at the office from the moment it opened in the morning until the last partner locked the door in the evening, no matter what time that was.

It was better this way, under the circumstances. He and Lucy had done nothing more than share an afternoon pot of tea—albeit on a regular basis—or play with the orphans together. It wouldn't do Lucy any good to get further involved with his difficulties.

⌐

On Friday, Lucy heard each tick of the clock, one anxious pause after another. Hours crept by, and no matter how much work she buried herself in, she knew the precise time at every moment of the day. Will rarely arrived at St. Andrew's before three in the afternoon, and generally by five she was on her way home, so they had only a few minutes to steal together. By four-thirty on this day, though, she gave up hope he would come. Whatever was happening at his firm was consuming and obviously required his best attention.

At a quarter to five, Lucy began to pack some papers in her satchel. The ranks of eight-year-olds at St. Andrew's were swelling for some reason, and the teachers were asking for more classroom space for this age group. Lucy had offered to try to sort out the challenge. She could easily ponder the dilemma at home. At five minutes until five, Lucy resigned herself to going home without seeing Will. She took her cloak off the hook, wrapped it around her, pulled up the hood, and stuck her head in Mr. Emmett's office.

"I'm going now, Mr. Emmett," Lucy said. "I've taken some papers to sort out the classroom question. I'll try to propose a solution next Friday when I come."

"Thank you, Miss Banning. That will be very helpful."

"It's my pleasure."

"Don't forget to look in on the dining hall on your way out," he said.

"Oh?"

"Mr. Edwards has taken the painting in hand with some of the older boys. They started about an hour ago."

The folds of her cloak hid her tremble. "Yes, I'll be sure to have a look."

"Good night, then."

Lucy turned and clicked down the hall to the dining room, pausing in the doorway to survey the scene. Will had his sleeves rolled up, with a can of blue paint in one hand and a brush in the other. Five boys ranging in age from eleven to fourteen stood at stations along the back wall listening carefully to Will's instructions about the direction of their strokes and the necessity of wiping up paint dribbles immediately.

Lucy went no further.

Clearly Will had been in the building for quite some time. If he'd wanted to speak to her, he would have. At least he had not abandoned St. Andrew's. At least for now, he wouldn't break Benny's heart. Blinking back stinging tears, Lucy resumed her path out of the building.

Outside, she could hardly believe her eyes. *Oh, not now!* There was Daniel, leaning against his carriage looking as if he were exempt from the cold.

"Hello, Daniel," she said evenly, fully intending to press past him.

"Hello, Lucy. I didn't realize I would run into you today." Casually, he stepped into her path.

Does he think I'm an idiot?

"Daniel, why do you follow me?" Lucy asked.

"What makes you think I'm following you?"

"Do you have business at the orphanage?" she asked, sighing.

"I promised my mother I would bring her donation."

"You could have just mailed a check."

"The personal touch is so much more meaningful, wouldn't you agree? Things don't get lost that way."

Things don't get lost? "Mr. Emmett is in his office. I'm sure he'll be grateful for whatever you can give."

"I understand Mr. Edwards has begun volunteering here as well."

"Yes, that's true." *Get to the point, Daniel.*

"I also understand he's run into some difficulties at his place of employment."

"You would have to ask him about that."

"Perhaps I will, the next time I see him." He gestured toward the carriage. "If you care to wait while I go see Mr. Emmett, I would be happy to escort you home. I won't be a minute."

"That's not necessary. I can manage."

"Yes, I suppose so. After all, you've been navigating the city for quite some time without my knowledge."

She held her response to his barb.

"Well," Daniel said, "I suppose it's a relief that your father's things were recovered."

Lucy raised an eyebrow. "He's grateful to have them back."

"No doubt. It's rather odd they should turn up where they did, don't you think?"

Lucy was silent, trying to read the face of the man she had once thought she would marry.

"That pen leaks," Daniel said. "I'm not sure why Samuel is so fond of it. You're fortunate it didn't leak on your things in the drawer."

"I didn't realize you'd heard all the details," Lucy said.

"Oliver," Daniel said simply. "He keeps me up to date." He looked at Lucy's face, unflinching.

Lucy nodded. *Oliver has been in New York for the last two weeks.*

"Perhaps I'll see you later," Daniel said, smiling in that way Lucy recognized as pleasure. "I may spend the night in town so I can be fresh for an early meeting at the bank. I have a new account, a firm seeking a loan to build a new office building. It just came up this week."

Daniel tipped his hat at Lucy and sauntered into St. Andrew's.

Lucy pivoted, suddenly in need of a robust walk. She would not even try to find a cab.

26

I do wish you would have agreed to a trip to Europe," Flora whined on Monday morning. "If we had left in mid-February, we could have been back in plenty of time for the fair's opening, and you would have had an adequate wardrobe for the spring and summer."

"I'm hardly in danger of going without clothes." Lucy's mother had been pushing for weeks to go to Europe—even after she knew Lucy was enrolled in a class at the university. "Lenae can make me anything I need. Besides, there's far too much to do for the women's exhibit before opening day."

"I suppose you're meeting with that architect again," Flora said.

Lucy's heart lurched, then fell back into place with the realization that her mother meant not Will but the architect of the women's exhibit.

"Her name is Sophia Hayden," Lucy explained—for the umpteenth time. "She has been unwell lately. I'm not sure if she'll attend today's meeting."

"The women's exhibit seems to have become your Monday ritual."

"The time suits everyone's schedule." Lucy checked the tilt of her hat in the foyer mirror. "There's a small group of us charged with making sure all the details are in place. Mrs. Palmer is quite particular, and we have only seven weeks left."

She smoothed her skirt one last time. The woolen cashmere suit, with matching blue skirt and jacket and a contrasting cream silk blouse, suited Lucy's tastes while meeting her mother's standards for quality of workmanship. Flora remained skeptical of the clothing of the "New Woman," but Lucy appreciated the practicality and flexibility the styles offered. If she got overly warm in her work, she could simply remove her jacket and still be appropriately dressed, an alternative not available with conventional two-piece suits. Charlotte had gently waved her hair and drawn it back into a small, high chignon, a style that pleased Lucy.

Penard stood by to open the front door for Lucy, and Archie had already brought the carriage around. Lucy's leather satchel contained her notes for the meeting. She kissed her mother's cheek, walked through the open door, and allowed Archie to assist her into the carriage.

Of course Lucy did not want to leave Chicago in the middle of a university term. And of course she would not abandon her duties with the women's exhibit and disappoint the Board of Lady Managers. She supposed those reasons were why her mother had not put her foot down and insisted Lucy go to Europe to have a wardrobe made. What Lucy would not say aloud to her mother, though, was that she would not leave Will behind—especially until she understood why he was being aloof.

⁓ᴄ⁓

Five hours later Lucy returned to Prairie Avenue, exited the carriage, and walked through the front door ready to toss her satchel on the foyer table and remove her hat. She had no sooner pulled out the first hat pin than Leo crashed through the door behind her.

"He's gone," he said.

"Who?" Lucy asked innocently enough, thinking perhaps Leo was looking for Daniel.

"Will. He's gone. I can't find him anywhere."

Lucy spun around to search her brother's face. "What do you mean, gone? Did he lose his position?"

Leo shrugged. "I don't know."

"Did you telephone his office?"

"They only said Mr. Edwards was not available."

"His rooms?"

"Empty. His landlady hasn't seen him since early Saturday morning. No one has."

"That means he's been gone most of three days," Lucy reasoned. "Surely somebody knows something."

"I have been trying all day to track him down," Leo said firmly. "We had plans this morning, and he didn't show up. Will doesn't know that many people in Chicago, so how many places could he be? No one has talked to him in days."

"Did you see his rooms for yourself? Perhaps—"

Leo was shaking his head. "No clues, Lucy. Everything is as it should be, but his valise is gone."

"So you really think he left the city."

Leo nodded. "I do. But I don't understand why, or where he would have gone."

"New Jersey?"

"That's a long trip to make without planning ahead. Why wouldn't he have mentioned something to me?"

Or me, Lucy thought. *Is this why he wouldn't speak to me on Friday?*

⸙

For three days, Lucy waited for word of Will, but Leo found nothing new. Lucy even inquired of Mr. Emmett if Will had happened to mention any upcoming plans. She went so far as to try to ferret something out of Benny.

No one knew where Will Edwards was.

By Thursday evening, Leo was fuming but resigned that he would have to wait for Will to contact him and explain himself. When Lucy walked into the parlor for the predinner family gathering, she nearly turned around and walked out.

Although Daniel still used his room at the Banning house for the convenience of staying near his downtown office at the bank, his appearances at dinner had become sporadic. Lucy knew Oliver and Leo still saw Daniel from time to time for a tennis match or a party, and she did not begrudge them the lifelong friendship, but given his recent penchant for turning up at odd times and places, she was content not to have him at the dinner table. But there he was, smiling and making pleasant conversation with her parents, whose affection for him was unabated.

At least it was Thursday, so Aunt Violet would be there. Lucy missed Charlotte, though, gone for her day out. She imagined the maid sitting on Mrs. Given's faded sofa with Henry on her lap, or throwing him in the air until he giggled, or taking him out in the buggy for fresh air, or rocking him to sleep before she returned to Prairie Avenue and a world where he was not welcomed.

"Hello, Lucy." Daniel's cheerful tone snapped Lucy back to the scene at hand.

"Daniel was just telling us about his new client," Samuel supplied.

"Oh? The office building folks?" Lucy hoped she sounded casual.

"That's right," Daniel responded. "I think we've come to an agreeable business arrangement."

Leo spoke up. "When Will got that commission, I thought Daniel could help seal the deal with a solid loan. And he could see what great work Will does and perhaps recommend him to others."

"I'm sure Will would appreciate that." Inwardly Lucy grimaced at Leo's unfettered trust in Daniel.

"Your friend seems to have disappeared from the picture, though," Daniel said. "My recent conversations about the funds required for the project have been with the owners of the architectural firm." He chuckled. "It would seem Mr. Edwards was careless about some detail and will have to prove himself trustworthy once again."

Lucy glanced at Leo, who tilted his head to consider Daniel's remark.

"Daniel," Leo said, "my intention was that a business arrangement between you and Will would benefit you both. I hope you did not misunderstand that."

Good for you, Leo!

"In any event," Daniel responded, "your friend seems to be unavailable to answer questions, and one of the partners has taken over the project. I don't suppose you know where to reach Mr. Edwards?"

"No, I don't," Leo admitted, moving toward the window and gazing out.

"So the project is moving forward successfully?" Lucy queried in an even tone.

Daniel nodded. "It would seem so. Just without Mr. Edwards."

"But he did the drawings," Lucy protested. "Twice!"

"Ah, but having to do them twice was the result of his carelessness."

Lucy clenched her fists against Daniel's smugness.

Aunt Violet stood up at that moment and glared. "Daniel,

you seem amused. Might I ask what you know about this alleged carelessness?"

Thank you, Aunt Violet!

Daniel waved a hand. "Very little, actually. The client expressed some rather strong opinions about what happened when it delayed the loan. That's all."

"Are you sure?" Violet prodded.

Daniel smiled blandly. "I don't take your meaning, Violet. I've said all I know."

Flora interrupted. "Must we have all this business conversation at dinner? I'm sure we can find something to talk about that is of more interest to everyone."

⟶ ⟵

Lucy had to call for Elsie to help undo the back of her satin gown. As soon as the dress was off, she dismissed the maid and sat down to brush out her own hair. Thursday evenings without Charlotte had become a peculiar time. After dinner she had managed a quick, hushed conversation with Aunt Violet in which the older woman made clear she thought Daniel knew more than he was saying. Lucy didn't know what to think. Now she wished she could talk to the only real confidante she had. Charlotte would know what to say to calm her nerves.

Where are you, Will?

27

Charlotte gave the rag a final twist and hung it over a hook at the back of the sink. Sunday luncheon was finally over, and the kitchen was scrubbed down. The rest of the day was hers, and Henry was waiting. He would probably still be napping when she arrived at Mrs. Given's house, but Charlotte loved to stand over his crib and watch his chest rise and fall. He slept on his back with his arms flung over his head and his tiny lips twitching with his dreams. Mrs. Given would offer her tea, and Charlotte would hold a steaming mug while she watched her son sleep, waiting for that radiant moment when he opened his eyes and she was the first thing he saw. Perhaps she would take him out in the buggy for some air.

Thirty-five minutes later, Charlotte rapped on Mrs. Given's door. No answer. She knocked again and called out.

Rather than the scrape of a chair or footsteps, Charlotte heard crying. Henry's crying—louder than she had ever heard before. She pounded on the door.

"Mrs. Given, what's going on? Open the door!"

Finally she heard fumbling on the other side of the locked door. Mary Given pulled the door open and greeted Charlotte with frantic exhaustion, her hair dropping from its pins and her eyes bloodshot.

Henry was not sleeping. He was screaming in Mary's arms. Charlotte reached for her son. "He's burning up!"

"He took sick on Friday," Mary explained. "I thought it was just a runny nose, but by evening he had a fever."

"That's two days!" Panic surged up in Charlotte. "How long has he been this bad?" She put her face against her son's hot cheek. Henry continued to scream.

"He's been inconsolable since yesterday afternoon. The fever rose suddenly and he's hardly slept at all."

"Does he scream all the time?" Henry was an easy-natured baby who never had been sick before. He fussed very little when his needs were attended to. Charlotte trembled as she held him.

"He screams some of the time and then the coughing sets in and I'm afraid he's going to stop breathing."

Charlotte turned Henry in her arms to look at his face, purplish and distended. "Has he actually stopped breathing?" She put her ear to his tiny chest to listen to his rasping breath.

"Only for a few seconds at a time," Mary answered quickly, "but I can't seem to comfort him, and of course I have the twins to look after. I knew you would want to come, but I had no way to get word to you. No one in this neighborhood has a telephone, and I don't have any spare coins to send a driver with a message."

Charlotte's heart pounded. She had seen babies sick before—she had three younger brothers, after all, and one of them had nearly died when he was not much older than Henry. But the thought of her own child in such distress without her knowledge was almost more than she could make sense of. It was one thing to leave him in the care of another woman when he was well and happy, and quite another to be so far away that she did not even know he was ill.

"I'm not leaving," she declared, plopping onto the sofa and arranging Henry in her arms. "I can't leave him like this."

"What about your position?" Mary asked.

"I can't think about that now. Henry is the only thing that matters. Can I have a cool cloth, please? I have to get his temperature down."

"Mar-mar," a little voice whined.

Charlotte looked over at both the bedraggled twins as one of them tugged on Mary's skirts.

"I'm sorry," Mary said. "They're hungry and tired. I couldn't keep the baby quiet last night, so no one slept. It's long past lunchtime, and they haven't had a proper nap, either. I didn't dare leave the baby in case—"

"Don't say it," Charlotte said. "I'm here now. I'm going to take care of my son and he's going to get better. Feed the twins."

<hr />

The week had been protracted torture. On Monday, Lucy attended the meeting on the women's exhibit and pressed through the papers she brought home from the gathering to review again the list of countries that would be represented in the exhibit. She attended her class on Tuesday and Thursday and completed the assigned reading on the nature of philosophical arguments. She spent Friday at St. Andrew's, updating records and overseeing the rearrangement of classrooms. The dining hall was half painted because Will had not come back to supervise the continuing endeavor. At church Pamela Troutman sat beside Oliver in the Banning pew, prompting speculation about their future. Over Sunday luncheon, Aunt Violet promised to stir up the ladies auxiliary to make quilts for the orphanage. Throughout the week, Lucy cocked her head, listening for Leo's step, his voice, his accounting of what he had discovered about Will. But the accounting never came, because Leo did not turn up any new information, despite diligent effort.

No one knew where Will was. By now he had been missing for a week. Lucy could hardly think straight.

Archie served the soup at dinner, and Bessie cleared dishes between courses, the routine of the Banning house undisturbed. Penard stood as always in the corner of the dining room, his watchful eye vigilant of every detail of the table service.

"I hear a good report of the Board of Lady Managers," Samuel remarked over the duck. "Yours may be the only building fully ready for opening day."

"Mrs. Palmer refuses to take no for an answer," Lucy joked. "Once she makes up her mind that something might be possible, she insists we bring it to reality."

"It's a shame about the lady architect," Leo said. "Imagine being the first woman to graduate from the Massachusetts Institute of Technology, being chosen to design a building for the world's fair, and then have such a bout of melancholy that she must withdraw from the preparations."

"Sophia Hayden did a wonderful job with the designs," Lucy said. "The building is a breath of Grecian beauty."

"Bertha Palmer can be a bit of a pill," Aunt Violet said in her usual get-to-the-point manner. "It would not surprise me one bit to find that she drove that poor girl to distraction."

"Violet, you are exaggerating as usual," Flora said.

"Just telling the truth. If you've ever met the woman, you know I am. I hear that the Board of Lady Managers is objecting to half the plans for the fair on moral grounds, and it's all Mrs. Palmer's doing."

Lucy controlled a smile as she glanced at Leo.

"The wheel Mr. Ferris is building looks more enticing every

time I see it," Leo said, changing the subject. "It's sure to be an attraction."

"I'm not at all sure I can bring myself to get on it," Flora said.

"I will, without reservation," Violet said.

Lucy laughed now. "I'll go with you, Aunt Violet." *You are so refreshing!*

"It won't be operating on opening day," Samuel advised. "I suppose the board of directors waited too long to approve the exhibit, and now it won't be finished by May 1, like a lot of other things. But it should be working for most of the summer."

Lucy couldn't help but remember the first time Will came to dinner and said he'd love to see the drawings for Mr. Ferris's wheel. She didn't recall he ever got that chance.

Dinner conversation drifted into other dimensions of fair preparation. Samuel was looking after fair business on an almost daily basis and reported that arrangements for the opening ceremonies in the Court of Honor were nearly final. At last dessert was served—Mrs. Fletcher's lemon raspberry pie was incomparable—and Flora and Samuel decided to take their coffee in the parlor. Lucy moseyed with them through the foyer. Just as they arrived at the parlor's arched doorway, she realized she must have dropped her embroidered handkerchief in the dining room and turned around to retrieve it.

She did not mean to overhear Penard's conversation with Mrs. Fletcher. Lucy was not in the habit of listening in on such exchanges. However, their voices seemed slightly raised, and in a room without the family present, words easily rang across the empty space.

"That girl knows she is to be back in the house by nine o'clock on Sunday evenings," Penard insisted. "It's well past nine-thirty, and she's not here to help with clearing and wash-ing."

"She's never been late getting back before," Mrs. Fletcher responded. "Perhaps she was delayed, or the streetcar broke down."

"We don't even know where she goes. We never hear a report of her friends or excursions. She's keeping a secret, I tell you. We have no way to tell what kind of shenanigans a girl her age is getting into."

Lucy cleared her throat and made her presence known. "I seem to have dropped my handkerchief."

Penard glanced at Lucy's chair at the table. "Yes, miss, here it is." He stepped over and picked it up and handed it to her. "Will there be anything else, miss?"

Lucy said evenly, "Please tell Charlotte I'd like to see her as soon as she comes in."

"Yes, miss. We expect her at any moment."

"I'll be in my suite. Please send her right up."

Lucy turned and ambled back across the foyer. She stuck her head in the parlor. "I've changed my mind about coffee," she told her parents. "I think I'll turn in early tonight."

"Are you feeling unwell?" Flora asked.

"I'm fine. I'd just like to do some reading before I go to sleep."

"I'll be on my way as well." Aunt Violet set down her coffee cup. "I've already been here far longer than I intended to stay."

Lucy kissed her aunt's cheek.

"Come for tea this week," Violet urged. "We'll have a catch-up."

"I'd love that," Lucy said.

Violet leaned in to kiss Lucy's cheek. "He'll be all right," she whispered.

Lucy left her parents in the parlor and went upstairs to

her suite. It was not like Charlotte to do anything to put her position at risk. Lucy sat in the armchair with a book in her lap, but she did not read a word. Instead, she watched the clock. Nine-forty-five. Nine-fifty. At ten she heard the gong of the grandfather clock in the foyer. Ten-fifteen. Ten-twenty-five. She got up and went to her vanity table to push the annunciator button.

"Yes, miss?"

"Has Charlotte come in yet?"

"No, miss."

She snapped the button off. Something was wrong. Lucy knew exactly where Charlotte was.

Ten-thirty. Ten-forty.

Lucy opened her door and stepped out into the hall. Richard and Leo's doors were closed, and she saw no light creeping out. Oliver's door was open, but his room was dark. He was still out with Pamela. Stilling the rustle of her skirt as best as she could, Lucy walked softly down the hall to the top of the stairs. A dim light was on in the foyer, probably for Oliver's sake, but the parlor appeared vacant.

Lucy returned to her room. Ten-fifty. Eleven. Eleven-ten.

Lucy's mind was made up. She rose from her chair, crossed to her closet, and retrieved her hooded cloak and a small pouch of coins. She couldn't risk calling for a carriage. The whole household would be up in arms at the suggestion that she should go out unaccompanied at that hour of the night, and she could not risk leading anyone to Charlotte. Yet she had to go.

Wrapped in her cloak, Lucy skulked down the stairs, slowly, alert for any sound of movement in the lower rooms. Satisfied there was none, she crossed the foyer and unlatched the front door. Even at this hour she would be able to find a cab on Michigan Avenue.

28

$\mathcal{D}$aniel stepped out of the carriage that had brought him from the train station to Prairie Avenue, after catching the last Sunday evening train from Riverside. An early Monday breakfast meeting compelled him to sleep at the Bannings' that night, regardless of the late arrival. He would let himself in with his key and go directly to his bedroom, requiring no assistance from the household staff tonight. As he reached into his pocket for coins to pay the cab driver, a flickering shadow caught his eye, and he turned his head to follow its streak.

"I've changed my mind," he told the driver. "Go around the corner over to Michigan Avenue, but take your time."

The driver shrugged as Daniel reentered the carriage. Daniel's eyes fixed on a shrouded figure he was sure was Lucy. On Michigan Avenue, the driver pulled to the roadside, and Daniel waited in darkness. She could not claim to be going to the orphanage at this hour, nor a class at the university, and he was quite sure she was not on her way to see Will Edwards. Audaciously leaving the house alone at this hour of the night meant she did not intend to be discovered.

He intended to discover her.

She got in a cab herself, one of the few still straggling along the avenue. Daniel saw her lean forward and slide the glass open to give an address, and he made the same motion.

"Follow that carriage," he instructed his driver, "but stay back."

His cab once again began to rock with forward motion. He watched out the windows as Michigan Avenue transformed along the southern route, shops and offices giving way to neighborhoods and businesses with less and less similarity to Prairie Avenue and transecting properties of factories and manufacturing plants. The stillness of the street, inhabited at this hour only by shadowed silhouettes, magnified the clip-clop of the horse's hooves.

The forward cab turned a corner to the west and slowed. Daniel's driver did the same.

"Stop here," Daniel said. Lucy's cab had come to a stop half a block ahead of him.

The driver descended to open the door for his customer and offer her a hand exiting the carriage, then waited humbly while she fished for the fare in her bag.

Lucy knew exactly where she was going, Daniel observed. Clearly she had been here before and did not hesitate to approach a less-than-modest narrow dwelling. She knocked on the door, and a curtain moved enough to fleetingly spill a yellow shaft of light onto the street. A moment later a figure allowed entrance. Daniel chided himself for not telling the driver to pull closer. Something was familiar about the form that greeted Lucy in the moonlight, but Daniel could not see the face.

"Are you getting out, sir?" the driver asked.

Daniel greeted the question with silence, then finally said, "No. Take me back to Prairie Avenue."

"Miss Lucy, you shouldn't be here!" Charlotte exclaimed. "What will Mr. and Mrs. Banning think?"

"It's Henry, isn't it?" Lucy said. "That's why you haven't come home."

Charlotte gestured to the sofa, where Lucy recognized the quilt. Rather than being wrapped in its comfort, however, Henry lay on top of it, awake but listless and pale. On a nearby table sat a ceramic bowl filled with water, a small cloth hanging over its rim.

"Where's Mrs. Given?" Lucy asked.

"I told her to go to bed," Charlotte answered, her own face haggard. "She was up all night last night with him, and the twins too."

Lucy undid the button at the neck of her cloak and flung the garment over a chair. Without it, she noticed that the fire in the grate barely warded off the outside chill. "How bad is the fever?"

"Very bad, since Saturday. If I don't put water on him constantly, it fires up again. He screams and pulls at his ear, or he lies there like this. I don't know which scares me more."

"An ear infection perhaps," Lucy suggested. "I've seen them at St. Andrew's."

"I don't think he's breathing right, either." A sob caught in Charlotte's throat. "I didn't think what would happen if he got sick and I wasn't with him."

Lucy stooped and laid her fingers against the baby's face. "Probably some sort of general respiratory malady." She stuck her hand in the bowl of water. "This is lukewarm. Doesn't Mrs. Given have any ice to cool him? She said she had ice when we first brought him here."

"It's gone. The iceman will be here before dawn." Charlotte picked up her baby and sat on the sofa with Henry on her lap, and Lucy leaned over them both. "I try to spoon some water into him, but he spits out most of it. He won't eat, he won't drink."

"We'll keep trying." Lucy picked up the bowl. "I'll get some fresh water from the kitchen pump. It's sure to be cooler than this."

The kitchen was small and sparse, and an odd experience for Lucy. If not for the handful of times she had helped in the kitchen at the orphanage, it would have been an entirely foreign setting. But thanks to St. Andrew's, she knew a small bit about a kitchen. She knew iceboxes had catch pans, for instance, for the water that drained off the melting ice. Lucy found the catch pan of Mrs. Given's icebox and transferred the water it held into the bowl before returning to the sitting room, triumphant.

"I've brought the water in the catch pan under the icebox," Lucy said. "It's still quite cold."

Charlotte held Henry upright in her arms, supporting his bobbing head against her chest, while Lucy put the spoon to his lips. When he opened his mouth to moan, she dropped the water in.

"He swallowed it!" Charlotte said.

"We'll do this all night if we have to." Lucy offered another spoonful of water. "You look exhausted. Are you sure you don't want to rest? I can look after Henry."

Charlotte shook her head emphatically. "I couldn't close my eyes for a second knowing he was like this."

"Come on, Henry," Lucy coaxed, "another sip."

"I can't believe you came," Charlotte said hoarsely, "to this neighborhood, at this time of night."

"Of course I came."

"Mr. Penard and Mrs. Fletcher must be furious. I was supposed to be home hours ago."

"Don't worry about them right now. You made the right decision to stay with your baby."

"They wouldn't see it that way. And I can't tell them I have a baby."

"No, of course not. We'll figure something out."

Henry took a deep breath and began to scream and cough. Charlotte sprang to her feet, holding him upright against her shoulder and patting his back firmly while she paced. Lucy dipped the cloth in the cool water, wrung the drips out, and placed it on Henry's head, then moved it gently over his face as she followed Charlotte's movements around the room. Henry drew air again and bellowed, and a second cry came from the children's bedroom.

"He's woken one of the twins again." Charlotte sighed. "Mrs. Given has been up and down with them three times already tonight."

"She can look after them," Lucy said. "There will be time to sleep later. They're not ill. For that we can be grateful."

Henry's face flushed red, and he writhed in his mother's arms. Charlotte paced more quickly, patted his back more firmly.

For another three hours, the baby alternated between screaming spells and quiet times, but he did not sleep. Lucy spooned water in his mouth and kept the damp cloth fresh. Finally, deep into the night, his eyelids grew heavy and his breathing smoother.

Lucy put her hand on the baby's face again. "I think the fever is breaking. He's cooler."

Henry slept at last. With her baby quiet in her arms, Charlotte sat in an armchair and put her head back, daring to close her own eyes. Lucy never closed hers. She laid the baby's quilt over sleeping mother and child and watched an hour's respite, praying with every breath.

Around four in the morning, Charlotte roused. "What was that?"

"What was what?" Lucy asked.

"I heard a sound, a horse in the alley, I think. It must be the iceman. He'll come to the back."

"I'll see to him." Lucy met the iceman at the alley door and made sure the new block of ice was installed in the icebox, a procedure she had never observed before. As she watched him leave, she knew she must soon follow. It would not help Charlotte for the Banning household to find Lucy missing as well.

Henry was still sleeping on his mother's chest.

"I have to go now, Charlotte, or there will be such a fuss at home I'll never explain my way out of it."

Charlotte nodded.

"I'll come back," Lucy offered, "after my meeting for the women's exhibit. I could catch a cab."

Charlotte shook her head. "I think it's over. He feels more like himself, and he's breathing so much better. I don't want to cause you any more trouble."

"It's no trouble," Lucy responded.

But Charlotte shook her head again. "If he rests for a few hours and seems all right, I'll come home."

"Stay as long as you need to."

―⁌⁍―

Prairie Avenue was still shrouded in gray when Lucy got out of the carriage. It had not been easy to find a cab to take her home. Mrs. Given's neighborhood was a destination for reluctant cab drivers, not the sort of place where they lingered in pre-dawn hours hoping for fares. But Lucy finally was home, and the household showed no signs of stirring. She turned her key in the lock slowly and opened the door as stealthily as possible, keenly aware that her parents' bedroom was only down the hall and her mother was a light sleeper.

Safely in her suite, Lucy mussed her bed and changed into nightclothes. But she did not sleep. She couldn't. She sat in the armchair and waited for dawn, and then for the avenue to awaken. At her normal rising time, she went to her vanity table and pushed the annunciator button.

"I'd like Charlotte to assist me, please," she said.

"I regret Charlotte is not available," Penard answered. "Will it be satisfactory if I send Elsie?"

"Yes, thank you." Lucy snapped off the button. She couldn't tell much from Penard's tone, but she had accomplished her goal of maintaining a semblance of normalcy.

An hour later, Lucy entered the dining room. Leo, Richard, and Daniel were feasting on eggs and fried potatoes with dried apricots, toast and jam, and a robust tea. Bessie was attending to their needs.

"Lucy, have you heard?" Richard popped a piece of toast in his mouth.

"Heard what?" Lucy kept her tone light while her stomach bore her anxiety.

"Charlotte's gone missing."

"Oh?" She raised her eyebrows. "Where is she?"

"If anybody knew where she was, she wouldn't be missing," Richard pointed out.

"No, I suppose not. Bessie, I'd just like tea and toast this morning." Lucy took her usual seat between Richard and Daniel and smiled across the table at Leo. "I was only told Charlotte was unavailable."

"Penard reported to Father a few minutes ago," Leo explained. "It seems Charlotte never came home from her half day off yesterday."

"Penard has that scowl he gets when he's unhappy but not supposed to show it because a professional butler doesn't show his emotions," Richard said.

Bessie poured steaming tea in Lucy's cup. Daniel had not looked up even once from his newspaper.

"Perhaps we should wait for an explanation," Lucy said, "before we jump to any conclusions about Charlotte. It's possible she couldn't get home for some good reason."

Samuel entered the dining room. "Good morning, Lucy."

"Good morning, Father. Have you eaten?"

"Yes, long ago. Richard, get your things. It's time for the carriage."

Richard stuffed one last bite of potatoes in his mouth. "I always miss the excitement. I'd like to be a fly on the wall when the maid gets home."

"There will be no excitement," Samuel said. "It's a staff issue, and Penard will deal with it appropriately."

"I'd better be going as well," Leo said. "Department meeting first thing this morning. Someone got hold of a listing of exhibits for the Manufactures Building at the fair, and we're going to have a preview."

Silence settled over the dining room. Daniel munched on a piece of toast, still absorbed in his paper. Lucy debated the merits of trying to make conversation to fill the empty space between her and Daniel that resulted when her brothers left the room.

"Leo is almost as excited about the Manufactures Building as I am about the women's exhibit," she said. "I suppose it will be an industrial engineer's dream to see the new machinery on display."

Daniel folded his newspaper, laid it on the table next to his plate, and looked at Lucy, his face deadpan.

"I'm sure the papers are full of articles about the fair these days," Lucy speculated. She took a sip of tea.

Daniel reached over and covered her hand with his. Lucy's breath caught.

"I know, Lucy."

She studied his face and saw it was true.

"I'm still working out some of the pieces," Daniel said. "I don't understand why you went there last night, but when I discovered this morning that the maid had not come home, I realized she was the one who let you in the door in that rattrap of a house."

Lucy refused to gasp. "You must stop following me, Daniel. If you don't, I'm going to tell my father—or yours."

"No, you won't." His tone was free of fear. "I know more than you think I know, and I'm confident you don't want the truth to come out. So you won't say anything, and I will do as I please."

Lucy froze to her chair as Daniel pushed his back, picked up his newspaper, and sauntered out of the room.

29

When Charlotte finally stepped off the creaking streetcar, she knew the worst lay ahead. She might well find her dilapidated carpetbags packed and waiting for her inside the female servants' entrance to the Banning home. There was little to gain by avoiding the encounter, however. The green trunk she opened in the small third floor room on her first day came to mind. It held the belongings of the previous kitchen maid, whose apron Charlotte inherited. As far as Charlotte knew, the girl never came back to claim her things. Perhaps she, too, dreaded going home after an unexplained absence and simply decided not to bother. Certainly she'd left behind nothing of any value. Charlotte at least wanted to retrieve her grandmother's Bible. She walked the blocks from the streetcar route to the Bannings', determined to hold her head high whatever awaited her. The only thing that mattered was that Henry was going to get well.

Charlotte approached the house with managed trepidation. Archie, the footman, flashed her a look when he saw her coming. He stood at the side of the road, polishing Mr. Banning's carriage.

"Well, look who's here!"

Archie was more jovial than Charlotte thought the situation called for.

She paused briefly to ask, "How bad is it? How much trouble am I in?"

Archie tilted his head to consider. "Mr. Penard mumbled all through the servants' breakfast that such defiance of his role would bring consequences."

"So he's going to dismiss me?"

"He didn't come right out and say that, but he could make up his mind at any moment."

"I see Mr. Banning is home." Charlotte nodded at the carriage.

"He called from the office to say he had a headache and wanted to come home. I just let him off at the front. I was about to go to the carriage house when I saw you coming. Are you all right, Charlotte?"

She swallowed. "As well as can be expected. I'd better face the music and get it over with." She took a step forward, but Archie caught her arm.

"Whatever it was, Charlotte, I'm sure it was important." He held her gaze.

He sounded sincere to her. "Thank you, Archie. It was."

She stepped under the arch and around the partial brick wall that shielded the female entrance from public view. Once inside, she heard the usual bustle of activity drifting from the kitchen. By now luncheon would have been cleared away and Mrs. Fletcher would have turned her attention to the formal family dinner to be served in five hours. Charlotte stood under the door frame, trying to discern if she were welcome in the kitchen.

Mrs. Fletcher looked up from the breadboard where she was kneading and said simply and softly, "Mr. Penard will want to speak with you." She tilted her head toward the butler's pantry.

"Yes, ma'am." Charlotte began to cross the room.

The door flew open and Penard stepped out of his pantry, glaring at Charlotte.

"I am certain you are aware of your transgression, Miss Farrow."

"Yes, sir."

"You are also aware of my authority to dismiss you for a flagrant violation of expectations."

"Yes, sir."

"What do you have to say for yourself?"

"I was faced with an emergency," Charlotte answered, launching into the brief speech she had rehearsed in her head on the streetcar. "Someone I care for was found seriously ill and required attention. I was the most suitable person to step in."

Penard, his lips pressed together, blew his breath out through his nose. "You have responsibilities here."

"Yes, sir, I realize that. I had to make a decision and trust your good graces upon my return." She only hoped he had some good graces stored somewhere.

"By someone you 'care for,' I presume you mean a man."

Charlotte was silent. She had said as much as she could safely say.

Penard scowled more tightly. "I will not have one of my maids bringing disrepute to this house by staying out all night in the company of a man."

"No, sir. I felt it was a matter of life and death."

Penard looked skeptical. "Is your 'friend' better?"

"I believe so. Another friend is now caring for him."

"Ah, so it is a man!" Penard shouted, triumphant.

Charlotte bit her lip and said nothing.

"You will return to your duties," he said, "and I will advise you of my decision as to whether you will continue your employment."

"Yes, sir." She did not let out her breath again until the butler had wheeled and left the room. Charlotte turned hopefully to Mrs. Fletcher. "What will he decide?"

The cook shrugged. "He's been fit to be tied all morning. Perhaps now that you're back he'll simmer down."

"I hope so. I never meant to endanger my position, but I had no choice."

"If you were with a man, I would understand," Mrs. Fletcher said unexpectedly. "After all, I wasn't always the widowed cook."

"What would you like me to do?" Charlotte changed the subject. "Shall I finish the bread for you?"

Mrs. Fletcher brushed her hands together, spraying loose flour across her apron. "You do that and I'll get the dinner roast started."

❧

Lucy came through the front door and dropped her bag and hat on the foyer table. She had hardly heard a word anyone spoke at the weekly women's exhibit meeting, nor had she eaten a bite of the luncheon Mrs. Palmer ordered from her husband's hotel so the group could extend its meeting time. Plenty of restaurants closer to the exhibit building would have sufficed, but Bertha Palmer would not miss a chance to direct every detail to her advantage and dramatically arranged for a Palmer House feast to be delivered with accompanying china and crystal. At least the committee had made forward progress. Between Will's disappearance, Charlotte's baby being ill, Daniel's threats, and the lack of sleep, Lucy had little energy available to object to anything Bertha Palmer suggested. She reserved her focus for the details she was responsible for.

Lucy now wandered into the late-afternoon emptiness of the parlor, hoping for a few moments of quiet before the family began to trail in to dress for dinner. Her favorite chair provided only temporary refuge, however. From her view in the parlor, Lucy saw Penard emerge from the dining room and cross the foyer before turning down the hall that led to her father's study. *Is Father home already?* she wondered. Lucy rose and moved smoothly to the arched doorway, where she could see Penard knock on the study door. Her father's voice bid him enter. Lucy crept down the hall, encouraged that Penard did not close the door behind him. She pressed herself against the wall beside the door, out of the sight of anyone in the study.

"The maid returned," Penard reported.

"Oh?" Samuel answered. "Did she offer a credible explanation for her absence?"

"Hardly. I am inclined to believe that she has become involved with a man."

"She spent the night with a man?"

Lucy cringed in the hall. *Don't believe it, Father!*

"She claims she was with a sick friend," Penard said, "and it appears indisputable that the 'friend' was male."

"But you have no actual proof," Samuel said, ever the lawyer.

"Even without proof of involvement with a man, her disregard for her duties is ground for dismissal."

"If you dismiss her, you'll have to find another maid quickly," Samuel said. "Flora won't stand for any interruption to the flow of work."

"I will contact the service, and I'm confident they'll have recommendations for someone with more experience."

"Do as you see fit," Samuel said. "I have a headache."

Lucy couldn't hold still another minute. She jumped into the doorway. "No, Father, you cannot condone dismissing Charlotte."

Her father looked startled. "Lucy, have you been eavesdropping? It's unbecoming."

"I'm sorry, Father. When I saw Penard come down the hall, I was afraid this was on his mind."

"You know very well I leave managing the household staff to Penard," Samuel said. "I can't get involved with these details."

"I'm not asking you to get involved," Lucy said. "I'm only saying Charlotte has pleased me more than any ladies' maid I've ever had, experienced or not, and I want to keep her on. If Penard does not want to use her in the kitchen, I'll take her on full time."

Samuel Banning looked from his determined daughter to his resolute butler. "Penard?"

"I will of course acquiesce to Miss Lucy's wishes to allow the girl to keep her position," Penard finally said, "though I will give the maid a stern warning that continuing this behavior will not be tolerated."

Lucy let out her breath. "That seems fair. In fact, I'll speak with her myself about the matter, if you'll be so kind as to send her to the parlor."

Charlotte stepped into the parlor, her eyes wide.

"Get your coat," Lucy said, her voice low. "I'll say I want to stroll over to one of the little shops on Michigan Avenue and require your assistance."

When they were clear of the house, Lucy burst with questions.

"How is Henry?"

Charlotte smiled. "His temperature was normal from the time you left until I came home—almost ten hours. He slept a lot, but when he woke up, he was hungry."

"So he's really on the mend! I'm so relieved."

"I would never have left him, no matter what the consequences, if I weren't certain he was all right."

Lucy put a hand on her maid's arm. "It distressed me no end that you had to go through this alone."

"I wasn't alone. You were there."

"I mean as a parent," Lucy said softly. "I've come to be very fond of you, Charlotte, and I hope you think of me as a friend."

"I do."

"As a friend, I can't help wondering about Henry's father. Wouldn't he want to know if his child is sick?"

Charlotte's steps slowed almost to a stop, and she looked away. "Must we speak of that, Miss Lucy?"

Lucy chose her words carefully. "I won't blame you if you simply say it's none of my business, but I do care for both you and Henry."

Charlotte sighed. "I have a husband under the law," she finally whispered, "but he is no true husband and can never be a father."

"You're speaking in riddles," Lucy said. "I don't understand."

"Please, Miss Lucy, trust me. Henry would be in danger if his father finds us. I can't let that happen."

"Does anyone know where you are? Your own family?"

Charlotte shook her head. "I can't risk it. For Henry's sake."

"We'd better keep walking so we don't arouse suspicion," Lucy said, glancing around and resuming movement. "Of course I would never knowingly do anything to endanger you and Henry, but I may have done so already."

Charlotte sucked in her breath. "What do you mean?"

"Last night. Daniel followed me. When you weren't in the house this morning, he figured out it was you I'd gone to see."

"Does he know—"

Lucy shook her head. "No, he doesn't know about the baby. And he doesn't know whose house that is. But he knows where it is now, and he knows you were there."

"If he follows me—"

Lucy nodded. "He's sure to discover Henry. I'm so sorry. I only meant to help you last night, and look what I've done."

Charlotte shuddered. "I can't bear the thought of staying away from my son, not after last night. What if Daniel approaches Mrs. Given directly?"

"We'll figure something out," Lucy assured her, "but we both must be very careful. Daniel is used to getting what he wants."

Charlotte turned and looked Lucy in the eye. "Do you think he has anything to do with Mr. Edwards leaving so abruptly?"

Lucy shrugged. "I don't know. But I wouldn't put it past him."

As the two women slipped into an obscure milliner's shop, Daniel noticed and smiled at his good fortune. Like last night, he hadn't even been following Lucy this time, and merely stumbled on her subterfuge in action. Nevertheless she confirmed his suspicion that something was going on with that maid. He was going to get to the bottom of things. Suddenly he decided not to catch the train to Riverside but to go to dinner at the Bannings'.

30

$\mathcal{A}$lone in the house, just the way he liked it. He hadn't had the pleasure for quite some time, but Thursday afternoon turned out perfectly. Flora was at her ladies' reading group, Leo was working long hours, Lucy was at her harebrained philosophy class. Penard had practically posted guard on Samuel's study since the return of his missing items, but Daniel saw the butler leave the premises twenty minutes ago. None of the family was home for luncheon, which meant the staff was feeling relaxed. Mrs. Fletcher and two of the maids would have their feet up somewhere in the servants' quarters while they did handwork. Charlotte, he knew, had the afternoon off, and he was pretty sure he knew now where she disappeared to every week. Perhaps next week he would surprise her, but today he was content to be alone in Samuel's study.

Daniel sat in the supple leather chair and soaked up the surroundings. He had loved this room since the day the Bannings moved into this house. The rich wood of the partners desk, the first editions collection, the charcoal drawings in tasteful frames, the matching fountain pens in their brass stand. Not everything in the room was valuable, but it was all sentimental. Samuel kept such interesting mementos of his contact with clients. Nearly every item in the room carried a story Daniel could tell as well as Samuel himself.

He ran his fingers through his hair, then laid one hand on top of the neat stack of papers on the lower right corner of the desk. With the other, he stood his briefcase on the desk and opened it.

Lucy was looking forward to a hushed house and a midafternoon respite. It would have been more convenient to learn that her Thursday afternoon class had been canceled before she got all the way down to the university, but at least Archie had not yet disappeared with the carriage. Now that her class attendance was no longer secret, she was free to use one of the family carriages at her convenience—and if she did not, her mother would accuse her of using the streetcar. The week had been stressful, and Lucy intended simply to go to the lecture and come right back home, so she had arranged for Archie to drive her. Generally Archie did not stray far, and Lucy was back in the carriage within ten minutes of discovering the lecture would not happen.

Drained by the week thus far, Lucy had no complaint about a reprieve from class. After staying up all Sunday night with Henry and pressing through Monday, Lucy had fallen prey to exhaustion at last on Monday night. In her waking hours, however, she was still unsettled knowing Daniel had seen her at Mrs. Given's house. Daniel had not reappeared at the Banning home since Monday evening, when he targeted her with several barbs meant for the others to perceive as humor. Lucy had once thought she knew him so well, yet in the last few weeks Daniel had become erratic to the point she could no longer predict his movements. Every tidbit of conversation with her family became of interest to her. Perhaps someone had seen or spoken to Daniel or knew something she did not know of his activities.

Charlotte was off the rest of the day, of course, since it was Thursday. Lucy had pressed some coins into Charlotte's hand with strict instructions that if anything was wrong—anything at all—she was to send a cabbie with a message. Lucy looked forward to hearing a good report on Henry's health at the end of the day. For now, though, she was grateful simply to have some extra time with no demands.

Archie let her off in the front of the house, opened the front door for her, then proceeded with the horse to the carriage house. Lucy went directly into the parlor, where she sank into the settee and let her head fall back. If she could just have twenty minutes, perhaps she could manage the stairs. After a moment, she removed her hat and unbuttoned the tweed jacket she wore over a blouse and skirt.

Her head rolled toward the door when she heard a sound she could not quite identify. Was that someone shuffling papers? A scratching noise? Shuffling steps? She listened again. The distinct sound of a book dropping emanated from her father's study down the hall, but why should anyone be in there? Surely her father had not come home early twice in the same week.

Lucy closed her eyes again.

Definitely someone was in the study. Penard perhaps?

Lucy leaned forward, then finally stood up and crossed the room. She was certainly not going to sit there pondering a mystery when all she had to do was step down the hall and look through a doorway in her own home to solve it.

"Daniel!" she said, surprised a moment later. "I wasn't expecting you here." She had the vague impression he'd been sitting in her father's chair. His leather briefcase with brass corner mounts stood open on the desk.

Daniel casually closed his briefcase. "Your father and I were supposed to meet," he said. "He has a client seeking investment advice and thought perhaps I could help."

"Father usually holds that sort of meeting at his office." Lucy guardedly moved around the desk. Was that book with the red binding out of place? "He didn't mention anything at breakfast."

Daniel shrugged. "I telephoned him at the office this morning. I suggested perhaps this would be more convenient, but apparently he was not able to get away after all."

"He's rather particular about these things."

"Miscommunication happens to everyone." Daniel smiled at Lucy—that smile she had stopped trusting a long time ago.

"I'm sure he'll be sorry he missed you." She smiled back.

"We'll reschedule. No harm done."

"Perhaps I could offer you some refreshment." Before Daniel could respond, she pushed the annunciator button behind her father's desk. "Mr. Jules and I will have some refreshment in the parlor," she said when Mrs. Fletcher answered.

"Yes, Miss Lucy," came the answer. "I'll send Bessie with the tea cart."

Lucy lifted her shoulders and smiled brightly. "Let's go to the parlor. I believe Mrs. Fletcher has been baking today. No doubt Bessie will bring us some delightful pastries."

"I'm afraid I don't have time."

"Maybe Father will turn up if you wait a few more minutes," Lucy suggested.

"It's already well past the appointed hour, so that seems doubtful." He stepped toward the hall.

Lucy fell in step with him to try another tack. "Daniel, perhaps we can talk about the other night."

"Is there something you wish to confess?" he asked.

"No, of course not," she answered quickly. "I knew Charlotte had gone to see . . . a friend . . . and when I learned she hadn't come home, I simply thought I'd see if I could help."

"Are you sure it's appropriate to get involved in the servants' private lives?"

"Of course I don't mean to intrude," Lucy said, "but Charlotte had expressed some concern for her friend and it weighed heavily on my mind."

"She shouldn't be troubling you. You're fraternizing entirely too much with the staff. No doubt it comes from involving yourself with the urchins at St. Andrew's."

Lucy flared. "Never mind. I thought perhaps you would understand, but I see I was mistaken."

They stood in the foyer, glaring at one another.

"Will you take tea in the parlor, miss?" Bessie asked, pushing the rolling tea cart across the marble floor.

"I won't be staying," Daniel announced, and he went out the front door.

"Miss?" Bessie queried.

"I'm sorry to have troubled you," Lucy mumbled. "I guess I don't need the cart after all."

Bessie wheeled the cart around to return to the kitchen, leaving Lucy sighing. She knew no more about Daniel's activities in the last three days than when she stumbled on him in the study.

But what was he doing in the study in the first place?

～⁓～

The answer came just before eight o'clock. Lucy dressed for dinner and waited in the parlor with her mother and her brothers as usual. Samuel stormed down the hall from his study.

"What the blazes happened to my drawing?" he demanded.

Lucy was instantly alert. "What drawing?" she asked.

Leo said, "I thought you got all your things back weeks ago."

"I had a new pen and ink drawing on the front of a card," Samuel bellowed. "It was a gift from someone on the Expo board of directors to show the work of one of the artists who will be exhibited."

"Calm down, Samuel." Flora stood and took his arm. "We'll sort it out."

"No, we won't," he said through gritted teeth. "You know perfectly well that my other missing items turned up under suspicious circumstances. It was not my imagination."

"That's true," Flora agreed, "but perhaps if we stay calm we can retrace your steps and determine the last time you saw the card."

"I saw it this morning," Samuel insisted. "I just received it a few days ago, and only this morning I laid it on my desk. Now it's gone."

"So it disappeared today?" Lucy asked.

"Yes! I want to know what happened to it!"

"Father," Lucy said, "my class was canceled today and I came home early. I found Daniel in your office."

"What was he doing in there?"

"I'm not sure," she admitted. "He said he was expecting you for a meeting."

"Nonsense."

"So you didn't have a meeting scheduled with Daniel today? He didn't telephone you this morning to arrange it?"

"Didn't I just say that was nonsense? Clearly he was mistaken."

"Daniel is rarely mistaken," Lucy mused. "But he *was* in your office this afternoon. Perhaps he found your drawing."

Samuel looked at his daughter as if she had suggested walking on the moon. "You suspect Daniel?"

"I'm only saying he was in your office today. Alone."

Leo jumped in. "You have to admit it's possible, Father."

"I can't believe it," Samuel said. "Why would Daniel take an ink drawing?"

"Why would anyone take anything from your study?" Lucy pressed. "Only a few weeks ago the finger was pointing at me. Surely you don't believe that."

Samuel's silence was disconcerting.

"Father," Leo said, "you can't seriously think Lucy took your things."

"Lucy's behavior has been odd the last few months in many aspects," Samuel remarked. "University classes, breaking her engagement, all that time at the orphanage."

"That hardly makes me a thief!" Lucy exclaimed.

Leo moved toward her and put a hand on Lucy's shoulder, but the gesture did nothing to calm her.

"Daniel took that card," she insisted, on her feet now. "I'm sure of it. Who is to say he did not take the other things as well? He's had the run of the house for years."

"He is the trusted son of our oldest friends," Samuel pointed out.

"And I'm your *daughter*!"

The clock in the foyer announced eight o'clock and Penard promptly appeared. Lucy lost her appetite.

❧ 31 ❧

*L*ucy had neither seen nor heard from Will for two weeks and four days. Not an hour went by that she did not wonder where he was, how he was—why he was wherever he was. In their leisure time, Will and Leo had been nearly inseparable since Will moved to Chicago. Even if Will pulled back from her, he would not pull back from Leo. The more time that passed, the less satisfied Lucy was that Will would leave town without telling Leo and make no effort to send word of his decision. As she sat in her philosophy lecture on Tuesday afternoon, Lucy made up her mind. As soon as class was over, she was going to Will's office and she was not leaving without answers. She would instruct Archie to drop her downtown and promise to take a cab home later.

She was right where he wanted her. He could not have arranged this encounter more satisfactorily. It was only a matter of time—only a few minutes—and Lucy Banning would regret a great many things.

Lucy presented herself in the stone lobby of the building

and studied the list of occupants. Will's firm was on the fourth floor. She marched to the elevator and told the attendant where she wanted to go. On the fourth floor, the glass doors with the brass handles intimidated her fleetingly, but she pressed through them. A young man behind the counter hunched over a typewriter, studying the impressions he'd just made. He looked up at Lucy over his spectacles.

"May I be of assistance?"

"I'd like to see one of the partners," Lucy said calmly, "or perhaps a manager."

"Do you have an appointment?"

"No, I decided to come on short notice." The young man seemed slightly suspicious, which made Lucy impatient.

"May I ask the nature of your business?"

"I am inquiring about one of your employees."

He squinted at her. "Can you be more specific?"

"I would prefer to speak with one of the managers," Lucy said.

"I would like to help you, ma'am, but I must understand the nature of your inquiry before I can direct you."

Lucy swallowed. "I'm inquiring about Mr. Will Edwards. My name is Miss Lucy Banning."

In response to her last name, the young man stood immediately. "I'll see what I can do. Please have a seat." He gestured toward a trio of green velvet upholstered walnut chairs.

Lucy selected a chair and sat stiffly, holding her gloves and satchel on her lap. The clock on the wall underscored how slowly time seemed to be moving. At last, the young man returned.

"Mr. Jensen has agreed to see you without an appointment," he said.

Not one of the names on the door, Lucy noted. "May I inquire what Mr. Jensen's position is?"

"He looks after the daily business affairs of the office.

It would seem the partners are occupied with clients at the moment. Would you like to see Mr. Jensen?"

Lucy stood up. "Yes, of course."

She followed the young man through a maze of small offices and drawing boards spilling rolls of paper in every direction. Young men sat on stools with fine pencils and straight edges in their hands. On one desk, Lucy saw a nameplate that said "Will Edwards," and her stomach flipped. He was still an employee.

"Right here." The young man gestured to an open door.

Lucy stepped into the modest office and met the eyes of a middle-aged man with gray hair and wearing a snug striped silk vest. She extended her hand.

"I'm Lucy Banning. Thank you for seeing me."

"Frank Jensen." He took her hand. "It's a pleasure to meet you, Miss Banning, though I'm not sure I can be of any assistance. I understand you're inquiring about Mr. Edwards." He motioned for her to sit.

"Yes, that's right." Lucy arranged herself on a high back slatted oak chair across the desk from Mr. Jensen.

"Mr. Edwards is on leave at the moment."

At least he had not been dismissed. "When do you expect him back?" Lucy asked.

"The leave is of an indefinite nature. The partners approved an urgent request."

"Do you know if Mr. Edwards left town?"

"I don't have any details."

"Has he contacted anyone at the firm while he's been on leave?"

Mr. Jensen shook his head. "I really couldn't say, Miss Banning. We have two telephone lines, but any number of people use them on a given day. The mail is distributed promptly when it arrives. We don't keep a central log of these matters."

"Of course not."

Mr. Jensen leaned forward on his desk. "May I ask if you have a particular concern about Mr. Edwards?"

How could she answer that question?

"He's a friend of my brother," she finally said, "and I was hoping to put my brother's mind at ease. He was distressed at Mr. Edwards's rather sudden departure after some . . . unfortunate miscommunication with a client."

"Ah, you refer to the missing drawings. Yes, that did cause quite a stir around here, and I admit it seemed prudent to remove Mr. Edwards from further contact with the client. His request for a leave came at an advantageous time for all involved."

"But he has not been dismissed?"

"No. At least not yet. He's clearly a talented architect, and the partners are most anxious for a successful arrangement, despite the current circumstances. My understanding is that he is welcome to take up his post again as soon as he has worked out his personal matters, though there may be additional supervision."

Lucy stood. "Thank you, Mr. Jensen. You've been most helpful."

In the lobby a few minutes later, Lucy paused to lean against a wall and gather her thoughts. She still did not know why Will would take a sudden leave of absence, but at least it seemed to have been voluntary, and his employers had every expectation it was temporary. This was consistent with Leo's inquiries at Will's rooms. In his initial questions, Leo must not have pressed enough at the firm to learn that Will's leave had been approved.

But what would take Will away? And why had he avoided her before he went?

"Hello, Lucy."

Lucy flinched at the sound of Daniel's voice and looked up at his face leaning close to hers.

"You look tired, Daniel," she observed—and meant it. "Have you been sleeping?"

His bloodshot eyes glared at her, and she stiffened.

"Why are you here, Daniel?" she asked softly.

"You know why."

"Do I?"

"Don't play me for the fool, Lucy."

She held her silence and intentionally slowed her breathing.

"Leo came by the bank yesterday," Daniel said, "with some silly notion that I might have an ink drawing that belongs to your father. I can't help but think you are responsible for his suspicion."

"You were in the study the day the drawing went missing. You had opportunity."

"That's as good as twisting a knife in my back." He leaned toward Lucy, then put one hand on the stone wall behind her.

Lucy's instinct was to duck away, but Daniel's second hand went up, caging her in against the stone wall.

"You were in the study, and the drawing did go missing." She spoke the truth flatly, then squeezed to one side and glanced around the lobby.

Daniel smiled and stepped to the side with her, preventing Lucy's escape. Abruptly he gripped her elbow to the point of pain. "Why don't we go somewhere and talk about this?"

"If you don't mind, Daniel, I was planning to go home."

"I do mind. I know you sent your driver home, so no one is expecting you. The hotel a few blocks away serves a wonderful afternoon menu."

"I'm not hungry."

He clutched her elbow and pulled her uncomfortably close to his side, steering her across the lobby toward a door at the back of the building. His hot breath broke over her neck in waves as she struggled to keep up with the pace he set.

"Where are we going, Daniel?"

"I told you, the hotel. It's not the Palmer House, but the food is well worth the effort of seeking it out."

"Why aren't we going out to the street?"

"The alley is much quicker." He pushed open a door and urged her through it toward the left. "Just keep walking. I'll tell you when to stop."

"Why would we stop before we reach the hotel?"

"You ask too many questions, Lucy. That's always been your problem. You don't understand your place any more than that insipid maid of yours."

Lucy twisted in an effort to get her arm free, simultaneously glancing around to find the way out of the alley. Daniel's muscular fingers never wavered.

"Daniel, please. I don't think this is the way to handle our differences."

"I'll be the judge of that."

Lucy gasped as a shadow rose behind them, and Daniel's grasp abruptly released her. She wheeled—and stared into the cobalt eyes of Will Edwards. With the advantage of three inches in height, he had Daniel's throat captive in the crook of his arm.

"Mr. Jules," Will said, his voice full of authority, "I believe I can show you the way out of this alley. It's really no place for a gentleman, and certainly no place to entertain a lady."

Will moved forward, taking Daniel with him and Lucy heaving with relief in his wake. At the end of the alley, Will nudged Daniel into the pedestrian traffic on the side street. "I believe you know your way from here."

Daniel glowered at Will and gave Lucy barely a glance, but he did walk away.

Lucy clutched Will's arm. "How did you . . . ? Where have you . . . ?"

Will kicked a tin can out of the way, took her chin in his hand, and examined her face. With his eyes inches from hers, Lucy forgot to breathe. Will lowered his face to kiss her slowly and fully on the mouth. Lucy raised quaking hands to his shoulders and returned the kiss. Finally he released her lips with a sigh and enfolded her in his arms.

"I'm sure you have a lot of questions," Will said. "I have a few of my own. But I have a feeling we've just begun to find the answers."

Lucy nuzzled his shoulder, her arms around his neck now. "I never imagined our first kiss would be in a dirty alley, but I've never been so happy to see anyone in my whole life."

"I wonder who has been imagining our first kiss longer, you or I." He kissed her again, deeply. When he finally broke the kiss—reluctantly, it seemed to Lucy—she wrapped her fingers around both his hands.

"I just got back to town on the train," Will said. "I was going to check in with my office when I saw Daniel taking you out the back door. I'm escorting you straight home, and we are going to talk to your parents about certain realities."

32

$\mathcal{L}$ucy clutched Will's arm as they strode back through the stone lobby of the office building and emerged onto State Street into welcome sunlight. Will hailed a cab and helped Lucy step up into it, then climbed in and sat beside her. For once, she was grateful for a carriage, and the practicality of a streetcar did not cross her mind.

"I've been worried sick about you," Lucy said after Will had asked the driver to take them to Prairie Avenue. "Before you left, you were avoiding me, and then you disappeared without a word."

"The first part of what you said is true," Will admitted, wrapping an arm around her shoulders and pulling her close, "but the second part went awry."

"What do you mean?" Without reluctance, Lucy laid her head against Will's shoulder.

"I began to wonder what I really had to offer you," Will confessed. "We come from different worlds."

"That's ridiculous. We're two people who care about each other. The rest of it is nothing to me." She reached for his hand.

"There's a lot you don't know about me," Will said.

"Does it have something to do with why you took a leave of absence so suddenly?"

He nodded. "In a way. Even Leo doesn't know about how I grew up."

"I don't understand," Lucy said. It was true she never heard a single story about Will's childhood, though Will knew a great deal about her youth. The stories he told her about his life before Chicago did not go back any further than his late teens.

"I never knew my father," Will explained. "My mother was a seamstress, but it was difficult for her to look after a child. I got into some trouble when I was eight and was nearly branded as a child criminal. She decided it was for my own good that I live somewhere with more supervision. I grew up in a place not so different from St. Andrew's. I was one of the lucky ones, though. My mother stayed in touch.

"Somehow I stayed in school till I was sixteen, though goodness knows most of my friends didn't. After that, I worked in a factory. One day some sketches I'd done of the building fell out of my coat pocket, and the plant manager discovered them. When he called me into his office, I was sure I was being sacked. Instead, he said I had talent and he offered to help."

"And that's how you ended up working for the architects?" Lucy said.

Will nodded. "I started as an errand boy of sorts. Cleaning up. Fetching things. Eventually they started giving me some simple drawings to copy. Once they realized I planned to stick around, they made me an intern."

"And somewhere in there you met Leo."

"One of the partners gave a party. His son went to school with Leo. We ended up across the dinner table from each other."

Lucy laughed. "And once you meet Leo, you're hooked. Everybody is."

"Leo is a great pal," Will said, "but your parents are another matter. They think I went to school in Princeton with Leo, and even that is not good enough for them. What if they find out I never set foot inside a college in my life? What if getting involved with me meant you could never go back to Prairie Avenue? I didn't want to take you away from everything you know. That would be asking you not to be Lucy."

"So you just left?"

Will shook his head. "No. I got a telegram saying there was an emergency in New Jersey and I should come home."

"Your mother?"

"The message said she had taken very ill and was not expected to live. Of course I arranged to go immediately and got on the first train east."

"Is she . . . did she . . . ?"

"No, that's not it," he assured her quickly. "My mother was fine. I should have known. If she was so ill, how could she send a telegram? And there's no one else who would have done it."

"But you did get a telegram."

"Yes, and I've tried to track down its origin. Someone went to a lot of trouble to make it appear as if it came from New Jersey, but now I suspect the source was right here in Chicago."

Lucy leaned back in the seat. "Daniel."

"After what I witnessed today, my suspicions are even stronger."

"He's changed so much in the last few months. I don't know him anymore, or what he's capable of. But if your mother was fine, where have you been all this time?"

"She *was* fine when I arrived," Will explained. "She was

so happy to see me that as long as I was there, I decided to stay for a visit. My employer had already given approval and I'd sent word to Leo about where I was going."

Lucy sat up straight again. "But Leo looked everywhere for you when he first discovered you were gone. He called your office and they said they didn't know where you were."

"They didn't. I said only that I had urgent personal business to look after. And it's possible whoever took Leo's call was not aware of the arrangement. It was made in haste."

"And your landlady?"

Will shrugged. "The rent is paid in advance, and she was not home when I left. I didn't want to lose precious time looking for her."

"You said you sent word to Leo."

"A messenger. A boy came to the office and picked up the letter on Saturday morning."

Lucy shook her head. "Leo never got it."

"Obviously. Of course, I didn't know that at the time."

"How could you?"

"I assumed Leo would pass the word on to you. Sending you a note directly would have ruffled feathers at your house. And then my mother twisted her ankle badly the day I was to return to Chicago, and I felt I should stay a bit longer."

"Wait a minute," Lucy said, "if the messenger did not deliver your note to Will, perhaps the messenger also did not deliver those drawings that went missing."

"I'm one step ahead of you."

"Daniel. He's been behind everything."

"I know you like your independence, Lucy, but I'm concerned for your safety. We must tell your parents what Daniel has been doing."

"They think the world of him, and we have no proof of anything."

"We have proof that he threatened you today," Will said. "I saw the way he was holding you against your will, and nobody in his right mind would take Lucy Banning of Prairie Avenue into an alley behind State Street."

"And why would someone like Daniel even know where the alley is? Why wasn't he at the bank where he should have been on a Tuesday afternoon? He even knew I had dismissed my driver."

"The time for secrets is over, Lucy. Your parents need to know the truth for your safety."

"And Daniel's parents should know for his safety."

They were almost to Prairie Avenue by then. Will's confessions of his past reeled through her mind as they got out of the cab and Will paid the driver. In that moment, Lucy knew she wanted no secrets between them.

But the last secret was not hers to tell.

Flora came in the front door from the ladies auxiliary meeting with great fanfare and found Lucy and Will sitting in the parlor.

"Why, Mr. Edwards, you've turned up."

"It turns out he was never really lost," Lucy said.

Will stood. "It's lovely to see you again, Mrs. Banning."

"Mother, what time do you expect Father home today?" Lucy asked.

"Around seven, I believe," Flora answered. "You know your father always comes home in time for dinner."

It was nearly five. "Do you think there's time to invite Irene and Howard to dinner?"

"Tonight? That's rather short notice. Perhaps on Saturday."

Lucy shook her head. "I'd like them to come tonight, and

I'd like Will to stay. We have something we need to say to the four of you."

Flora looked from Lucy to Will with dubious eyes. "Lucy, dear, I can't imagine what dealings Mr. Edwards would have with Irene and Howard."

"Please, Mother, just telephone them. I'd do it myself, but I don't think they would come for my sake just now. They will for you, though."

"How will I explain the urgency?" Flora was unconvinced.

"It has to do with Daniel. They'll come if you say that."

Flora sighed. "This all sounds rather ominous."

Lucy did not deny the description. "There's still time to catch a train from Riverside."

"I'm sure they'll prefer to bring a carriage. Oh, all right, I'll telephone. But whatever is going on had better be worthwhile."

"And perhaps you should arrange for Richard to have his dinner in his room," Lucy suggested.

Howard and Irene were stunned. Will looked back and forth between their faces, aware that what he had just described must have sounded ludicrous to them. Even Leo's eyes were wide.

"You are making some serious allegations, Mr. Edwards," Howard Jules said, his eyes dark with confusion. "By your own admission, you've only met my son a handful of times in passing. What grounds do you have for these charges?"

"I can imagine what you must be thinking," Will said. "Mrs. Banning's telephone call must have sounded mysterious. I appreciate your coming to dinner."

"I have little interest in the menu," Howard said. "What does it matter what the roast is or whether it is served with potatoes or rice in the face of these accusations?"

Progress of the meal came to a standstill before the soup and fish had been cleared away.

"I'm sorry my account sounds like allegations," Will said. "I'm afraid it's all true."

"This explains a lot of things," Leo said. "Daniel is my friend, but if these things are true—"

"It's all true." Will was keenly aware how shocking his statements sounded, but he was not about to minimize the significance of Daniel's behavior that day. "You're quite right that I cannot prove—yet—that Daniel interfered with my messages or sent the telegram, but I am quite certain of what I saw this afternoon. His intentions toward Lucy were far from kind."

Samuel looked at his daughter. "Can you verify this, Lucy? Did the events happen as Mr. Edwards has described them?"

She nodded. "I'm afraid so. This is not the first time Daniel has shown up out of nowhere, but it is the first time he pressed me to do anything against my will."

"Did he hurt you?"

Lucy shook her head. "No, but I really thought he might."

"Were there any witnesses?" Samuel probed.

"Do you doubt my word, Father?" Lucy asked. "Or the account Mr. Edwards has given of what he himself saw?"

"It would not stand up in court," Samuel mused. "Hardly more than hearsay evidence that cannot be confirmed."

"You have my word that I never received the message Will sent me," Leo pointed out.

"But we have no evidence that Daniel sent a message," Samuel countered, "and we have only Mr. Edwards's word that he received a telegram."

"With all respect, Mr. Banning," Will said, "this is not a court of law and we are not seeking to press charges. My concern is the safety of your daughter."

Lucy jumped in. "And mine is Daniel's welfare." She looked around the table. "Surely you can all see that he has become unwell."

"Of course Daniel is not unwell," Irene Jules insisted, "at least not in the manner you imply. You broke his heart when you broke the engagement, and he has suffered some melancholy, as is to be expected."

"It's more than melancholy," Lucy challenged. "And seated around this table are the people who care for him most. If we won't help him, who will?"

Silence.

"We'll speak to him," Howard finally said. "No doubt he'll be home when we get there, since he hasn't come here."

"He sometimes comes in rather late," Leo pointed out. "Perhaps I'll see him at breakfast."

"If you see him before we do," Irene said, "please do not alarm him. Just ask him to telephone his mother."

"In the meantime, perhaps Lucy should have a companion whenever she goes out," Will suggested. "Her Aunt Violet or one of the maids. At the very least she must have a coachman or footman with her at all times." He did not dare suggest himself as a suitable companion. Despite the afternoon's events, the Bannings would surely regard such an offer as inappropriate.

The meat was served, then the vegetables and finally the salad. Will pushed food around on his plates in between sparse bits of conversation. For the most part, everyone lowered their hands to their laps to indicate they were finished nearly as soon as the last person had been served. No one ate, and Will wondered why they were going through the motions of being served. Charlotte moved among the guests, removing plates that were barely touched.

Will saw the maid glance at Lucy just long enough for

Lucy to return the look before picking up her water goblet. He laid his knife across his bread plate as he considered the significance. It was a secure glance—familial, a glance friends would share over a confidence. Lucy knew something she wasn't telling him, he was sure of it.

By general consensus, dessert and coffee were omitted, and Howard and Irene returned to their luxurious carriage. By ten o'clock, Will said good night to Lucy as well—standing in the foyer in the presence of her parents and Leo—and exchanged a glance with her himself. Daniel had not appeared, and Will hoped he would not have the gall to present himself at the Bannings'. However, Daniel's state of mind was dubious. He'd been doing a lot of things no one would have imagined.

After Will closed the door behind him and stepped away from the house, he turned for one last glance through the window. The others had moved away from the foyer, but Lucy was still there, speaking with Charlotte, their heads curiously close together.

33

*L*ucy did not see Daniel for the next few days. None of the Bannings saw him, and the servants reported each morning at breakfast that he had not used his room on the second floor. Perhaps his parents had been able to talk some sense into him after all, Lucy reasoned.

On the other hand, Lucy saw Will as often as she could. They had managed a few minutes together on Wednesday after he finished his workday, and she had brought him home for dinner on Thursday, much to Violet's delight. On Friday, she spent the day at St. Andrew's as usual, marking the hours until he would arrive to spend the evening painting with the boys. Lucy stayed late to cheer them on. She took a pile of papers that needed sorting to one of the tables in the dining hall, staying well away from any open paint cans or loose brushes. Several of the younger children helped her shuffle papers around until they were called to their own supper. However, most of her attention went to watching Will's patient instruction and encouragement with the boys. Finally, around six-thirty, Lucy knew she must go home if she were going to be changed in time for dinner.

"Are you sure you don't want to come to dinner?" Lucy

pleaded as Will walked her out of the building to see her safely to the carriage.

He chuckled and raised a finger dotted in blue. "Your parents still are not quite sure what to make of me. Let's give them some time to recover from having me at their table twice already this week."

"Will I see you tomorrow?"

"The moment I can leave the office. I do have to catch up on a few things."

He glanced around, then kissed her just as Archie opened the door to her carriage. She would rather have been looking for the streetcar, but Will insisted she not put herself in situations where she could be caught off guard. Archie's instructions from Samuel Banning himself were to wait for Lucy as long as necessary.

Lucy entered the front door and, as usual, put her things down on the foyer table.

"Oh, there you are," Flora said, coming from the parlor. "Finally!"

"I know I'm late, but I promise I'll be changed in time for dinner," Lucy assured her mother. By now Charlotte would have already laid out a gown to replace the sporty-looking brown broadcloth suit Lucy had chosen for a day at St. Andrew's.

"Irene telephoned," Flora said. "She wants to know if you've seen Daniel."

"Why would I see Daniel? After what happened the other day—"

"That's just it," Flora said. "After what happened the other day, it seems no one has seen him at all. He never went home that night. Irene and Howard assumed he stayed here. Today they discovered that he hasn't been to the bank since Monday. Yesterday he missed a critical meeting with a new manufacturer the bank managers were counting on him to woo."

"Slow down, Mother," Lucy said. "Are you sure no one has seen him? Not since I saw him on Tuesday?"

"He hasn't been here, he hasn't been home to Riverside, and he hasn't been to the bank. That's what I'm saying. His poor parents are out of their minds with worry."

Lucy turned her palms up. "I haven't seen him nor heard from him."

Flora gave an exasperated sigh, and Lucy started up the stairs. She didn't know what her mother expected she could do, and frankly, she was relieved not to have any notion of Daniel's whereabouts.

As she expected, Lucy found a gown and accessories laid out on the bed. The damask fabric was overlaid with netting in the bodice and embroidered with delicate flowers in three shades of pink. Charlotte had chosen a silver locket to accent the scooped neckline, and Lucy was pleased with the selection. However, the dress included tiny buttons in two rows up the back, so Lucy would need help. She pressed the annunciator button to inquire if Mrs. Fletcher might spare Charlotte from the kitchen.

When the maid entered, she smirked playfully. "Mrs. Fletcher is none too pleased with my being pulled away so close to serving time."

"We'll be quick," Lucy promised, stepping out of her skirt. "Just get me buttoned up."

Charlotte picked up the gown from the bed and held it ready for Lucy to step into. "Did you see Mr. Edwards today?"

"I just left him. That's why I'm so late."

"I've been thinking, Miss Lucy," Charlotte said quietly.

"About what?"

"About you and Mr. Edwards. I don't want to be between you."

"What do you mean?"

"The baby. And what you've done to help me. I've decided that if you trust Mr. Edwards, then I trust him."

Lucy swiveled to look her maid in the eye. "Are you sure?"

Charlotte nodded, then moved behind Lucy once again to tackle the buttons. "Your mother has been full of questions today." She pushed the first stubborn bead through its loop.

"Do you mean about Daniel? She waylaid me the minute I walked in the door."

"I think she's worried."

"She loves Daniel," Lucy said simply. "Apparently his mother telephoned."

"I heard Mrs. Banning take the call. Mrs. Jules sounded frantic. It was all your mother could do to calm her down enough to understand the problem."

"Daniel will turn up, and when he does he'll have an explanation. He always has an answer."

Charlotte was silent and tugged at three more loops.

"What is it?" Lucy prodded. "I can tell when you have something on your mind."

Charlotte shrugged. "Has he ever gone missing before?"

"Well, no, not to my knowledge."

"Then something *could* be wrong. When Mr. Edwards went missing, you were frantic yourself."

"That's different. Will and I have come to care for each other." *To love each other.* "I was worried something had happened to him."

"That's how Mrs. Jules feels—and your mother. He's gone missing and they don't know if he's going to be all right."

"It does seem irresponsible of him not to inform the bank

of his plans," Lucy admitted. "And he looked positively fright-ful the other day."

"So you can understand why they're worried."

Lucy tugged at the shoulders of her gown. "Charlotte, get me out of this monstrosity."

"Miss Lucy!"

"I know where Daniel is," Lucy said. "Tell Archie to get the big carriage ready, and two horses. Quick, undo those buttons!"

Minutes later Lucy was downstairs again in her brown suit and a warm cloak and flying out the front door. "Archie, take me back to St. Andrew's. That place really needs to get a telephone."

At the orphanage, Lucy jumped out of the carriage without waiting for Archie to open the door and ran into the dining room.

"Oh, good, you're still here," she said when she spotted Will cleaning brushes. "I need you. Daniel is missing and I know where he is."

Will looked skeptical. "Lucy, can't someone else find him? Are you sure you want to put yourself in his path?"

"I decided not to marry Daniel, but that doesn't mean he's the enemy," Lucy said. "I grew up with him and was engaged to him. I know him better than anyone else. He needs help. If you're with me, I know I'll be all right."

She held her breath, willing him to speak.

"Of course I'll come."

At Lucy's urging, Archie kept the horses moving at a can-ter, especially after they left the confines of Chicago traffic.

"You really believe he's at the lake house?" Will asked.

"He loves it up there. He always said he could think

clearly when he was there." She hesitated to say more. "It's where we first kissed, and where we first talked about getting married."

"And he proposed there last summer. Leo told me about the Fourth of July hoopla."

"Daniel adores his work at the bank, and he loves Chicago. But if he is going to disappear anywhere, it's going to be at their lake house."

"Which is right next to your family's lake house."

"I'm worried about him, Will. It would be easy to put him out of my mind after the way he's been behaving, but what if he can't help it? What if he's truly not himself? How can I walk away from him?"

Will put his arm around Lucy and squeezed her shoulder. "You can't. This is the right thing to do."

"It's at least a three-hour trip. We usually make this journey in daylight. The roads are not well lit."

"It's nearly a full moon," Will said. "That will help."

They cantered through the communities that had sprung up north of Chicago. Ravenswood, Lincolnwood, Wilmette, Northbrook, Highland Park. The burgeoning web of railroad tracks allowed people to live in outlying areas and still enjoy the benefits of being near Chicago. Gradually, though, the towns grew more rural, hugging the shore of Lake Michigan between Chicago and Waukegan.

Two lanterns hung from the front of the carriage, lighting the road before them as it narrowed and curved through the thick trees. When they passed through Lake Forest, the last town before the stretch of exclusive lakefront property where the Bannings and Juleses owned land, Lucy leaned forward, feeling her pulse race.

"I hadn't realized how black the sky is away from Chicago," Lucy said. "The view of the lake is spectacular, though it will be hard to see much tonight. I always imagined bringing you up here on a fine summer day, not the middle of a frigid night."

"We're here for Daniel," Will said, "not the view."

Finally Archie slowed the carriage and turned on a familiar lane. Lucy knew where the ruts were on this road and braced herself by gripping the carriage seat.

"Can you hear the lake?" Lucy asked, cocking her head to listen to the water slapping the ridge of rocks at the end of the lane. "We're almost there."

The carriage stopped behind two houses with floor plans that mirrored each other.

Will gave a low whistle. "Those structures are not exactly rustic cabins."

"We bring most of the household staff when we come," Lucy explained. "We share the pier between the two houses."

Will reached across Lucy's lap and pulled on the door handle just as Archie appeared to open the door from the outside.

"Shall we check the house first?" Will suggested.

"All right," Lucy said. "Archie, perhaps you'd better come with us."

"Yes, miss."

"And bring a lantern."

"Yes, miss." Archie unhooked one of the lanterns from the front of the carriage and turned toward the path.

Will grabbed the other lantern. "Better safe than sorry."

Will led the way and Lucy crept behind in the shifting yellow sliver of light. Archie followed.

Lucy stopped abruptly and slapped herself on the forehead. "I didn't think about the keys. He might have locked himself in. We have a man up here who looks after the place in the off-season and has everything ready when we come. I have no idea where to find him."

"One thing at a time." Will led her forward. When they reached the Juleses' house, Will gripped the handle on the main door. It gave. "We're in. Do you have electric lights up here?"

"No," Lucy answered. "Gas lamps, but they'd have to be lit. There's no central line."

The trio huddled in the main sitting room, peering into darkness by the lanterns' twin shafts of light. Lucy noticed nothing out of place.

"Would he be sitting somewhere in the dark, do you think?" Will asked.

"Daniel!" Lucy called at the top of her lungs. "Daniel, are you here?"

No answer. "We'll have to check every room," Lucy said. "Archie, you check the downstairs rooms. Mr. Edwards and I will go upstairs. Be sure to check the closets and large cupboards."

"Yes, miss." Archie turned toward the kitchen, his lantern hanging from an arm extended straight in front of him.

Lucy led Will to the stairs, and they climbed together holding hands, listening for a stray creak from the rooms above them. "Daniel!" Lucy called every few steps.

They pushed open one door after another and found nothing. Everything was as it had been when the house was closed up in September. The bedding was stripped off and packed away, and long cloths kept the dust off the furniture, which seemed to have contorted itself into ominous shadows.

"I don't see any sign anyone has been here," Will said finally. "No tracks in the dust, nothing uncovered."

"No, he's not up here," Lucy agreed. "Nothing has been disturbed."

They made their way back downstairs, where Archie shook his head.

"We'll check outside," Lucy said. Then suddenly, "The pier! Why didn't I think of that sooner?" She quickened her steps toward the door facing the lake and stepped out onto the railed porch that wrapped around the back of the house.

Will was right behind her. "Look," he said, pointing. "Blankets."

Lucy gasped. "The nights are freezing up here at this time of year. If he's been sleeping outside—"

"Miss Lucy!" Archie exclaimed, lifting his lantern.

On the pier she saw a silhouette in the nearly full moonlight, squatting with his arms wrapped around his knees and wearing no coat.

"Daniel," she whispered. "Oh, Daniel, what happened to you?"

They moved closer as quietly as possible, stepping off the porch and onto the still icy path that led to the pier. Away from the house and trees, the moon's light bounced off ice and water. The wind gusted, and the lake's laps morphed into waves crashing against the rocks on the shoreline. Lucy put a hand on Will's arm to stop him when they reached the pier entrance.

"I'd better go alone," she said. "I'm not sure how he'll react if he sees you."

"It's unsafe, Lucy," Will insisted.

She shook her head. "I don't think so. I'm not afraid."

Will studied her face in the lantern's light and leaned in to kiss her forehead. Finally he said, "At least take the light. I'll be watching every minute."

Lucy nodded and took the lantern from Will's hands. The wooden slats of the pier creaked beneath her feet, as she knew they would. She walked slowly enough that the sounds should not alarm Daniel. He sat motionless, staring at the churning waters, and showed no reaction when Lucy stood behind him.

"Daniel." She laid a hand on his shoulder. "I've come for you."

"I wonder what it would be like to just slide off the pier into the lake," he said matter-of-factly. "The brushes would be lathered in black and shades of blue, and frosty bits of white in shapes that have no names."

What is he talking about? "That sounds like a lovely painting, Daniel. Maybe you should take up your art again. It's not too late."

"But I would be in the lake," he said, "and I could not keep the canvas dry."

"So you want to be in the painting?" Lucy guessed.

"I want to be in the lake."

"The lake is icy at this time of year. You know that."

"It won't matter."

He still had not looked at her.

"What won't matter, Daniel?" As she spoke, Lucy glanced at Will.

Daniel unfolded his legs from underneath him, scooting away from her touch to dangle his feet over the side of the pier. "None of it matters."

"Let's go back to the house, Daniel. We'll talk and get you warm."

"But I'm not cold. I should have my shoes on. It would be faster that way."

Lucy realized for the first time that Daniel's feet were bare and scratched. She glanced at Will and Archie again, relieved that Will understood her silent plea and moved forward cautiously. Lucy sucked in her breath and lowered herself to sit beside Daniel at the end of the pier. She set the lantern within easy reach and put an arm around his shoulders.

"We used to sit like this when I was little." Calmly, she moved her free hand to take one of his. "I was amazed at how much you knew about the lake. What kind of fish swim around here, what weather makes the biggest waves, how to tack and turn a boat in the wind."

"Some green."

"Green?" Lucy echoed.

"Black and blue and green."

"Yes, of course, the algae on the rocks," Lucy supplied. She did not dare turn her head to check Will's progress. "And you always knew the constellations. I've forgotten most of them. You'll have to teach me again, and I promise to be a better student this time."

Finally Daniel's head cranked toward Lucy. "No. I'm not going to do that." He turned his gaze back to the swirling lake.

"All right. Of course you don't have to."

At last the sound of creaking boards grew closer. Behind her, Lucy felt the presence of men's shoes, and a moment later Will and Archie gripped Daniel by the elbows and helped him to his feet. He did not resist them. Huddled and tangled, the four of them moved away from the end of the pier and toward the house.

"There's no telephone here. I think we should go straight home," Lucy whispered, and Will and Archie nodded. Together they steered Daniel directly to the carriage.

34

For the first hour, Daniel sat erect and stared at Will across the carriage, while Lucy sat next to Daniel and held his hand. By one in the morning, though, the trotting sway of the carriage had lulled him to sleep, his head bobbing gently against Lucy's shoulder.

"You did a wonderful thing." Will spoke in the hushed deep tones of night.

"I couldn't have done it without you."

"All that mumbo jumbo about being in the lake. If you hadn't been there and he slid off the pier . . ."

"Let's not focus on that. He's ill. I don't understand the mind as well as I'd like to, but I know this is not the real Daniel, and I want to believe he can get better again."

"You were the first to understand something was wrong."

"I should have seen it sooner. I was too busy avoiding the reality that I had to break our engagement." She glanced down at Daniel's chest rising and falling.

"He began taking your father's things long before you decided not to marry him. None of this is your fault."

"I know. It's no one's fault." She paused, then added, "Will, there's something else I need to tell you about."

"I've had a feeling there might be. Something about your ladies' maid?"

Lucy's eyes widened. "How did you know?"

"Because I've come to know you well, Lucy Banning, and I can tell when your heart is torn up about something."

"She has a baby and I've been helping to hide him." Lucy spoke in clip-clop rhythm set by the horses. "Daniel was on the verge of finding out. On the one hand I've been relieved not to see him these last few days. On the other hand, I've been on pins and needles wondering what he might do if he discovered the baby."

Will inspected Daniel's sleeping face. "I have a feeling you're not going to have to worry about that now. And you don't have to carry the secret alone any longer."

"Thank you, Will." She sighed heavily. "It was Charlotte, you know, who said I could tell you. She said, 'If you trust Mr. Edwards, then I trust him.'"

"I'm honored at her confidence."

"I do have a question," Lucy said. "You knew I wasn't at the orphanage on Tuesdays and Thursdays, but you never asked where I was. Then you knew something was going on with Charlotte, but you didn't ask me what. Why didn't you ask?"

"That's not the way trust works," he said simply. "Or love."

They soaked up each other's features in the silence.

"You must be exhausted," Will finally said.

"I am, but we have a long night ahead of us. I'll call Howard and Irene as soon as we get home. We can't leave Daniel alone even for a moment."

"We still have a couple of hours before we get back to Chicago," Will said. "Why don't you put your head back and doze. I'll watch him. It's not as if he can go anywhere."

"He might try to jump out of the carriage."

"I won't let him," Will said. And Lucy believed him.

Lucy did not think she would sleep.

She did.

It was well after three in the morning when Archie pulled the carriage up to the front of the Banning house on Prairie Avenue. Daniel had hardly stirred in more than two hours. Lucy woke when the carriage slowed and roused him enough to cooperate while she and Will walked him into the house, his arms slung around their shoulders.

Charlotte was waiting in the parlor, still fully dressed, and jumped to alertness when the odd trio came through the front door.

"You found him!" Charlotte said in full voice.

Lucy put a finger to her lips.

"Everyone was in such a tizzy at dinner," Charlotte whispered. "I didn't know what to tell them because I didn't know where you'd gone—only that you went to find Mr. Daniel."

"Everything's fine now," Lucy whispered, "or it will be."

"Mr. and Mrs. Banning retired about midnight," Charlotte said. "I knew I couldn't sleep. I've been sitting here waiting for you and haven't heard a sound from down the hall."

"Perhaps that's best. Archie is putting the horses away. Will, maybe you should go upstairs and wake Leo."

Charlotte and Lucy settled Daniel on the settee in the parlor. He was dozing again before Lucy could spread a coverlet over him.

Leo entered the room, pulling his chocolate-colored silk robe closed, his eyes full of questions. Will was right behind him. Speaking in low tones, Lucy gave a quick summary of the night's events.

"I have to call his parents," she finally said.

"I'll find the number." Charlotte moved quickly to the desk where Flora kept a small carved board with jewels embedded at the top. It held about twenty addresses and telephone numbers.

"Good," Lucy said, "then I want you to find Archie. He's probably still in the coach house cooling the horses. Take a fresh horse and the small carriage and go for Dr. Carson. He has rooms above his surgery on Wabash Avenue. Tell him I sent you and he won't ask any questions."

"Yes, miss. Here's the number for the Juleses." Charlotte was out of the room in a smooth motion.

Leo and Will were both gawking at Lucy with their jaws gaping.

"What's the matter with you two?" she asked.

Will found his tongue. "How is it that you know a doctor who won't ask any questions when you send for him in the middle of the night?"

"Just to clarify," Leo added, "this Dr. Carson is not our usual family physician."

"It's a complicated and not very interesting story," Lucy replied, "about something that happened at St. Andrew's last year. Suffice it to say, I am counting on the Banning name to mean something in these circumstances."

Will expelled his breath. "I'm sure it will."

"I'll make that telephone call now."

Lucy was back a few minutes later. "They're on their way. They should be here in about an hour."

"How much did you tell them?" Leo asked.

"I didn't want to frighten them," Lucy answered. "It's difficult to explain on the telephone. It's better if they see for themselves when they get here. By then we should have a doctor on hand as well, and he may be able to explain things."

Slowly the house came to life, whether Lucy meant for it to happen or not. A groomsman from the coach house had seen Archie's movements and felt Penard should be alerted. Once he understood the situation, Penard woke Mrs. Fletcher to prepare coffee and rolls. Despite Lucy's efforts to keep things peaceful, Flora and Samuel heard the commotion in the parlor from their bedroom just down the hall and appeared in their robes, insisting that they had not slept a wink. Even Oliver and Richard found their way downstairs, and before Lucy could contain the tumult, Bessie and Elsie were up as well.

Lucy shooed everyone out of the parlor, except Will and Leo, and insisted that the lights be kept dim. Daniel was sleeping, and she wanted him to continue sleeping at least until the doctor arrived. She had no way to know what he would do if he woke in the midst of the hubbub. The rest of the Bannings moved to the dining room to speculate on what Daniel's behavior meant, while Lucy stood guard at the parlor window that looked out on Prairie Avenue. The street was motionless, empty, dimly lit. Lucy's ears still tolled with the rhythmic waves of Lake Michigan outside Lake Forest, where the water slapped the rocks countless times a day. *Water will never be a soothing sound to me again*, she thought.

When she saw Archie arrive, she had the front door open before Dr. Carson could get out of the small carriage. Charlotte followed the doctor up the short walk to the front door.

"Dr. Carson, thank you for coming." Lucy welcomed him to the foyer.

"I only hope I can help. Your maid has given me a brief summary of recent events. I'd like to examine the patient."

"He's right in here." Lucy motioned toward the parlor. "His parents are on their way."

The doctor encouraged Daniel to wake up and converse. Charlotte brought Daniel a glass of cold water to help him rouse. Lucy read the concern on the doctor's face in response to the disjointed answers Daniel gave to his questions. The answers rarely matched the questions, and sometimes Daniel merely stared in silence until Dr. Carson tried another question. In between questions, the doctor felt for Daniel's pulse, looked into his wide eyes, and listened to his heart. Charlotte quietly rolled a tea cart into the parlor and began pouring coffee. Lucy was once again standing guard at the window, watching for Howard and Irene.

It was after four-thirty—closer to five—in the morning when they arrived, frantic and grateful at the same time. Leo let them in the front door, and they burst into the parlor and fell upon their son, calling his name and asking questions. He did manage to say, "Hello, Mother," at one point, but otherwise did not respond to their efforts.

The family members banished to the dining room emerged with a fresh endeavor to discover the details of what was going on.

"If I'm going to be up in the middle of the night, I at least want to know why," Richard complained.

"Nobody forced you to get up." Lucy turned his shoulders back toward the dining room and herded the others. "I promise I'll come and explain everything as soon as I can. Right now the last thing Daniel needs is a mob scene."

"We're just concerned, dear," Flora protested but retreated to the dining room.

Lucy stood with her hands on the pocket doors, ready to pull them closed. "Mrs. Fletcher, perhaps you might as well make a hearty breakfast despite the early hour." It was the first thing she could think of to keep them all occupied. Eating would give them reason to stay in the dining room.

Returning to the parlor, Lucy motioned that Howard and Irene should step into the foyer with the doctor, leaving Daniel under the vigil of Will and Leo.

"He's obviously disoriented." Dr. Carson twisted his stethoscope in his hands. "I don't find anything wrong physically. I believe he has a basic awareness of where he is and who is present. However, he doesn't seem to understand the circumstances that brought him here and is not able to answer questions in a meaningful way."

"What can you do for him?" Irene asked. "Is there a medicine you can prescribe?"

Dr. Carson shook his head. "These kinds of cases are complex. A young Austrian doctor named Sigmund Freud has done some work in the field of what happens in the mind, but the truth is, we understand very little of it. I don't have a compound to recommend."

"We'll take him home," Irene said. "He needs to be in his own home, to sleep in his own bed."

"I'm afraid I can't advise that, Mrs. Jules," the doctor said. "I believe your son needs to be in a sanitarium where he can be properly observed and evaluated."

"You mean a lunatic asylum?" Howard asked. "Has he completely gone round the bend, then?"

"I'm not saying that," the doctor responded carefully. "I'm simply saying that I don't think he's going to snap out of this with a few days of bed rest, and his behavior is likely to be unpredictable. I've read a number of journal articles about Dr. Freud's 'talking cure.' I can suggest several facilities that would serve your son well with this approach."

Lucy saw the blanched, stricken faces of Howard and Irene and said, "Dr. Carson, I'm sure you appreciate the need for discretion."

"Of course. I know of a place in Wisconsin that takes particular care to guard privacy. We can make the arrangements first thing in the morning. It might be a few days before we can transport him, though. I would not suggest trying to move him on your own."

Lucy glanced out the window. "From the look of the sky,

first light is not far off. He can stay here until the arrangements are complete. Please telephone as soon as you can with instructions, and ask to speak to me."

Dr. Carson took down the telephone number for the Bannings, and Lucy dispatched Archie to take the doctor home.

"Let's make Daniel comfortable in his room upstairs while we wait for the arrangements," Leo suggested. "We'll pull in some armchairs for Howard and Irene and make sure they have everything they need."

"Thank you, Leo," Lucy said, and Howard and Irene murmured their appreciation.

"Come on, Will," Leo said. "You're in too deep to back out now." Leo turned back to Daniel.

Will stepped close to Lucy to whisper, "When this is all over, remind me to tell you how wonderful you are. Oh, and I love you."

She turned her face up for a kiss, not caring that her parents were behind merely a pair of pocket doors.

35

Through the window of the train, where Charlotte sat across from Lucy in a private compartment, Charlotte's eyes feasted on the budding greens as bushes and trees along the track established themselves for a brilliant summer. March had been such a difficult month, the likes of which Charlotte hoped not to see again for a long, long time. By the third week of April, she had been part of the Banning household staff for six months and her position seemed secure. Henry was thriving, and she saw him on Thursdays and every other Sunday. When Lucy rang for her, she felt the warmth of friendship, not the dread of what might go wrong. Finally, only a week ago, she had taken her grandmother's Bible out of the carpetbag in the closet and laid it, open, on the table next to her bed. Did she dare acknowledge she was beginning to feel safe—even hopeful? This train journey could not have been less like the one that had carried her to Chicago six months ago.

"Mr. Daniel seemed well." Charlotte searched Lucy's eyes for confirmation. Only a few minutes ago they had left the sanitarium after a visit of two hours.

Lucy nodded. "I was not sure what to expect after the way we found him three weeks ago. The doctor didn't think he should have visitors before now, but he seems to be making progress."

"He seemed glad to see you."

"I believe he was," Lucy said.

"Will you visit him again?"

Lucy tilted her head thoughtfully. "I don't know. I would not want him to misinterpret my attentions. That would only make his recovery more difficult. And I don't want to draw attention by frequent trips to Wisconsin and have the wrong person discover why I go. So far we've managed to keep this out of the papers."

"Even the rest of the staff don't know where we went today," Charlotte assured her. Lucy had kept Charlotte's secret for six months. Charlotte would guard anything Lucy asked her to, including where Daniel was. The missing ink drawing had turned up in Daniel's briefcase, just as Charlotte was sure it would. The bag contained assorted other drawings Daniel apparently made himself, though no one was quite sure what they represented.

"They saw what Daniel was like that night," Lucy said, "so of course they can guess what sort of place he's in. It's just better if they don't know the location."

"Mr. Penard made it clear to all of us that we would never find another position in service if he discovered any of the staff told a soul about that night."

"I certainly hope it won't come to that. The important thing is to recognize he's ill and pray he gets better. Even Will wants that for him."

Charlotte smiled slyly. "Mr. and Mrs. Banning seem to be warming to Will."

Lucy made no effort to disguise her grin. "Yes, they are, and it's about time."

"They thought you were marvelous, the way you looked after Daniel," Charlotte said.

"And they saw that I can be quite stubborn! I love Will, and I'm not giving him up."

Charlotte nodded, wondering silently why it had taken Lucy's parents so long to understand how tenacious she was.

Two days later, Lucy's Friday at the orphanage sped by. Late in the afternoon, Benny, who recently had turned seven, wandered into the volunteers' office.

"It's time for Mr. Will," Benny said. "Why hasn't he come?"

Lucy glanced at the clock. It was indeed past the time Will usually arrived.

"You've learned to tell time so well!" Lucy said to the boy.

He shrugged. "It's not hard. Where is Mr. Will?"

"I'm not sure," Lucy said. "Perhaps someone he didn't expect called for him at his office, or some urgent work came up."

"But it's Friday. He's supposed to be here."

"I'm sure we'll hear from him," Lucy said. As the boy, still grumpy, turned on his heel and walked out, Lucy looked at the clock again.

"Thank you for seeing me, Mr. Banning." Will shook Samuel's hand in his downtown office. He could not judge from Samuel's expression what kind of mood the older man was in. Their interactions for the last several weeks had been increasingly congenial, and Will was counting on that foundation for this conversation as he took a seat in an overstuffed chair.

"What can I do for you?" Samuel arranged a blank page in front of him and picked up a fountain pen. "Have you come on a legal matter, some agreement you wish to enter?"

"As a matter of fact, I have," Will answered. "You know by now that Lucy and I have become quite fond of each other."

"My daughter has made that plain these last few weeks. What is the legal matter on your mind?"

Will decided he might as well get right to the point. "I love Lucy and I'm sure she loves me. I've come to ask for her hand in marriage."

Samuel's eyebrows lifted briefly, then fell back into place. "I concede that I am not entirely surprised. I assume you are predisposed to think Lucy would accept this offer?"

"We have not spoken of it directly," Will said. "I felt I should come to you first. But, yes, I do believe she will accept."

"So you've come to ask me to give you my daughter's hand in marriage."

"Yes, sir."

Samuel turned his head to one side and laughed. "Mr. Edwards, I would have thought that by now you would realize Lucy's hand is not mine to give you. Goodness knows it took me long enough to figure that out. She has a mind of her own."

"Yes, sir."

"You understand she is utterly determined to earn a college degree."

"I do, and I think it's a fine idea."

Samuel nodded. "Yes, it seems less far-fetched to me than it used to. I'm glad to hear you express support. Anyone who is married to Lucy will have to be ready for anything."

"I want whatever will make Lucy happy."

"Then I suggest you take this question directly to Lucy."

"Yes, sir. I presume I have your blessing to do so."

"If you feel you need it, yes."

"Thank you, Mr. Banning!" Will jumped out of his chair, grabbed Samuel's hand again, and pumped it.

Samuel tilted his head toward the door. "If I'm not mistaken, Lucy is expecting you at St. Andrew's by now. She doesn't like it when people turn up missing. Not one bit."

Will shot out the door and ran for the streetcar.

The diamond was small, but Lucy did not care. She wore it only because Will insisted on giving her an engagement ring. If she had her way, they would be married in short order, ring or no ring. Even Flora had not argued when Lucy insisted she wanted no part of an extravagant wedding that took months to plan. She simply wanted to be married to Will Edwards—soon.

Small though it was, the stone glinted in the reluctant sun on the cool, misty morning of opening day of the World's Columbian Exposition. The Bannings, as well as many of their Prairie Avenue neighbors, had been wrapped up in planning the fair for two years. It hardly seemed real to Lucy that opening day had come at last—months after the dedication ceremonies. Lucy, of course, had seen the progress of the fair during construction because of her involvement with the women's building. Nevertheless, she was not prepared for the breathless panorama of May 1.

Grandstands on the Court of Honor accommodated dignitaries from around the globe, including the Duke of Veragua, a direct descendant of Christopher Columbus, and Grover Cleveland, recently inaugurated to serve for the second time as the president of the United States. Will, Lucy, and Leo stood together amid a throng of excitement.

"With dignitaries from around the globe sitting up there," Leo joked, "I wonder who is running the world today."

Lucy laughed and raised her voice to be heard above the crowd. "It's time the little people get some credit!"

Will squeezed Lucy's hand. "There must be a hundred thousand people here. They just keep coming!"

The Court of Honor opened a vision of fourteen stunning buildings covered with the same spectacular white stucco—the White City. Altogether the fair had more than two hundred buildings. Before wandering into the maze of a city within a city, visitors were greeted by a large reflecting pool with an elaborate fountain and an immense gilded statue, *Republic*, rising a hundred feet in the air on its stand and bursting with American spirit.

"It's unfortunate Sophia Hayden is not well enough for this day," Will said. "She would have a great deal to be proud of."

"I will personally make sure she knows how impressive her work is," Lucy responded. Millions of people would pass through the Court of Honor and into the fair over the next six months. Lucy was confident the women's exhibit would hold its own against any other, showcasing the aspirations and accomplishments of women around the world, as well as the desperate plight of women in some places.

"Time for the speeches," Leo said. "I hope they keep them short."

The director general stood at the front of the grandstand to give a welcoming speech. However, the crowd's eyes were on the next speaker, President Grover Cleveland. After a short congratulatory speech just before noon, President Cleveland moved a golden lever on the table in front of him and the White City transformed into its glory. Simultaneously, flags from around the world unfurled and flapped in the breeze, water sprang up from fountains and soared into the sky, whistles blew as machines cranked into action, vessels in the nearby harbor fired salutes, bands began to play. The World's Columbian Exposition was officially opened!

"I want to see the Manufactures Building," Leo said

immediately. "If we press our way through now, we can get ahead of the crowd."

Lucy looked up at Will, who smiled. "Sorry, Leo. Our first stop is the women's exhibit."

"Are you taking orders from your wife before she's even your wife?" Leo chided.

"Just making sure she knows I believe she can do great things."

And Will bent to kiss Lucy full on the lips in the middle of the crowd.

Author's Note

*A*lthough the main characters in the Avenue of Dreams series are fictional, the primary historical markers are true. Supporting details come from the daily reports of these events in the *New York Times* and *Chicago Tribune*, as well as accounts in publications by scholars and experts available through Google Books. For instance, the wealthy families of Prairie Avenue were the driving force behind bringing the World's Columbian Exposition to Chicago and breathed life into the fair with leadership and financing, so the Banning household is in the middle of that process. There really were a thousand little girls dressed in red, white, and blue at the parade reviewing stands at the fair's dedication in October 1892, so Lucy could have spoken to one of the children. The Calumet Club did burn down within thirty minutes on a frigid January day in 1893, costing a young maid her life. George Glessner did have a fascination with fire and often went to the sites of fires, so it's entirely conceivable he would have been at the Calumet Club fire, just blocks from his home, to run into Lucy Banning. Sophia Hayden, the architect of the women's exhibit, did have a breakdown that kept her from participating in the final preparations.

In some cases, the choice was to be faithful to the times but use information in the best way possible for this story. For example, the Chicago Orphan Asylum was located on South Michigan Avenue, and we have information about the work and services of this institution that cared for six thousand children during its existence. In fact, there were a dozen such orphanages in Chicago by 1890, and many Prairie Avenue families contributed financially. This series creates a fictional orphanage to use its characters and setting without violating the history of a particular institution. However, the plight of orphans and the response of the wealthy are true to the times. The fictional Banning family lives in a block where their house could not have existed because the lots were occupied with other structures, but having them close to the richest of the historical families helps to immerse the reader in the times.

Acknowledgments

People often ask me where I get ideas for novels, and I say the ideas are everywhere, ready like cherries for the picking. The seed for this one came from Stephen Reginald, an old publishing friend, when he became a volunteer docent at the Glessner House Museum in Chicago, at the corner of Eighteenth and Prairie Avenue. I thank him for his unflagging belief in me as a writer for the last two decades. He generously chose me to partner with him on this gem of an idea and threw himself into the research necessary to bring it to life.

Thanks also to William H. Tyre, director of the Glessner House Museum, for answering questions of minutiae and allowing me a private tour.

Thanks to Vicki Crumpton for her careful review of the manuscript and the team at Revell who helped turn a pile of words into a book.

Elisa Stanford, savvy fiction reader and friend extraordinaire, read raw chapters as I churned them out. Her enthusiasm kept me pecking at the keys. Rachelle Gardner, literary agent, believed it was just a matter of finding the right project, and now we're off and running. The rest of our book group gave rah-rahs at needful moments and constantly remind me that excellence is out there, because they are busy setting the bar. I love them all.

Olivia Newport's novels twist through time to discover where faith and passions meet. Her husband and two twentysomething children provide welcome distraction from the people stomping through her head on their way into her books. She chases joy in stunning Colorado, at the foot of the Rockies, where daylilies grow as tall as she is.

Meet
Olivia Newport
at
www.olivianewport.com

to read her blog, connect with her, and
learn more about the series.

Connect with Olivia on

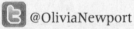 @OliviaNewport

 www.facebook.com/OliviaNewport

• • •

To mail Olivia a note, please send your letter to
Revell, a division of Baker Publishing Group
6030 E Fulton
Ada, MI 49301

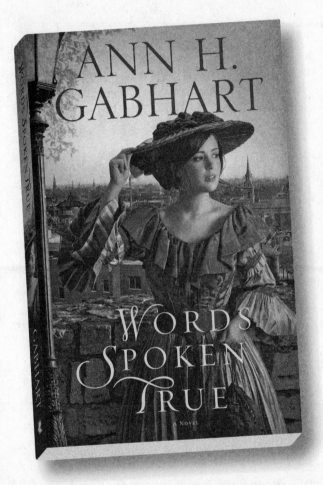